The
LIGHTKEEPER

A NOVEL

Sherry Shenoda

ANCIENT FAITH PUBLISHING CHESTERTON, INDIANA

Published by:
    Ancient Faith Publishing
    A Division of Ancient Faith Ministries
    P.O. Box 748
    Chesterton, IN 46304

ISBN: 978-1-944967-89-5

Library of Congress Control Number: 2021936313

Printed in the United States of America

To Veronica, warm Hearth
To Andrew, bright Light

Acknowledgments

ANNA, HELENA, LAURA, SANDRA, VERONICA. Thank you for being my sisters, supporting and cheering my work, and allowing me to live life with you. I love you so much.

Katherine, Melinda, Lynnette, and Matt. I am so grateful to work with such a generous, big-hearted publication team. Thank you for being beacons through this process.

Mom, Dad, Michael. I love you to the moon and back. Father Bishoy, my father, always. Basil, who forewent many LEGO building sessions while Mom worked on "poetry," and Tobias, who will never know how much brainstorming went on while he thought he was just nursing. And as always, to *mi media naranja*, Andrew, who knows why.

Special thanks to Dr. Ramez Mikhail for his beautiful translation of the work of Rainer Maria Rilke.

Author's Note

All lighthouses mentioned are real, with the exception of the Loon-Call and Rake-Point Lights. Hannah Thomas was a real lightkeeper at the Gurnet Point Light.

PART 1

You, Beloved, who were lost

from the beginning

who never came

I do not know which songs are dear to you.

RAINER MARIA RILKE

~: 1 :~

As the old saw says well:
every end does not appear together with its beginning.

HERODOTUS, *THE HISTORIES*

Loon-Call Light, Maine, 1938

THE LIGHT HAD BEEN KEPT by a large, solitary man with faded eyes the color of the sea in midwinter. She arrived, her left foot still bare on the warm sandy beach of a more pleasant assignment. She sighed, stepped forward, and felt the last few grains of warm sand fall away as her foot was firmly encased in a sturdy leather boot. *A death,* she thought, *and my vacation is over.* She glanced at the man, wrapping the musty coat that had materialized on her shoulders more firmly around her to ward off the chill. Wherever she was, it was definitely North.

She had come from a remote island Light complete with balmy breezes, warm sandy beaches, and solitude. She had been covering the Light for a truant young Lightkeeper who had abandoned his post to seek his true love, or some such rot. She'd read his note to the Company, full of angst and remorse for leaving a massive beacon unlit and unmanned. At least he'd folded his uniform and left a note.

She wasn't unsympathetic. Loneliness she understood. She could have written that story. Irresponsible desertion, though, she had no patience for. She rolled her eyes into the top of her head at his gross negligence, sighed, and kept the Light lit in his absence, which turned out to last about a month. A glorious month of living in a shift, barefoot, her straight hair whipped by warm sea breezes, dining on fresh fish and coconuts. She'd wanted to stay forever.

Forever, she thought with a huff. *Whatever that means.* She shifted in her recently boot-clad feet. The boots pinched, and she wanted to be finished with whatever had to be done here so she could be warm again. Of course that errant keeper down south had returned a month later, his tan fading, a great, ridiculous grin on his face and a bride in tow. She saw them coming in the distance, from the high watch of the lighthouse, and climbed down to meet them on the road. It would have been immensely gratifying to give him a talking-to, but she was never granted that particular pleasure. No, she had to content herself with the thunderstruck look on his face as he saw that the Light was lit. *And well lit, too*, she thought smugly, but by then she had begun to feel the Change, and nothing was as sobering as that. She took a few more hurried steps up the path as they rounded the bend in the road up ahead.

The man dropped the hand of his bride and broke into a run, frantically waving his hands above his head. She sighed, for she had already felt the chill of the North circling around her skirts, and she slowed her pace with the dread of certainty. Between one stride and the next the warm sand slipped away, the seascape changed, the errant keeper and his bride faded, and she was here—cold, hair in a practical bun, wearing a damp coat that smelled faintly of old fish. She brought a sleeve to her nose and wished she hadn't. Oh, and this keeper was not taking a vacation or a nap.

She took a long, measured breath. *Time to get back to the real work,* she thought. Some days were worse than others. She wasn't normally so callous toward death, but this transition had been more jarring than most. Her heart softened as she looked down on the man slumped forward at the small table tucked against the curved wall of the Light. She instinctively reached out and carefully closed his eyelids, her fingers lingering for a moment against his leathery cheek. They curled back in surprise at the warmth of his skin.

He must have died only recently. She found her fingers drawn back, sifting through his soft white hair and passing down to his broad shoulders and back, only a little bent by age. His body was bowed over the keeper's log, which she carefully eased from under his right hand. It was surprisingly heavy, that hand, though her mind didn't register the fact until later. Her gaze fell on her own hand next to his: hers ageless, smooth, and unmarked, the log beneath it. His was heavily veined, spot-marked with age, the nails square and the pads calloused. She curled her own hand into a momentary fist.

She glanced over the log with detached interest, as a doctor might conduct an examination. The last few nights had been uneventful. The keeper had developed a mild cold earlier in the week. *Pneumonia, probably*, she thought, glancing down at the top of his head. Her eyes fell on the last entry, reading it without interest at first, then again, more slowly, her heart rate quickening.

She picked up the hefty book and rifled back a few pages. He had an uncramped, careful scrawl that was easy on the eye. She often made character judgments—rather unfairly, she knew—from a keeper's log, and she decided immediately that she would have liked to know this old man. He was a meticulous author, descriptive but not tediously so.

Cold wind from Nor'easter last week. Fresh breeze, moderate waves. Sighted two ships starboard. No visitors.

Glad I missed that, she thought. *Fresh breeze, moderate waves—Beaufort 5*, she thought automatically, translating the keeper's language into weather shorthand. A glassy sea was a rare zero, and hurricane-force winds were a malevolent twelve. She had been through enough storms to develop a proper respect for a dread Nor'easter.

She turned the page.

Moderate breeze, small waves breaking. Relieved for two nights by SS while away in town. Supplies acquired. No visitors.

Beaufort 4—oh stop it! she thought, annoyed with the reflex. This was followed by a list, in his carefully measured handwriting.

She flipped back a few pages, but there was only page after page of uninteresting, stock keeper-log material. This made the last entry particularly befuddling.

His handwriting was the same, and he hadn't written it in a hurry, as the man-child on the island had written his letter to the Company. It looked like every other entry, but instead of commenting on the weather or the number of ships, it simply read:

Welcome home.

The hair on the nape of her neck rose in response, and she startled as something brushed against her skirts. She glanced down to find a large grey-white cat twining itself familiarly around her ankle. It glanced up at her, wide blue eyes set in a silvery moon-shaped face, and blinked. The Keeper blinked back, and the cat turned and leapt lightly onto the table, crouching next to the slumped figure. She sniffed his hand and gave a plaintive meow.

The Keeper's gaze followed the cat, then caught on an object in the man's palm. She left the log lying open and with her thumb and pointer finger tried to slip it free, while the cat meowed encouragingly. He held the item securely, even in death, and when she lifted his hand to open his fingers, her mind finally registered that his hand was heavy, substantial. She yelped and let go, his hand thudding dully back onto the table.

"Curious," she murmured aloud, and the cat tipped its head at her.

She frowned down at the man in confusion. She wasn't afraid, not really. Nothing could hurt her here. She was, however, wary, and even more improbably, she was interested. The Keeper paced beside the man a moment in the small space, and then tentatively touched his shoulder. Solid. He was as solid as she was, and she shuddered. The humans never felt this way to her.

She had buried a keeper just the week before, a middle-aged man without a family, on the colder, eastern shore of Ireland. She fished him from the sea and knew right away, from the waterlogged feel of his body and the cold, sea-blue tinge he had taken from his watery grave, that all that was left of him was a body. Cradling his slight weight against her and absorbing the seawater against her dress, she lifted him gently from the sea. She wished uselessly, as she had a thousand times before, that there was more she could do, that something could be done other than to treat a body with respect while she laid it to rest.

She floated that keeper in her arms from the sea, knelt with him by a little plot of soil with a view, and dug him a grave. It was the tail end of winter, but the frozen ground parted easily under her hands as though she were planting a seed in spring sod. She staked the ground to mark the site and tended to the Light. It was sixty-eight steps to the top, and after lighting it, she had taken an uncharacteristically defiant step off the side of the beacon. Burying bodies always made her a little testy.

She landed with the slight crunch of—not bones, despite the great height—but just a little snow beneath her boots. She remembered a flock of white-crowned widgeons gliding overhead. She had rolled her shoulders, turned up the collar of her long coat, and glanced back to see the Light burning brightly. She recalled her lifted eyebrow, the unspoken *anything else you need me to do?* just before she translated. *That was routine*, she thought. *Easy.*

Her eyes fell again on the keeper's hand and the thing he was loosely gripping. She had a suspicion that this keeper's death was not going to be easy. She ignored the feeling of wrongness at the weight of his fingers and gently pried them from the object he held. Her breath caught as what he had been clutching tumbled into her hand. She cupped it carefully and passed her thumb back and forth over it, one corner of her mouth lifting reluctantly. She hesitated for only a moment.

The cat folded its paw like a sphinx. "Don't give me that look, cat," she muttered, and tucked the small object into her pocket.

She stepped lightly to the lantern glass and pushed the small door open to step outside. She gasped against the cold, smiling as it stung her cheeks after the warmth of the lantern room. She took several deep breaths of the winter air and tilted her face up to the Big Dipper and the Little Dipper above her. The waves crashed against the shore below and she counted them silently, as she often did, to calm herself. Some beaches were what she thought of as threes: every third wave was a larger wave. Some beaches were sevens for the same reason. She counted. It was a threes-beach.

Calmer, she turned back into the heat of the lantern room, and to her task. Then a long, horrible wail pinned her where she stood. She froze while the haunting sound sliced through the clear winter night. "It's just a loon-cry," she chided herself aloud. Nevertheless, the sound held her until the last note died away. She shook her head and reached for the door, chilled.

This will be no ordinary night, she thought with a grimace, gazing down at the slumped figure. She sighed, and rolled her shoulders once again. She sketched the Sign in the air over him and began to unbutton the cuffs of her stiff coat, to push and roll the sleeves up to her elbows.

A slow snow began, each flake seemingly suspended for an eternity in the unnatural brightness of the courtyard lit by the lighthouse beam.

She went into the cottage and stripped the bed sheet from his bed. Back outside, she awkwardly lowered his body into it. The bumping journey down the spiral staircase of the Light had been unspeakable, and she decided immediately to forget the sound his body made on each tightly stacked step.

She began dragging the body across the yard, her hair on end and feeling like a raw nerve, her quick, panting breaths white in the dark night air. The sheet made the going only marginally easier, and she kept uselessly muttering "I'm sorry" to the body behind her. They cut a large skid mark across the yard away from the base of the Light as she painfully made her way to the large apple tree that partially shaded the cottage.

The journey was a revelation to her, who thought herself both a woman of the world and entirely imperturbable. By the time she had reached the tree, she didn't feel much like either. She paused more than once, dragging her forearm, gooseflesh and all, across her face. Her cheeks and nose stung from the bitter cold.

She steeled her heart against the man whose body she couldn't bear to look at. "I hate this," she informed him, since there was no one else to listen. "Why can't I lift you? You're so heavy."

She couldn't understand why he was so substantial, why this was so painful and difficult. They were normally all so easy to lift. *Why you?* she asked silently. There was no answer, just the silence of the moon-faced cat, which didn't seem inclined to leave her alone.

His weight didn't make it easier to give him a decent burial. She leaned a moment against the apple tree, glancing down at the body in the sheet. He looked peaceful, undisturbed. She was the one disturbed by this incident. He was gone, had no cares here, and she momentarily considered simply stopping, leaving him where he was. *Who is there to see?* She shook her head violently at the unbidden thought and pushed away from the tree. She chose a spot, hoping she wouldn't come across anything in her digging, and went to look for a shovel.

It was no easier to part the earth than it had been to carry his body. Every clod of dirt seemed to resist her efforts, and she nearly despaired as a dusting of snow fell around her, not sticking, but melting as it reached the ground. She longed to be inside, with tea, and warm in bed.

The wind picked up, and she pulled the stiff coat around her, closed her eyes momentarily, and then slowly emptied her mind of everything unbearable, as she had taught herself to do from time to time, in order to do things that could not be borne. She acknowledged the cold and discomfort, and then dismissed them. She took the things she liked and buried them deep, until she was just a live body, burying a dead body.

She opened her eyes. Her boots squelched in the mud beneath the tree as she counted. One, two, three, four, five, six, seven feet long. Three wide. Her hands knew how and worked methodically, one shovelful of earth at a time, the hole deepening around her as the night darkened above her. She worked into a rhythm, one boot on the shovel, stomping it into the hard ground, arms shaking with the effort to scoop out the earth. If she could have wept from sheer exhaustion and misery, she would have.

It was close to morning by the time the hole was long enough and deep enough, and she finally looked up, noticing that the sky had lightened. She looked briefly down at herself and started. She sniffed delicately. "Did you see her hem?" she murmured. "Six feet deep in mud!" Her bark of laughter sounded hysterical even to her own ears. The cat peeked over the side of the grave, eyes wide, and gave her a questioning head tilt. "Not a fan of Austen, are you?" asked the Keeper, then rolled her shoulders once more before beginning to climb out of the grave. Her face came momentarily on the same level as the dead keeper's. *Not for me, this grave*, she thought, and hoisted herself out.

There was no one else there, and the keeper didn't seem to have family to mourn him save the cat, so she collected her thoughts, found what compassion remained within her after the long night, and before she lowered him as gently as she could into the grave, tried to honor the white hair on his head and the crags that lined his face. She knew not what he worshipped, so she invoked the One she worshipped and made the Sign again over his resting form, and over the newly turned earth in which she laid him. As the cold, windy morning began to break with the faintest of light, she kissed his leathery cheek, blessed his brief, difficult life, and, under the scraggly apple tree, laid him in the ground.

She stepped back for a moment before beginning to shovel the dirt back into the hole. Her grimy hands, seeking warmth, reflexively sought her pockets, and the fingers of her right hand brushed against the object the keeper had been holding. She felt a twinge of guilt. It was clear that it was beloved, and she nearly pulled it out to put it back in his hand. She had never understood why humans buried beautiful things with their dead. She hesitated, her dirty fingers stubbornly tightening over it. *No*, she thought. *This doesn't belong in the ground.* The cat meowed beside her, as if in approval.

Turning away, the Keeper emptied her mind once more, picked up the shovel, and began replacing the earth, one shovelful at a time. The night had been interminable to that point, but now it picked up speed, seeming to make up for its previous glacial pace. Afterward she vaguely remembered making a grave mound and leaning the shovel against the tree. There was a water closet and bath, and the welcoming warmth of the keeper's cottage. She remembered kicking the door closed behind her, prying off her boots, dropping her sodden clothes to the ground by the bed, bathing hastily with a cake of soap she found next to the tub, drying off with a small towel she found in the kitchen, wrapping herself in a quilt, and tumbling into sleep before her head hit the pillow. The cat had followed her inside as though it owned the place, so she made no fuss when it curled beside her head like a dream. *Perhaps this whole night is a dream,* she thought wearily. Her last thought was a vague hope that the Light was still burning, because she had no strength left.

❧ 2 ❧

Circumstances rule men, men do not rule circumstances.

HERODOTUS, *THE HISTORIES*

S HE WOKE IN LATE AFTERNOON with a mouthful of cotton and a feeling in her head akin to what she felt the morning after she had discovered an unmarked bottle of sweet cider in one keeper's larder and helped herself liberally while reading *Moby Dick* by the fire. It had not been cider, as she'd discovered the next morning, and her relationship with Captain Ahab and his ill-intentioned whale had been irrevocably altered. This morning, she burrowed under the quilt in the keeper's bed, trying to figure out where she was and how she had gotten there.

Her first thought was *Ah, yes*, pulling the covers up to her nose. *Warm, balmy island. Translation. Cold, inhospitable outcropping, dead keeper.* She felt a tightening in her chest for the keeper who had died so alone and unloved. *What a world this is*, she thought. He had probably been a perfectly respectable sort, and even if he hadn't been, it always pained her to know someone had died alone. She felt that this keeper had been a respectable sort. *His handwriting, for one*, she stubbornly asserted. *And his cottage.* She pulled the covers down slightly and looked around, still cocooned in the quilt like a wet-winged butterfly, gathering strength to emerge.

Her second thought was quick on the heels of the first, and it came on a flash of anger. She disliked waking in the same place after the task was complete. It gave her orphaned soul a taste of what home would feel like, and she resented it. Every assignment was temporary, and she had long ago stopped hoping for anything else, such as waking in a warm bed in a cozy house.

She was only too familiar with the sinking despair of having hoped in vain, then being snatched away to another Light once more. If she had fallen into that trap a single time, she had fallen a hundred times. "Stop it," she said aloud, trying for sternness, but only accomplishing the croak of the first words of the morning.

Many of her translations required her to stay after the task was completed. She had reasoned that this was because many of the Lights were remote, and once the Light went dark in a keeper's absence or illness, it would take some time for relief to arrive. She often found herself in the same place for several days, whiling away the hours with a book, if one was available, counting waves, and listening to the cries of seabirds until she was suddenly whisked away. Sometimes she saw her relief arriving, as the keeper had with his bride at the most recent tropical Light. More often she was taken away without any help in sight. She imagined her ghostly presence fading moments before a ship rounded the far bend at the breakers, or a pair of boots rounded the nearest blind corner before sighting the Light. She could only imagine the surprise she left in her wake with a well-lit Light and no keeper in sight.

In any case, it might be but a matter of minutes before she was taken away from this cottage. *Take me away,* she pleaded halfheartedly. It was comfortable and warm, and she thought, wistfully, that it felt like it could be home. *Is it possible to be nostalgic for a place I've never been?* She lay in the warm bed a while longer, but she had never been one for lying about, and sighing, she pushed the covers back. She looked around for the silvery cat, but there was no sign of her.

The house was divided into two rooms. There was a main room, which she had seen in a half stupor after stripping out of her clothes and bathing in the outdoor bathhouse the night before. The main room contained a heart-stopping number of books, as well as two large armchairs. An attached kitchen was likely connected to the large cisterns beneath the house that stored rainwater to be pumped in for use. She was in the second room, a bedroom with a hardwood-framed bed, soft pillows, and clean sheets. *Bless him.* A window above the headboard of the bed looked out onto a small garden, chicken coop, the apple tree, and beyond that, the sea. The Light was on the far side of the house and not visible. She propped herself up on an elbow to look out the window behind her.

A small menagerie of hand-carved wooden animals lined the ledge. There was a clever little fox, a bulky bear, and a series of birds: kind eiders, sandpipers, and a pair of loons. She smiled, reaching for the loons and feeling a sense of loss that she had not met this keeper before his death. *A dreamer put this window here,* she thought. A man who, despite the difficulty of keeping warm in the winter, had deemed this a necessary addition. She ran a finger down the smooth back of a loon until her gaze was pulled inexorably to the apple tree, and she felt her heartbeat quicken at the sight of the freshly turned earth. *Time to get to work,* she thought, eyeing the deepening shadows.

With some effort she unfolded herself from the bed and put one bare foot after the other on the cold wooden floor, stretching her limbs, then opening the wardrobe against the wall. Hanging next to a few pairs of neatly mended pants, shirts, and uniforms, in the far corner of the wardrobe, were three dresses. Her outstretched hand stilled. Had she buried a man who had family somewhere who would return to find him gone? Then she fingered the fabric and knew the dresses hadn't been worn in some time. *Pity*, she thought. *I could have at least buried him next to her, had I known where the grave lay.*

She glanced back out the window at the approaching dusk and then hurriedly picked a dress, a pretty thing, though practical by the feel of the sturdy flannel, and put it on. It was a near fit, if a little loose here and there. She found her mud-caked boots by the kitchen stove and stepped into them as though donning armor. Her hands hovered over her stiff coat. It hung on a hand-carved wooden peg next to a man's thick coat. She hesitated only a moment, then reached for his coat, smelling it as she pushed her hands through the long sleeves. She rolled them up a few folds so her fingers were liberated. The coat smelled clean, like the sheets, but more human. She automatically slipped her hands into the pockets and fingered the two objects within before drawing them out. In one pocket was a small chisel, and in the other an oblong piece of smooth cherry-wood. With a pang she slipped them back into the pockets, wondering what project he had been about to begin when his time had come.

She braced herself at the door, then pushed into the world outside, gasping, a smile on her face, as a wall of cold air struck her. Her teeth began to chatter lightly. She didn't mind the cold when she knew she could go right back inside, curl under a blanket by the fire, and read a heavy book. It was just the glacier's tip of winter, and the first frost hadn't been long ago. The front door opened onto a walkway that ran a ways to the end of the drive, which split into two paths. One, presumably, led to town, and the other to the Light. She took the latter, picking her way in the crisp air through light snow flurries that barely powdered the ground, to the towering Light, where she set to work lighting the beacon. The cat, which had wandered away earlier, returned, and now watched her with supervisory eyes while she tended to the Light.

The keeper's cottage was at the intersection between the river and the sea, and the lens was a fourth order, by the look of it. It was a medium-sized lens of a few hundred pounds. She liked the lens of this particular Light, and more importantly, she liked the solitude that it afforded. Not only could a smaller lens be kept by just one keeper and his family, obviating the need for an assistant keeper, but the smaller lenses were much less of a draw for visitors.

The Fresnel lens was a piece of brilliant applied mathematics that took a regular lens, cut its curvature into pieces, and attached them in concentric circles to a smaller, lighter lens. The result was a stronger beam that rotated to shine out over the water for nearly twenty-five miles. Best of all, there was no whale oil involved. She detested the smell of whale oil. There was just a beauty of a suspended lens, crystalline and magnificent, beaming out over the water.

She began her vigil by warming the ten-gallon bucket of vegetable oil and carrying it up the wrought-iron spiral of the lighthouse tower, counting the steps aloud. *Forty-two. The answer to life, the universe, and everything.* She smiled. It had been a good day long ago, in the future from this time, when she discovered a dog-eared copy of Douglas Adams' book on the desk of a keeper and stayed up all night reading, blessing Edison and electricity. She'd never encountered a lighthouse with forty-two steps before; she liked this Light already.

Her steps were slow and measured, for her skirts were long, the stairs narrow, the pail heavy, and the oil hot. She actively blocked the remembrance of the feel of a heavy body hitting each successive step behind her in that tight spiral, and squared her shoulders. She strained the oil into a reservoir under the lamp within the lens, and once the lamp was lit, kept the flame low while she worked, so there would be no dramatic change in temperature to crack the glass. On her tiptoes, she pulled back the curtains that ringed the inside of the small tower room. She had learned long ago that the lens worked both ways, and if it wasn't shielded during the daytime, it could act like a powerful magnifying glass to concentrate the rays of the sun and perhaps set the beacon on fire.

The same long, mournful cry she had heard the night before, like that of a lone wolf under the full moon, pierced the chill early evening air. It caught the Keeper with her hands still full of the curtains, and she froze. The cry came again, and the silence after it was more pronounced in its wake. She gathered the curtains and, casting about for a tie, made short work of the job.

Backing a few steps down the narrow staircase, she stepped out onto the small, high ledge with its iron gate below the lantern room. After the heat of the lantern room the cold air was welcome on her flushed face, and she waited, ears strained. The sound came again a moment later, a high, keening, lonely wail far to her left, down toward the river. This time, it was followed by a second wail. Her skin pebbled along her arms, and she wrapped them around herself to keep that sound from entering her body. *In all the world,* she thought, *there is no lonelier sound than a loon searching for its lost mate.* Another resonant wail broke out, this time from not so far away, and was answered more quickly. She glanced up at the lantern and knew her time was up, so she rubbed her arms, and willing the loons to find one another quickly, ducked back into the tight spiral staircase to the warmth of the lantern room.

The Keeper could hear the wail in her mind, long and sorrowful, as she checked to make sure the curtains were securely tied. She slipped a linen apron that had hung in the keeper's storage room over her head. The white gloves she found were less than a precise fit, but she made do. She turned the flame up a little as the glass warmed, and straightened to her task. The prisms of the lens caught and held every color of the rainbow, and she loved this part of the work best of all. She could put up with hot oil, narrow staircases, and foghorns for this. The lens was a beauty, and she lost herself in cleaning the concentric rings with a feather duster, one curve at a time, occupying herself with trying to remember the exact opening lines of *A Hitch-hiker's Guide to the Galaxy*, since that was a cheerier thought than lost loon-mates.

"Are you ready, cat?" she asked. The cat tilted his head to one side and eyed her placidly.

"Far out in the uncharted backwaters of the unfashionable end of the Western Spiral arm of the Galaxy lies a small unregarded yellow sun." She worked her way from the outside of the lens in tightening circles, though there was not a speck of a dust mote to be seen.

"Orbiting this at a distance of roughly ninety-eight million miles is an utterly insignificant little blue-green planet whose ape-descended life forms are so amazingly primitive that they still think digital watches are a pretty neat idea." She grinned, and the cat meowed, unimpressed.

One day, she thought, *I'll meet someone who appreciates this talent of mine.* On the heels of that thought was the firmly grounding thought that if she did, she would likely have to explain what digital watches, the galaxy, and hitchhiking were, not to mention who Douglas Adams was, which would make it all rather less humorous for the explaining. She gave an impatient huff at her wandering thoughts. *Never mind that*, she chided herself, and ducked her head to her polishing.

By the time she was finished polishing, she could turn the flame up entirely and trim the wicks. The cat had disappeared. All that was left was to wind the cable below the lens that operated the weighted rotating apparatus and . . . she ducked as the first brilliant flash of light sliced out above her head. Her heart always caught at that first flash of light from a beacon, though it always nearly blinded her. It didn't matter how many times she'd seen it. That first flash had a presence, a sound, as it cut a path out over the water. She felt that it beamed out with all of her anonymous goodwill to whoever was on the other side to see it, and that in some small way, she was not com-pletely unseen in the world because of it.

Nonsense, she muttered, and smiled self-consciously. *Still*, she thought, glancing out at the strong beam across the water as it flashed again, *it is supremely satisfying*. She would check back on the Light later, but she didn't feel the need to sit by it all night as she did with some Lights. She was confident the amount of oil she had added would keep it lit for hours, and the rotating mechanism seemed sturdy. Timing her exit between flashes and tugging the apron off over her head, she slipped down the staircase and out into the dusk of the evening. She craned an ear for them, but the loons were silent.

She headed back down the path toward the house. The keeper had kept a garden, carefully tended out front next to the chicken coop, and she went there first, rummaging about until she found some leafy green vegetables. The bright red of a perfectly ripe straggling tomato stopped her in her tracks. It was miraculously undamaged after the first frost, and she smiled as she bent to twist it gently from the vine. "My wages," she murmured, straightening from a crouch. She had few qualms about helping herself to her wages, wherever she was.

She had often wondered how many hundreds of keepers she had tended the Lights for had awoken—just seconds after she had toiled to relight a beacon, or fought the whole night against strong rain, wind, lightning, disentangling humans from the fingers of the ocean—only to find that a crust of bread they were about to eat, a piece of cheese they had set aside for later, or the last sip of wine in their glass had been finished.

Her fingers stilled next to a weed insinuating itself among the green vines. She itched to pluck it from the earth as she had plucked the tomato, but she did not. She was only a visitor here. Her job was the Light. The old irritation rose up inside her. She grasped the tomato in her hand and marched indoors, stomping up mud in her wake.

She wandered around the small cottage, pulled water from the well, and turned on a burner under the teapot. The cat reappeared just as she brought a tin of tea to her nose and noted with surprise the combination of dried lavender, chamomile, and lemon balm.

"That's an odd choice for a lone lightkeeper," she told the cat, who studiously ignored her.

The Keeper had the sudden, overwhelming desire to be sharing this cup of tea with someone. Anyone, really. Instead, with immense satisfaction, and not a little wistfulness, she went through the ritual of making a single cup of tea. She carefully steeped a tisane and inhaled deeply of the scent. She had the sense for the second time in as many days that if she could weep, she might. Far off in the distance, she heard the cry of the loon again, and she gasped aloud with the loneliness of it. *This place might break me wide open after all this time*, she thought.

She took her teacup and settled back in one of the two armchairs next to the fire, the cat leaping with feline possessiveness into her lap. The room had a woman's touch, though there was no evidence that one lived there now. For surely *it* had been made for *her*, whoever she was. She pulled the small object out of her pocket and held it up to her face. The cat sniffed it and the Keeper settled a hand over him, feeling the small bones of his spine, the skin warm beneath the soft flesh. A purr vibrated beneath her fingers.

The object was carved from smooth hardwood, oak perhaps. It was small, about the width and length of two fingers, and clearly the work of a master craftsman. A smile free from irony tugged up the corners of her mouth, surprising her. The sweetness of the object touched her in a way she couldn't understand. Here was a man who obviously lived alone and had skilled hands, and yet chose to make a tiny four-pronged feminine hair comb. And if that wasn't enough, he'd carved it with an intricate pattern of curling waves on one side and a pretty vine with tiny curling leaves on the other. She thought again that she might have buried it with him, but was glad she hadn't. What use was there in putting this in the ground? Still, she couldn't bring herself to presume to do what she really wanted to do, which was to pull back a section of her stick-straight hair and sink the smooth prongs among the strands.

She leaned back in the chair, and rubbing the small comb between two fingers, scanned the wall of bookshelves. The keeper's library was carelessly extravagant: books lined the shelves of an entire wall, but they also spilled onto tables, sat in haphazard piles by every window in the room, by his bed, and on the kitchen counter. The house was orderly save for the books. They seemed to be afforded a luxury denied every potentially wayward rug, towel, pot and pan.

She tentatively looked over the treasure trove, briskly extinguishing the warmth that had started to spread inside of her—that treacherous feeling she had felt before. She picked up a book of sonnets— all she would likely have time for before help arrived—looked with a practiced eye around the room, and tucked herself back into what was obviously a reading chair by the fire. She propped her stockinged feet on the armchair opposite, the little comb still tucked in the palm of her hand.

She kept the Light that night and made up his bed in the morning, slipping between the sheets with a sigh and rolling herself into the quilt again. With regret she set the small comb on the stand by the bed. There was no use in translating with it—what a fine waste that would be! She looked longingly around at the small cottage, believing she would wake in a far place. She allowed herself a moment, then mercilessly dampened the small flicker inside again.

"Good night, little Moon," she told the cat, who yawned and curled beside her head once again.

She slept peacefully that day and woke in the afternoon with a start to find that she had not moved. Perhaps she would be given some time here, as she had at the last assignment.

In any case, aside from the cold, which she didn't mind terribly, bundled as she was in the keeper's coat, she rather liked it here. She bathed—running water and electricity were always a welcome addition—and walked out the back door of the cottage.

So what if she tried yet again to knead bread—that unconquerable task in her life!—and put it aside that night? Or that she restarted a book—*The Histories*, by Herodotus, no less!—as she sat next to the Light? It was not her home, nor would it be, but it seemed she was being allowed to keep it for a time. There was no use in putting her life on hold for uncertainty. She hadn't always felt that way, but she was learning to. So she weeded the garden the next afternoon, taking her mild aggression out on the weeds that dared to trespass in the keeper's absence, and then wielded soap against the pile of dirty clothes she had created the first night.

All throughout the day she argued with herself about going to see the town nearby. The cottage was well stocked and she didn't need supplies. Truth be told, she was scared. Scared in the same way one feels tiptoeing by a great giant. She felt in a vague way that she had been mercifully forgotten, and though she learned later that it was not true, she did not quite yet want to be remembered.

❧ 3 ❧

All men's gains are the fruit of venturing.

HERODOTUS, THE HISTORIES

O N THE FIFTH NIGHT SHE readied herself to go into town in the morning. She had used up the remaining flour in her quest to bake edible bread, and she felt an inkling to try again. She slept early, giving the Light one last glance over her shoulder and speaking a prayer out over the water before slipping into the bed. She woke early, banked the fire in the fireplace, fed the chickens, laced up her boots, and helped herself to a handful of coins from the jar on the mantelpiece, carefully tucking them into her coat pocket.

She eyed the bike that leaned against the wall in the entryway. *One of these days,* she promised herself. The Keeper picked her way on the narrow leaf-littered path, past the bifurcation to the Light, and on up the road in the grey morning, the ground squelching with cold mud beneath her booted feet.

She wondered how the Light would fare during the long winter to come, and whether it stayed lit year-round. In the far reaches of her memory was a translation to the Saint Joseph Light on Lake

Michigan. The Light had stood as solemn as a frost giant, hulking in its white stillness, blanketed to its lantern room in thick, impenetrable ice. Even the walkway to the Light had been frozen stiff, huge icicles longer than her arms hanging its entire length, making the walk to the Light treacherous and nearly impassable. She'd walked the long, slippery plank in spike-soled boots, her body entombed in a down jacket, inching along step by slick step until she had reached the end of the walkway. Time slowed. Clearly the Light had been shut down for the winter, and there was not a soul in sight. The sub-zero winds screamed all around her, scraping down her exposed cheeks, and though she stood there in that icy world for but a few moments, she had only to close her eyes, whenever she was in time, to conjure that indelibly imprinted image and feel a shiver of true cold shudder down her back.

If there had been a soul within that Light it would have taken explosives to blast a path through the tons of ice blocking the way. She still didn't know why she had been sent to Saint Joseph's, because there was neither a Light to keep nor a keeper to assist, but her respect for the abiding depth of winter had been born then. Some of her assignments were like that: a tendril of an experience, connected to a Light, with no clear purpose.

Hunched against the stiff breeze, she followed the road as it sloped up and down and wound side to side, cutting across the stark landscape beside the river. It was there she found the loons. They seemed well settled in the area, and she passed a small flock of them along the riverbank. Their slick ebony heads with sharp, pointed beaks bobbed above elegant black-and-white spotted finery that gave the impression of a ballroom mid-waltz as they glided in the water. The effect was only diminished by their unsettling red eyes. The loons called comfortable, familial hoots at one another, and she was grateful that there was no searching wail to chill her today.

She thought of a poem by Mary Oliver that she loved and recited it under her breath as she passed by. It spoke of a loon that had "cried out in the long, sweet savoring of its life." She smiled and remembered the poet admonishing her to "tell no one" where the loons sang.

I have no intention to, she vowed, the loons' hoots fading as she rounded a bend in the road.

It took her under an hour on the narrow path to reach the center of town. The town was a soggy, sleepy place, with a post office to the north, a church to the east, and a bank to the south. She crossed the town green and saw the western corner lined with small shops. She passed a greengrocer, a baker, a fishmonger and a smith before she reached a general store, and with an efficient step strode inside.

She had realized long ago that there was something about her that made it difficult for people to see her. She wasn't invisible, precisely, but she was as insubstantial visibly to them as they were physically to her. She was difficult to remember, and she could come and go fairly unbothered. The Keeper had been walking alongside humanity for a very long time, and this had always been the case. It seemed that she was meant to leave no trace. It had bothered her, initially, to be so unseen. Unseen meant unknown, and unknown meant, *Well, never mind that,* she thought. She had realized over the years that she could either focus on being unseen, with all its accompanying isolation, or on the fact that it allowed her to live among others and learn everything that could be learned without arousing suspicion.

The owner of the dimly lit general store introduced herself as Willow Wendell, and the Keeper could have sworn the smartly dressed woman jumped when she saw her, but she recovered quickly and bustled around, though she glanced at the Keeper out of the corner of her eye several times. After efficiently retrieving the flour the Keeper requested, the woman looked the Keeper full in the face and smiled. The Keeper tilted her head to the side and thanked her. There was a twinkle in the owner's eye and a small smile on her lips that seemed unrelated to her surroundings, which were largely dried bulk items, candle wax and textiles, but as she said nothing out of the ordinary. The Keeper simply smiled and stepped back out into the cool breeze on the sidewalk, the package tucked under her arm.

She found her feet drawn to the bakery, enticed by the smells wafting into the street, momentarily masking the earthy smell of horse manure. The woman behind the counter was Dahlia Thorne, "How do you do?" and her shop was a wonder of sights and scents. The Keeper passed over the sweet pastries laid out like baked treasure and set her sights on a homey loaf of hearth bread. Dahlia wrapped it in brown paper and asked her where she was from. "Oh, I'm just visiting a relative in town," she said vaguely, and then quickly asked Dahlia about herself, having found over the years that this was the single most effective way to change a subject. Most residents of the planet could be diverted by being asked to talk about themselves, and Dahlia didn't disappoint.

"We live over on the other side of town, my Horace and I," she said. "Never had any children, but the good Lord has blessed us in other ways. My Horace is a banker. Works over on Main Street. That's how come we were able to open this shop. I've run the shop for years. Gives a body something to do in the middle of the day, you see?"

"Indeed!" enthused the Keeper, holding up the hearth bread. "And such beautiful hearth bread you make, too!" It was easy to be either pleasant or disagreeable when one was anonymous, and the Keeper had long ago realized she liked being anonymously friendly, as long as she could retreat to a quiet place afterward.

The shopkeeper sniffed, fingers hovering over the coins the Keeper had proffered, but she only said, a little stiffly, "Well, I make the pastries, you see. I don't bake hearth bread. Too coarse for my hands." She paused in making change and, looking down on her hands, inspected her nails momentarily. She shrugged a slim shoulder and smiled a secret smile that had nothing to do with their current conversation. Dahlia handed the change back. "Claire the hearth-witch makes them and brings them in here in the mornings." The Keeper waited. Another trick she'd learned: almost everyone was uncomfortable with silence. Again, Dahlia didn't disappoint. "She lives on the edge of town. Just keep going past the train tracks and you won't miss it."

Perfect, thought the Keeper, *the town witch will know everything.* "Thank you again for this lovely loaf," she told Dahlia, and waving with the paper-wrapped bread, stepped out onto the sidewalk, feeling decidedly lighthearted.

The hearth-witch, Claire, lived on the other side of the train tracks, literally and figuratively. The sight of a stranger in a town this size would normally cause people to pause and stare, but glances didn't linger overlong on the Keeper as she walked. This had likely saved her from a tight spot more than once. She thought of a couple of times in the colonies, in Massachusetts, when one or more bored schoolgirls would have loved nothing more than to accuse a ghostly Lightkeeper of witchcraft and send her to the gallows. She shook her head at that. *Superstitions.* She hated superstition. *In any case, it seems I'm off to see a witch.*

The Keeper turned off the main road onto the path to the home of Claire of the hearth, as she was called. The path evened out almost immediately, the gravel giving way to hard-packed dirt that seemed as if it had been swept. Less than a quarter of a mile up the road, a clearing opened up and she was suddenly there.

It didn't look like the house of a witch. It looked like the house of a whole coven of jovial witches. The Keeper's smile started down in her chest and expanded upward. The house was painted an unapologetic red with white trim on the door and windowpanes. The broad panes, one on each side of the second story, looked like two large eyes, and the door a broad, friendly mouth. A brown chimney puffed steady plumes of cheery white smoke. Wind flutes were strung around the clearing, and she could see the field beyond. A sizable garden separated the clearing from the house. The front stoop was flanked by a low brick wall, upon which sat several plants potted in mismatched, colorful crockery.

The door swung open and a short, silver-maned woman of medium build stepped out. She shaded her eyes for a moment and then broke into a trot. The Keeper, in mute confusion, was swept into an embrace as light and insubstantial as the short woman before her. She dropped her packages.

Well, she thought. *A friendly witch.* Perhaps she got so few visitors that they all received an enthusiastic greeting. Aloud she only managed a startled "Oh!" and brought her arms up to lightly pat the woman on the back. "Hello," she said, carefully, stepping back out of the woman's embrace.

Claire's face was shining. "Bless you," she breathed, her eyes darting over the Keeper's startled face. Behind the thick glasses Claire's brown eyes shone with a sheen of tears. She shook her head and laughed, then embraced the Keeper again. This time she was prepared and allowed her eyes to close for a moment. She so rarely received any affection, and it felt *good*, stranger or no.

Claire drew back, her hands cupping the Keeper's shoulders. "You are so young, my dear Aine. You have no idea who I am, do you?" She laughed then, a clear, joyous peal that sounded nothing like a witch's laugh, and took the Keeper's hands in her own, holding them warmly for a moment. She sighed, a long and contented sigh, and then said calmly, "Welcome, my dear. May I offer you a cup of tea on your journey?"

Bewildered, the Keeper followed Claire toward the house. *Have I been here before?* She ransacked her memory, to no avail. A green and blue wind chime hung over the door, and as the Keeper passed under it she looked up and saw that it was in the shape of a starburst. The entryway was comfortably crowded with hats, scarves, and coats on the wall-pegs. The walls were hung with colorful paintings and fabric. The painting closest to the door depicted a blue cat curled around a stack of books. *I would've remembered that.*

Claire's eyes followed her gaze and she smiled. "My daughter Willow painted that." *Maybe Claire is not so alone then,* thought the Keeper.

An odd assortment of comfortable armchairs, couches, and low tables was strategically placed to hold mugs of tea. The front door opened onto a sitting room, to the left of which lay the kitchen. The smell of cinnamon and baking bread emanated from this beating heart of the hearth-witch's house.

The sink was clean, pots and pans hung from the ceiling, and colorful bowls sat on the open shelves. The kitchen was built for comfort and warm meals. A kettle already sat on the stovetop when the Keeper hung her cloak on a peg and wiped her feet on the mat.

Off the kitchen was a small, glass-enclosed room full of what looked like a tangle of green plants. It was warmer than the rest of the house and seemed to serve as a sort of greenhouse for more delicate plants.

The Keeper followed the woman deeper into the house, musing over the exuberant greeting she'd received. *Perhaps I remind her of someone,* or, equally likely, *perhaps she's a little batty.* Either way, she seemed harmless enough for tea and a chat. The Keeper had come for information, and she had instinctively known the town outcast's kitchen would be the best place to get it. And the woman would forget the conversation had ever occurred. *Hopefully,* she added. She smiled at her hostess, not quite as warmly as she was being smiled at, but warmly enough.

She took a deep breath of the warm, yeasty smell of bread baked earlier that morning. "That reminds me," said the Keeper. "Thank you for the hearth bread. I'm looking forward to it." She motioned to the supplies she had brought into the entryway out of the cold. Claire looked over her shoulder as she stood next to the kettle, rummaging in a cupboard overhead.

"Yes," she replied with an absent smile. "You like that bread."

The Keeper felt that she was definitely being confused with someone now, but didn't comment. She often reminded people of someone they knew. A black and white cat sidled up to her and twined itself momentarily around her left ankle before sauntering away.

"That's Twitch. He is a complete C-O-W-A-R-D, but good for warming your feet when you're deep in a long book and a pot of tea." Claire spelled it out behind her hand in a whisper, as though the cat could spell, and furthermore, take offense at the affront to his honor. The Keeper's eyes widened as she stood warming her hands by the fire. "There's another around here, an orange tabby. She's Mistress. Looks sweet, but a ferocious mouser." Claire started the kettle and took out a pair of china teacups, ushering the Keeper into a high-backed chair by the fire.

"Now," said Claire, settling in. "Tell me."

"Well," began the Keeper, "I wanted to stop by and get an idea of . . ." she trailed off. "You know, the times," she finished vaguely. Claire's blue eyes were sharp and searching behind her glasses. The Keeper waited, but Claire said nothing.

The Keeper waited some more, letting the silence stretch out as uncomfortably as possible, but Claire of the hearth didn't seem to be blinking, let alone cracking. *A worthy adversary*, thought the Keeper, admiringly. Just as she thought she herself might be feeling some discomfort with the stretched silence, the kettle started to whistle impolitely. Claire finally blinked, and with a small, secret smile padded into the kitchen to pour the tea. She came back with the tea and a few generously buttered slabs of bread and arranged the tray on the low table between them.

She didn't ask how the Keeper liked it, but it was a perfect cup, smooth and fragrant, the steam curling just so against her face. She wanted to tuck her feet beneath her, but the era called for perfect posture, so she sat as unhappily straight-backed as she could.

"Well," started Claire, "the year is 1938, October. You're in Maine, in the United States of America. The town has a population of about five hundred, give or take." The Keeper sat, immobile, every muscle frozen, alert.

Claire continued as though she hadn't said anything unusual. "The biggest gossips are Dahlia Thorne, the confectioner, and Mae Caldwell, the other banker's wife." The word "confectioner" had rolled off her tongue with a hint of bemused affection. "Oh," she added, "they're harmless, though. The real gossip to watch out for is Oliver Caldwell, Mae's husband. He's an oily one. Reels you in thinking he's trustworthy, and the next thing you know . . ." She trailed off mysteriously.

"Thank you," said the Keeper. She hesitated. "I won't likely be here for long. I'm not sure how you knew . . ." She also trailed off, not knowing how much to say.

"You'll be back," said the hearth-witch, with certainty. Then something seemed to strike her forcefully and a shadow of fear crossed her face. Claire set her teacup down with a shaking hand, and it clattered against the saucer, tea sloshing from the rim. She looked quite suddenly troubled and withdrawn into herself like a wary animal. The Keeper couldn't understand what she had said, if anything, and made to set her own teacup down, ready to excuse herself, when she found the other woman's hand settling lightly upon her own. It was a small, wrinkled hand, and the Keeper could tell at a glance that it was often in the soil of a garden. It was a good, strong hand, but it still felt like a tiny patch of warm light against her own.

The Keeper looked up to find the woman's eyes sorrowful and knowing. "He's gone, isn't he?" she asked softly, her eyes brimming with tears.

"Who?" asked the Keeper, realizing as she was saying it whom Claire was asking about. "Oh," she said immediately. "Yes. Yes, he's gone. I'm sorry," she said automatically, unsettled that Claire seemed to know why she was there. "Were you related to him? I didn't know who to tell." She said this into her teacup, the words rushing out of her, and when she looked up she saw that Claire of the hearth had leaned her head back against the armchair and silent tears were leaking out of her tightly closed eyes. "I couldn't find a wife, or family, so I buried him a few days ago." The hand that lay gently on the Keeper's tightened momentarily.

Finally Claire reached up and dashed a hand across her eyes, then tilted her head to look at the Keeper. Her eyes held no recrimination, only sadness. It was the sadness of a friend lost, but there was something more. "Were you and he . . ." began the Keeper hesitantly.

"Oh no, my dear," said Claire quickly. "Ronan of the Light belonged to only one woman. But he was a good friend to me."

"Ronan," said the Keeper, testing out the name. She felt at ease with Claire and felt her defenses loosening. "It's harder somehow, knowing his name," she said absently, in an uncharacteristically open manner.

Claire murmured "Merciful God," but didn't elaborate.

"What was he like?"

Claire composed herself over the rising steam of her tea and answered quietly. "He was a monk at heart, I think. He probably belonged in that monastery in the wood. He had a couple of great tragedies in his life," she added.

"Oh?"

Claire said nothing for a moment, and the Keeper thought that perhaps she wasn't going to answer. After a time she said, "His sister, Margaret, drowned long ago. I didn't know him at the time, but they say he was in anguish over her loss." She took a deliberate sip of her tea. "He walked around talking about a selkie he'd seen and nearly lost the lighthouse commission. They thought he'd lost his mind."

There was nothing much to say after that, so neither did. Eventually, the Keeper glanced at the open window and noticed the afternoon shadows lengthening. "I'd better get back."

Claire stood with her and attempted a half-smile. She reached a hand out again and placed it on the Keeper's shoulder. "You'll come again," she said unquestioningly. The Keeper nodded, and thanked her for the tea. The cat Twitch sidled up to her once more, wrapping her right ankle fleetingly as she prepared to depart.

She had the whole long walk back to the Light to think about Claire of the hearth, and what might have been one of her oddest encounters with a human. She tripped once in the darkening afternoon, the toe of her boot catching painfully on a slab of granite protruding into the path. She stopped and examined the slab. It was long and vaguely rectangular. As she worked it free of the dirt, she continued to ponder the problem of Claire of the hearth. The woman seemed to remember her resoundingly unmemorable self, if that was possible. Her mind turned to the Light and its recently departed keeper as the granite came up easily into her hands. It was heavier than it looked, but she had no trouble lifting it into her arms, beneath her other packages. It would make a fitting headstone. *For Ronan*, she thought. *Ronan of the Light.*

~ 4 ~

Of all possessions, a friend is the most precious.

HERODOTUS, *THE HISTORIES*

S HE WENT BACK TO SEE Claire of the hearth the following week, setting out in the early morning after sleeping a couple of hours overnight. She didn't need food or sleep, but she liked the taste of food and loved the warm oblivion of being asleep.

Claire, thought the Keeper. *Claire is different, somehow.* Claire seemed to enjoy her company, but the Keeper was certain there was something important Claire knew that she wasn't telling. She couldn't shake the thought that somehow, impossibly, Claire remembered her.

Claire met her out in the clearing once again, as though she knew she was coming. Her hair was a silver halo, and the fog around her booted feet blanketed the light dusting of snow that had fallen and stuck that morning. She smiled readily, though her eyes held a hint of sadness as she wordlessly folded the Keeper in her arms. She smelled of bread, chamomile, and lavender, and felt like coming home. Claire ushered her past the whistling wind flutes into the cozy kitchen,

39

where the kettle was already shrilling. "No bicycle?" she asked, looking around.

"I don't know how to ride one," replied the Keeper.

"You will," Claire assured her, and the Keeper shivered at her words. "I thought you might come today."

"Really?" said the Keeper, an eyebrow lifting before she could tamp down her mischief. "I didn't even know I was coming."

"I said thought, not knew," reproved the hearth-witch, her eyes twinkling back.

She took the Keeper's cloak and waved her into the chair by the fire. Turning away, she poured the tea and then settled into the opposite armchair. She looked at the Keeper, then slipped her feet out of her shoes and tucked them beneath her in the chair. "There," she said. "That's better." She glanced over to see if her guest wanted to similarly divest herself, and shrugged when the Keeper stared blankly back at her, feet firmly booted.

They chatted for a few minutes about the town, who was up to what, and why, and with whom—the usual friendly gossip one could count on from the town hearth-witch—and then Claire's eyes sharpened, and she got down to business. "What have you learned while you've been here?" asked Claire, and for a moment the Keeper felt like she might have been a schoolgirl in a classroom at some point in her life, though she couldn't remember ever being that age. *So we're beyond the formalities already.*

She thought for a moment, and closed her eyes. This was a safe place, she was sure of it, though there wasn't much she was sure of. She knew Claire of the hearth was trustworthy, and she hadn't talked to anyone in so long it hurt. She realized she was going to tell her too much, but if she didn't speak to someone, she might burst. She sent up a silent prayer that the hearth-witch would forget everything she was about to say and began, tentatively. "I've had time to think," she started slowly, almost to herself, without looking at Claire. "I've learned something new of myself, after all this time. I love the ocean, still, despite the lives it has taken from me."

"Who has the ocean taken from you?"

"Oh," she said, taken aback. "I don't usually know their names. Keepers, sailors, women, children. Whenever I arrive somewhere and I'm too late to save someone in the water." She paused, struggling to explain. "They don't belong to me in the traditional sense. They're not relations of any sort." She wavered and tried again. "I know I have no right to feel that they are mine, but it feels personal nonetheless." Her right hand had clenched itself into a fist, and she glanced down and deliberately uncurled her fingers.

She peered over at Claire, but there was no judgment on the woman's face. The Keeper hoped she wasn't breaking some rule with this conversation, but she couldn't bring herself to stop the flow of words. "Try as I might," she continued, "I can't remember being a child." She paused again. "And while the perfect afternoon is still fruit, cheese, a pile of books, and the freedom to read them, I miss human companionship, if I ever had it. I can't remember," she said, her face blank. "Before you, the last I'd spoken with anyone was months ago."

Claire opened her mouth to say something, then closed it. She delicately cleared her throat and asked "When?"

"Months ago."

"I know, but when?" repeated Claire.

The Keeper looked over at her new friend, across their steaming mugs of tea and across an even farther distance. Claire of the hearth didn't blink, and they reached a silent understanding.

The Keeper took a deep breath. "In the fifteen hundreds, I think," she replied, her face expressionless. She waited for Claire to flinch, to react in some way, any way, but she simply nodded and sipped her tea quietly, and then looked up, waiting.

Extraordinary, thought the Keeper. She didn't sense danger, and nothing could harm her here. She wanted to spill her words as quickly as possible, for this had never happened before. She half expected Claire to disappear in a puff of friendly smoke.

"I'm not sure how you know, or how much, or even if this is allowed," began the Keeper slowly, dragging out her words to give Claire an opportunity to volunteer some information, or disappear. *I'm going mad*, she thought.

She sat gawking at the hearth-witch until Claire adjusted her position and gently prompted, "Fifteen hundreds or thereabouts?"

The Keeper couldn't help a slight smile. "Yes," she said. "Or thereabouts. It was a typical assignment for me, only an hour or so, and I exchanged a few words with the daughter of the keeper on my way out. The keeper of that Light never saw me, but his daughter did. I'm never certain if they see me because I interact with them directly, as I'm doing with you, or if they see me because there is something about them that sees." She looked at Claire expectantly, but the woman remained silent.

The Keeper's eyes looked into the middle distance, and as Claire of the hearth watched, she folded into her memories.

Kõpu tuletorn, Hiiumaa, Estonia, 1541

That girl had been a tiny thing, a few years old, and she had had no other family. The Keeper had looked into the wide, almond-shaped eyes of the child and smiled, and she had received a tentative, shy smile in return. The little girl followed her with wide eyes as she tended the Light, and the Keeper, wary of startling her, had left her to herself while she carried out her task. She fed small pieces of wood to the bonfire atop the tower while the child's father slept deeply, heedless of her quietly carried-out movements. She looked out to sea. Sometimes she could see the particular ship she had been called to keep the Light for in that particular moment in time, but more often than that she was called to keep the Light without ever seeing who it was for, or if it was for anyone at all.

She finished tending the Light and sat on a low bench to wait until her time came. The little girl watched her from the other side of the room, taking in her every movement, her clothes, her face, and her hair. The Lightkeeper smiled at her and asked gently, "What is your name?" Words had always been given to her, both to speak and to understand. She didn't know why, but it had always been this way: she both understood and was understood in any tongue.

"Alina" was the shy answer.

"Alina," murmured the Lightkeeper. "That is a beautiful name." The little girl blushed beside her, wide-eyed. The Keeper thought of the great Estonian composer Arvo Pärt, so far in the future, who would write a song for another Alina, and of how she wished this little girl could hear it. "Alina, make sure your father is well rested, for the Light nearly went out," she said softly.

The girl nodded solemnly, and so low that it was difficult to hear, she murmured, "He has not been sleeping." She bowed her head and did not meet the Keeper's eyes. "He cries for Mama."

She crossed the room and knelt to place her hand on Alina's shoulder gently, meeting her somber eyes. The child's shoulder felt slight, like a small bird, under her hand. They all had bodies that awaited death, that felt as though they would just ascend from beneath her fingers. Her hand tightened on the girl's shoulder, as if to anchor her to the earth, and to life. "You must be brave," she heard herself say, "and help him keep the Light." Did a task make grief more bearable? She didn't know.

She walked outside to clear her head, turning the corner around the small hut, her hand burning with the feel of the small bird-boned child, her body aching to take her up in her arms, tell her that all would be well, that her sleeping father would emerge from his fog of grief, that her childhood would not be forever pockmarked by her mother's death and that her life would matter. But as it was, she saw, glancing around, even running water was a few hundred years away. Her life will be difficult *and brief, she thought. At least it won't be difficult and interminable.*

She shivered in her cloak, and between one step and the next trans-lated to a new Light, its embers flickering, a young man asleep on a strong arm at his desk, and she was off at once.

"Alina," murmured Claire of the hearth. "A life lived a long time ago."

"Yes," said the Keeper. "A very long time ago. And it is so easy to become attached to them, to want to *stay*. To want to keep and be kept." Her voice was tainted with longing, and she heard it and cringed at the sound. "I know better," she said, hoping the bitterness wasn't as obvious as the longing. Her hand unconsciously touched her throat as though it still burned with the memory. She tugged her scarf aside.

Claire's eyes sharpened. "What is that?"

"A lesson," said the Keeper, "not to try to keep anything. It's one of my earliest memories."

She had landed along a coast in what was likely Cornwall, the Light stark white against a sky of ash. She tended the sick lightkeeper for a long, dreary day, while the very young children played out of doors, their mother away at market. He was delirious with fever and called her an angel while she bathed his face with a cold cloth, one eye on him, a weather eye on the sea and the Light, and the two in the back of her head on the children.

It was a whale-oil lamp, and someone had clearly mixed some of the less pure summer press into the store of oil, possibly to save money. It had been thick and hard, and the whale oil had congealed, needing to be warmed before she could use it in the spider lamps. It was dirty, stinking work, and when she finally got the lamp lit it sent plumes of smoke into the lantern room so that she was driven out of the structure, coughing the whole way down the winding staircase.

By the afternoon she was great friends with the children, though even that early on she had learned not to be too friendly or get too attached. She hated to think what she left behind. The memory of a waif hovering around the Light, likely smelling faintly of oil, ghosting in and out of lives. In her vanity she hoped the trace she left was more pleasant, but she strove to make as few ripples as possible, wherever and whenever she landed, knowing the memory of her presence faded as she left.

That gloomy summer day, when she heard footsteps up the path and the children hesitated a moment before turning to run to their mother, the youngest took the necklace of woven pink heath flowers from her own neck and handed them with a shy smile to the Lightkeeper. Hoping the child hadn't seen her hesitation, she smiled widely and accepted them. She turned from her and slipped the flowers over her head. She took two steps and found herself on a new shoreline, the sun shining brightly, her coat gone, and her hair in a braid. The heath-necklace, which she had hoped would fare well through the translation, had not only been crisped to ash, but its outline had been etched in a permanent circlet on the skin of her neck.

"So here they are," she said, unable to keep the bitterness out of her voice then. "Small, dark heath flowers in a chain about my neck for however intolerably long my life—" She stopped.

"Flowers from a child," murmured Claire. "You aren't allowed to keep even that." The Lightkeeper noticed that it wasn't a question, but said nothing.

"I've tested that particular rule many times," she said with equal parts frustration and resignation. "I've concluded that it has to do with intention. I think. I once doodled a little lighthouse and kept it in my right skirt pocket, intending to keep it." She gave Claire a defiant smile. "It's etched onto my right hip."

Claire laughed. "How do you know it has to do with intention?"

"Well, this left me cold with dread at the time, but I can laugh about it now," the Keeper started. "I realized mid-step between two Lights—between times, while I was translating, that is—"

"Translating?"

"That's what I call it when I'm taken from one Light and deposited at another. It takes less than a moment, and I never know where I am going. I can't stay once the Change happens, no matter how much I want to. Sometimes I go back to the same Light in the same time, but it happens rarely. More often I'm at different Lights or different times. I've been tending Lights as long as I can remember."

"Tending them?" asked Claire.

"I am called to a place and time to care either for the Light or for its keeper. Sometimes there's a life to be saved at sea," she said, as if reciting a lesson.

Claire looked as though she wanted to comment, but said nothing for a moment, and then gently prompted, "You were mid-step."

"Yes. Mid-step between translations, when I realized I had a leatherbound copy of *Moby Dick* in my hand."

"No!" exclaimed Claire.

"Yes," she laughed. "And I cannot abide *Moby Dick*, for reasons entirely to do with me, and not so much to do with Melville. My options were rather"—she paused, delicately—"limited at that keeper's house, and I'd tried for the third time to read it all the way through, failing yet again. There wasn't time to drop the book, though even *Moby Dick* I would have felt awful about leaving on a shore, exposed to the elements."

Claire sat, eyes wide, a grin on her face.

"I could feel the cold wind of my new assignment on my face, but I couldn't bear to open my eyes. I thought I would have the whole of that interminable novel tattooed on my body," she said, laughing.

They laughed together for a moment. "But you didn't?" said Claire.

The Keeper screwed her eyes together tightly for a moment. "I couldn't bear to look," she said. "But yes, my face blessedly didn't read 'call me Ishmael.'" They laughed together again, trying to shake the sadness from earlier. As though an unsettling thought had occurred to her, the Keeper added more softly, "A little whale did appear on the instep of my foot, though. I found it in the bath later that day, and it faded as soon as I saw it." They both sat quietly for a moment. "Whoever or whatever controls me," she said slowly, "has a sense of humor, at the least."

"And justice," added Claire. The Keeper nodded her assent, if grudgingly.

"Yes. I've grown up a bit, I think. I haven't always been as you see me now," said the Keeper.

"What do you mean? You mean you've grown older?"

"No. I don't think so. I haven't changed in what feels like decades. I mean I've grown here." She put her pointer finger to the middle of her forehead. "At least I hope I have. I used to hope for a home, a family, but not anymore. Now I just want rest," she told Claire honestly. "I hope you remember none of this," she added, glancing at the woman beside her. Claire said nothing, but she suddenly seemed interested in the contents of her teacup.

"I've been traveling like flotsam through time, tending Lights, for what seems like ages, and unsure of why. Why I tend Lights, why I travel, why I have no home." She paused for a moment, spent. "So many whys. Why you feel like a specter to me. Why the last keeper didn't feel that way at all," she said softly.

Claire leaned forward in her seat a little. "The last keeper?" she asked.

"Yes. Ronan, you called him. He was solid. Most of you—all of

47

you—feel like light to me. Except him. It troubles me." Sitting at Claire's hearth and being honest about so many things made her realize this had been weighing heavily on her mind, though she hadn't openly acknowledged it to herself. Claire nodded, but continued to say nothing.

"Why I have no choice," continued the Keeper, as though she hadn't noticed.

That caught Claire's attention. She cleared her throat. "Don't you?" It was a question, but not exactly.

The Keeper's hands fisted in what might have been remembered pain. "I tried once to do nothing," she said. "It was during a particularly terrible month. It was cold and wet and interminable, one assignment after another, all cold and miserable. I arrived during a storm and couldn't find the keeper. He was neither asleep, nor sick, nor dead. He was just missing. And I stood there at the base of that flickering Light and looked out to sea and saw the ship that was foundering." She paused, catching her breath, composing herself. "I was just so tired of doing something about everything, you know?" she said, a note of entreaty in her voice. She sighed audibly.

"So I did nothing, Claire. Don't ask me how I know that there were one hundred and twenty-seven souls aboard that ship. I just do. No sooner had I spat on the base of that Light in defiance than I was translating to a new shore. Claire, I wasn't given time to reconsider!" The other woman's gaze didn't falter, and she waited while the Keeper composed herself.

"I can imagine them, slipping around that slick deck, trying to secure the ship, straining to see the Light that was barely flickering above me. I know it guttered and died, and that they died. Don't ask how I do, but I can hear them sometimes. They didn't matter to me then, but they do now." She couldn't count how many times those voices had screamed and broken against imagined rocks, bolting her upright in whatever bed she found herself in. She had failed them an eternity of times in her dreams after that day. "In any case," she finished, "I understood the message. Do the task, or it won't be done."

The Keeper, perhaps feeling as though her confession of guilt finally meant the end of formalities, reached down to pry her boots off, then tucked her feet under her as Claire had done. The cat Twitch felt that this gave him leave to lightly pounce onto the arm of the chair and settle himself on the Keeper's lap with imperious condescension. The Keeper stroked a hand into the warm fur above the steady heartbeat, feeling the cat's small, regular breaths, and then his contented purring.

They drank an entire second cup in silence. Finally, Claire of the hearth asked, "Do you have peace now?"

The Keeper considered this while she sipped the last dregs of her tea, now lukewarm, over Twitch's head, while the sun waned. "Not yet," she admitted quietly, "but soon." Having lived with herself long enough, she knew she was close. Something was about to perfect her. She sighed into the empty cup. Knowing what she had learned so far, she knew it would not be comfortable in the least.

She went into town several more times during those weeks. She spent time in Claire's kitchen, drinking tea by her fire and talking about herbs and gardening. They didn't mention Ronan, and they didn't talk of the Light again. Claire had listened to all she had wanted to share, and there was only more of the same, as far as the Keeper was concerned. Instead, they had cozy chats about laying by seeds for winter and shared tricks for dealing with the peckish hens in the yard, while the Keeper continued to keep the Light into early December, when the world was a monastery of silence.

~: 5 :~

The saddest aspect of life is that there is no one on earth
whose happiness is such that he won't sometimes wish
he were dead rather than alive.

HERODOTUS, *THE HISTORIES*

S HE COULDN'T HAVE IMAGINED A more perfect situation. There
was running water, piles of books on every surface, deep armchairs by the window, a truly remarkable supply of tea, and the endless generosity of the chickens. *Well, the internet would be an improve-*
ment, she thought. *And some science fiction and fantasy. Or an actual*
man. But this'll do.

Astonishingly enough, no one came for this keeper. There was
no appearance of an assistant one. No one sent a greeting, a message, or supplies. No one inquired about his health. And the winter
weather kept the tourists away. She continued dipping into the jar
he kept on the mantle for the small amount of supplies she wanted
from town, the memories of the townspeople closing up behind her
like a sewn seam, with the exception of Claire of the hearth. She
liked going into town and chatting, even if it was with Dahlia for a

moment, before she bought the hearth bread made by Claire.

As for Claire, she still didn't know what to make of the woman, though she was grateful beyond words for her. During their last conversation, the Keeper had finally worked up enough courage to ask Claire directly if she somehow remembered her. It had taken courage because, as the Keeper had finally admitted to herself, she was afraid of the other woman's answer. *What if she knows me? What if she doesn't?* Both answers could be equally terrifying. Claire had answered very simply that yes, she knew her, from years before, and that she didn't think it wise to say anything else.

Claire had hesitated and looked uncharacteristically vulnerable then. The Keeper sat with a racing heart, torn between wanting to shake an answer out of the woman in front of her, and wanting to do something about her friend's obvious discomfort.

"Forgive me, my dear," said Claire finally. "I understand this must be frustrating for you. But please trust me that it's best this way." She hesitated again.

"What is it, Claire?" asked the Keeper, angling her body toward the other woman's chair.

Claire shook her head. "When you see me next," she started, then stopped and cleared her throat. "I was a bit . . ." She trailed off. "Lost. I was a bit lost when you next meet me."

The Keeper didn't know what to say to this, so she nodded. After a while she quietly asked, "Is there anything you want me to say to you?"

Claire smiled, an involuntary tug that was genuine and unguarded. "What a wonder it is to know you, my friend," she said, and the Keeper felt that she meant it. "No, nothing in particular. Just be patient, if you can."

The Keeper couldn't imagine being anything less with Claire of the hearth. They finished their tea in silence and Claire walked her to the door, waiting while the Keeper bundled herself into a scarf and Ronan of the Light's coat for the walk back home. Claire raised an eyebrow at the coat, but the Keeper only shrugged unapologetically. "It looks good on me," she said, eyes twinkling.

Her friend smiled back. "Yes, it does," she agreed.

The Keeper turned toward home, but a thought stayed her hand on the doorknob. "Claire," she began, "I may be called away suddenly. Do forgive me, if I don't come one day. It wouldn't be because I chose—" There was a thick feeling in the back of her throat, and for what seemed like the thousandth time in her life, she felt as though she *must* cry, or the dam within her would burst. Claire reached out and put a hand on her shoulder. It had the same light, ascending feel as all of them, and though the Keeper had felt that hand before, this time it brought a pang to her heart. *Not you too, Claire.* It suddenly struck her that Claire would die one day, and the thought was unbearable, until she found herself caught in a tight embrace.

That embrace lingered with her on the walk back home, and while she tended the Light. She realized later that it had been good-bye.

The Light was just remote enough to be a bother to reach, but still necessary enough to keep ships from smashing themselves on the unforgiving coast. *He was too self-reliant*, she thought. And if anything, she knew how to keep a Light lit well enough that no one realized anything was amiss.

In the course of that brief interlude in her life—one season, no more—she made him a grave marker, batted around the idea of writing down an account of her travels, dismissed it, and tended his garden instead. His headstone, which she chiseled herself into the slab of granite she had found, simply read "Ronan of the Light." She always thought of it as *his* garden, not hers, and had to remind herself that the old man was not coming back, and that she was likely tending it for the next occupant. Eventually, she gave in and jotted down a few thoughts here and there, and left them tucked safely into the copy of Herodotus that she kept by the teapot in the kitchen. No one read Herodotus much, which she had long ago concluded was in large part responsible for the state of the world. She was sentimental about that copy.

She finally gave in to her desire to slip the beautiful little comb into her hair while she was awake. She knew it was selfish and that if she translated it would be lost, but it was such a pleasure for her to trace the smooth curly waves and small leaves. She dressed in the mornings and slipped it into her hair like a talisman before facing the day, fingers alighting on her hair to feel for it.

After two months it became *the* kitchen, *the* garden, *the* Light. Not *his*, but *the*. And though she hated herself for the small flicker of warmth within her, she no longer knew how to kill it, which made the going, when she went, that much harder. She hadn't just sent out tendrils, but had rooted herself into the earth of the place so deeply that when she was up-earthed, it was a hard lesson, for one so worldly, in the dangerous recklessness of hope.

One moment she was walking toward the house from the garden, a bunch of rosemary in her hands—

Start Point Light, Devon, England, 1865

—the next she was wearing a coat crusted with sea salt, standing on another shore during a thunderstorm, the cruel-fingered wind raking across her face, her eyes squinting out to sea, where she was sure someone was battling the waves to take back a life. She reached up into her hair to feel for it, knowing it wouldn't be there, but hoping against hope. Her hand met no comb, but a wild profusion of curls, oddly, for her hair had never held a curl in her life, and she who had no prayers left that day sent up a word that it had fallen out before she translated. She couldn't bear the thought of it destroyed by her selfishness. She spared a thought of thanks that she had left her cottage—for that is what it had finally become—on a clear night when the Light would not be particularly needed, and then the small flame within her went out and stayed out.

The cold numbed her sufficiently that her feet churned toward the waves, the slicing wind a suitable foil for her pain and rage. *I knew it*, she thought bitterly, putting one foot in front of the other in the cold sand. *Why didn't I prepare myself for this? How could I let myself think*—she stopped. *Hope.* She had let herself hope. *Stupid*, she spat. *Negligent.* She hated herself for that. *Reckless*, she thought desperately.

Far above her from beside the Light she heard the deep mournful blast of the station's foghorn. She felt a chasm open up within her, deep and dividing. She felt marooned, as though she stood on a high cliff on an island, separated from the mainland by a dark churning sea, and no bridge in sight. Her hem was quickly soaked by the salt water at the ocean's edge, and as she squinted against the dark she glimpsed the keeper, not far from shore, clinging to the remains of a small skiff.

As she stepped into the water she realized that she no longer wanted to live. It was not much in the way of a revelation, but it was truer than anything else just then. She didn't want the guilt of the hundred and twenty-seven, or the innumerable others she had failed. She missed her one friend, the only one who remembered her and cared about her. "Claire!" she choked out.

She was cold and tired. She hated being cold. She felt as though she would never be able to sleep long enough or be warm enough ever again. As she came upon the keeper, the sorrowful sound of the foghorn reached her again, marking the passage of a full minute. The man looked at her as though at an apparition and floated eagerly into her arms. He weighed nothing, and she felt like a lead weight in contrast as she easily pulled him to shore. She floated him the last few feet and watched for a moment, treading water as he washed up onto the sand. *Just like a dead weight,* she thought. She watched him vomiting seawater and knew he would live.

It would have been the work of a few powerful strokes of her arms and a mere moment to swim to shore, but she continued to tread water instead, her skirts heavy around her legs. The foghorn sounded again. *I'm so tired,* she thought, and in a moment of sorrow as deep as the ocean she thought she might drift off in the cold for a bit. *No one is waiting for me at home,* she thought. *Home. The cottage and Claire.* She would never see them again. The thought made her despair complete. She trod water for a moment longer, and then stopped.

It was cold, and the water came up over her head, filling her ears. She tried to think of where she would rather be, and she mentally placed herself in the armchair beside Ronan of the Light's fire, with the blanket Claire had knitted for her over her knees, a book in her lap, her mug of tea steaming beside her. She held onto that image as her eyes and mouth filled with the tang of seawater. She thought in a moment of panic that if there was a chance she could go back there, she might not want to die quite yet. The foghorn blasted once more, as if a final warning, and then she was pulled down, down, into cold darkness.

∴ 6 ∾

Whatever comes from God is impossible for a man to turn back.

HERODOTUS, *THE HISTORIES*

For within her is a spirit intelligent, holy, unique, manifold, subtle,
active, incisive, unsullied, lucid, invulnerable, benevolent, sharp,
irresistible, beneficent, loving to man, steadfast, dependable,
unperturbed, almighty, all-surveying, penetrating all intelligent,
pure and most subtle spirits; for Wisdom is quicker to move than
any motion; she is so pure, she pervades and permeates all things.
She is a breath of the power of God, pure emanation
of the glory of the Almighty.

WISDOM OF SOLOMON 7:22–25 (JERUSALEM BIBLE)

SHE WAS ON A NEW shore, her hair clean and her sopping gown
dry. She looked down. She was wearing a gown of sea green,
and it was light and airy around her body, floating in the warm foam
at her bare feet. The sand was as white as the heart of the fire, but
dry and soft on her skin. The wind playfully picked up strands of
her hair as though it enjoyed lifting them gently from her neck. She

had felt moments before that nothing could really warm her, that she had been in too many cold, miserable places, worn too many sodden gowns, been exposed to too many stiff ocean breezes to ever be properly warm again, but this sun overhead warmed her easily. The darkness and the cold were swept away as though they had never been. The sight of the sand and the blue of the sea cleaned her vision, purified her lungs, and she felt light and alive. Most incredibly of all, she realized, looking up and down the shore, there was no lighthouse.

She knew with the certainty of dreams that there was no one to rescue from the sea in this place. The sea, indeed, had a different spirit here. It *has* a spirit, she realized with a start. It was no less wild, but it would not dare—nor indeed did it desire—to harm any soul. In fact, she could feel, as it lapped at her ankles, that it simply wanted to greet her. It was like a wide, deep, warm mother, holding all of life within her, and had no need or desire to claim any human life. *I'm careful not to*, the foam corrected her gently. The Keeper startled at the deep, assured voice that resonated against her chest from the sea. Wide-eyed, she stared out at the sea, but it did not speak again.

There is no one who needs me here, thought the Keeper. Was that a strange weight that was lifted from her shoulders, or a heaviness that settled on her heart? After all, wasn't the need for her existence the only reason she was alive, flitting from one shore to another? *If no one needs me, do I cease to exist?* The thought filled the emptiness within her with a deep sadness.

The foam at her feet touched her differently, with what felt like empathy, and though she had no memories of her mother, she imagined this was what a mother's arms would feel like, keeping tragedy at bay. She wanted to lie down in the sand and let the ocean cradle her and make her as weightless as she had been after rescuing the last keeper and drifting to her death. *Is this death?* she wondered again, and then felt the foam at her feet quicken.

57

She sensed a powerful presence and a bright light warmed her back. She turned, drawn to the warmth, but it was too bright, and she winced away. Blinded, she squeezed her eyes shut and dropped to her knees in the sand.

Instantly, the light dimmed, became a column, and when the Keeper tentatively squinted her eyes open, she could just make out an outline. It was the shape of a person. *A Woman*, she thought. The Woman walked toward her and continued to dim until all that was left of her brightness was a faint warm glow beneath her golden skin.

The Keeper briefly imagined the warmth of this Woman erasing the cold of every grain of sand from every beach of every assignment in her long existence.

The Woman was tall, her steps majestic, and she picked her way unhurriedly along the sand. Both her hair and her gown shifted around her like waves, sliding and cresting on an unseen wind.

The Keeper saw her face and held the breath she had drawn in. If anyone had asked her later how the Woman looked, she would have puzzled over colors and shapes but said definitively that she was like a gentle breath, or the surface of a stirred sea. The Woman's face was like an immovable stone in that moving sea. It did not waver, and the Keeper knew that even if everything around her moved, the Woman would be a haven in any storm. She exhaled her caught breath, and the Woman's face filled her with an indescribable peace.

"And so must you be," said the Woman. Her words crested over the Keeper, whose eyes closed, absorbing the power of her voice.

Almost helplessly, the Keeper said, "I—I think I just tried to kill myself."

"Yes, you did," replied the Woman simply. Her eyes were full of compassion. The water swirled reassuringly at the Keeper's feet, and the Woman's face broke into a sad smile. It stopped her breath. It felt like Love itself was gazing at her, and finding her somehow worthy of itself. "I am Sophia," came the strong voice. "I am the Wisdom of the King outside of Time, and I keep all Lights."

The Keeper's knees weakened and she felt herself falling to the sand, but in an instant Wisdom had taken two strides and was bending beside her, lifting her with a firm grip to her feet once again. "First, take this." She stretched her right hand above her, and her fingers seemed to reach far, far up into the bright expanse of the sky above. She reached and reached, and the Keeper was certain she had reached all the way up to the sun overhead.

Her fingers didn't burn or smoke as she cupped some of the light of the sun in her palm. Her fingers fisted over the light, and she brought her hand back down to the Keeper. An orb of light glowed brightly, shining like the rays of the sun through Wisdom's fingers, and the Keeper couldn't look directly at it.

"Open your mouth, daughter," Wisdom said, and the Keeper did, without hesitation. Wisdom placed the glowing orb on her tongue. It tasted of sunny apricots, and the Keeper felt the long, warm slide of it down her throat as she swallowed. It settled in her middle and burned there with comforting warmth, like the small sun that it was, and she felt warmth spread through her chest, giving her life and strength.

Wisdom watched her as she savored the sun, then in an unhurried voice that belied the urgency of her words said, "Next time, remember what you have." The Keeper looked at her, confused for a moment, but with the apricot taste on her tongue, her thoughts were somehow sharper than they had ever been.

I have time, she thought silently. The All-Keeper nodded encouragingly at her. *I have this body, which doesn't bleed or break.* Another nod. *I have . . .* Her thoughts trailed off, and her imagination temporarily failed her.

Wisdom didn't look disappointed, just gently said, "Think of it when you can. Now come. Let us walk together, you and I. You have questions." The Keeper silently fell into step beside Wisdom as she walked along the seashore, the sun warm on their backs.

There was no pressure from the sea or the Woman at her side. She took her time, and long minutes passed before the Keeper said anything. What did one ask first, after all, when she wanted to ask everything at once?

Who am I? Why am I pulled through time? Is the only reason for my existence to keep the Lights? Why do I not remember being a child? Who are my parents? Do I have parents? Why do I not age? Why do I have no control over anything? Why am I not allowed to keep anything? Why am I not allowed to die?

She blurted suddenly "Am I dead?" and instantly regretted the unworthy first question, until the Woman at her side turned to her with a smile that loosened the knot in her middle. She wanted to appear poised in front of the Woman and to please her, as one would want to please a beloved mother. She looked down at her feet.

"Not now," answered Wisdom quietly.

The Keeper said nothing. She wanted to assure Wisdom that she wouldn't do anything like *that* again, but she had no words. There were hardly words for the stone in the heart that had allowed her to try to die, and there was only a void of words in the aftermath. Wisdom said nothing, merely walked beside her on the shore of that strange sea, which continued to ebb and flow gently against her ankles in comfort.

There were too many questions to ask, some foolish, she knew, but there was one question that had been on her mind recently. "Why is it," the Keeper asked, "that most people are able to see me, but almost none remember me?"

"Why do you think?"

"I think they see me when I interact with them. When I stop, the memory fades." She continued, her confidence growing. "And I think few people remember me. Maybe just Claire. I think she may be my friend."

The All-Keeper considered her for a moment. "Yes. She is your friend. And yes. They see you when you interact with them. The ones that remember you do so because they are paying attention and see truly. You linger in their memories because they have some knowledge of you."

The Keeper felt the light that she had swallowed like a warm fire in her belly. It felt like it was spreading, climbing up her throat, expanding until it reached all her limbs, and suffusing her with light. She suddenly thought that her time with Wisdom was running out. She frantically thought of the next few questions she wanted to ask: the big *why*, why was this happening? Who was she? Where did she come from? What happened next? How much time . . . but she could feel the Woman beside her fading, or maybe she was fading. She closed her eyes for a moment, absorbing the calm of the place, the peace of the Woman beside her, and the warmth of the sun.

A moment later she was back in the cold ocean. She could hear the keeper she had rescued on the shore retching violently, trying to expel seawater. The foghorn sounded far above her, its sound less ominous than it had been moments before. She didn't feel the cold then. She felt the warmth of the light from the sun she had swallowed, warmth in every part of her body. She trod water and thought, *I have the warmth of the sun.*

Her arms and legs swept out into the cold water around her for a few moments while she thought of the answer Wisdom had given her. So it was the people who saw her and knew her that remembered her. *What does that mean? That since nobody remembers, nobody sees? Do I walk around all day, speaking with people, and they with me, but we don't actually see one another?* She thought of Claire of the hearth, and how, though she did not know her well, she saw her, knew her, and remembered her. *That's why she remembers,* she thought. "I have a friend," she whispered aloud, and feeling more alive than she had been in a long time, she stopped treading water, sank beneath the water for a moment, and rose with the ease of a seal, her dark curls slicked back from her face as she swam back to shore.

~: 7 :~

*The longer the span of someone's existence, the more certain he is
to see and suffer much that he would rather have been spared.*

HERODOTUS, *THE HISTORIES*

Bodie Island Light, Nags Head, North Carolina, 1876

THE KEEPER MATERIALIZED ALONG A coast in mid-morning, a hint of spring in the air. Roughly twenty feet from her a young woman stood defensively before two men, whose backs were to the Keeper.

The men might have been bulky sailors, and from the way they were dressed, they had either arrived from a shipwreck or were recent customers of a pub, for their clothes were torn and wet, with only one intact shoe between them. They stood close together. The Keeper glanced at the woman, and a chill ran down her spine at the hunted look on the woman's face.

The woman was petite, dark haired, brown eyed, with a pointed chin. She was wearing a gown that had been carefully mended so as to not show that she lived in near poverty. *I don't like this at all,* thought the Keeper. Time seemed to rush forward in a torrent.

One of the men barked something at the woman, she shrank away, and they pursued her to the base of the Light, where they were upon her in an instant. One man grabbed the woman roughly by the forearm. An animal cry tore from her throat, waking the Keeper from her dazed disbelief.

The woman cried "Matthew!" The Keeper looked, but there was no one around. *What do I do?* she thought, watching helplessly.

"Matthew!" cried the woman again. The first man yanked her back against the Light, pushing her roughly against the stone structure. She fought and cried wildly while the Keeper watched in horror.

"Stop," a voice croaked, and the Keeper knew it was hers. *There's no one else to help.*

The woman saw her, and her face held confusion, hope. One of the men glanced back at the Keeper, and his glance slid over her like oil.

"Help!" cried the woman, and the second man turned back toward her, viciously slapped her with the back of his hand across the face. The Keeper saw blood.

She heard her own heartbeats, one after another, agonizingly slow, pounding in her head, and as she heard them she felt a tide of pure rage rise up within her. She hated these men. She hated that the woman before her was helpless before them because she was a woman alone. She hated that they thought they could do as they liked because she was weak and they were stronger and could take what they wanted. She hated that this was the way women lived in this world. She hated the powerlessness of the woman in front of her, and then she didn't feel powerless anymore. The anger swelled up in her like a tide, and she felt it unfurl darkly within her heart until it moved her feet forward.

The Keeper's voice came from the same depth as her rage. "I said stop!" she roared, and was upon them in an instant, whacking the first man's arm away as she approached. Coming upon the second man, who had his hand up around the woman's mouth, she grabbed his arm at the wrist and squeezed. There was a sickening sound, and then one heartbeat of stillness between when the woman's screaming ceased and the man's screaming began.

The Keeper's vision cleared and she looked at the man. He was holding his forearm, which now ended in a bloody stump. She looked down at her own hand. It was slick with blood and clenched in a tight fist. On the ground between them lay the rough hand, dirty fingernails curled into the palm, as if holding a secret.

The Keeper took one look at the abject horror on the woman's face and, stepping quickly forward, caught her slumping body in her arms. She lightly hefted the woman, then turned to the men, both crouching on the ground. The man clutching his arm was still screaming, though his gaze on her was full of pure hatred. She wanted the sound to stop. She took a step forward, and the men, as one, fled from before her.

The Keeper slung the woman over her shoulder and glanced at her own bloody hand. She had never hurt anyone in her life. A wave of revulsion rose up inside her, and she felt a sinking in her stomach. She found a water pump by the side of the house, and hurrying to it, ran wave after wave of cold water over her hand, scrubbing with the cake of soap by the cold metal pump until the water ran clear and her hand was red from scrubbing.

The woman still slung over her shoulder, the Keeper made quick work of burying the severed hand behind the house, the ground parting easily under her fingers. She dusted them off just as the woman was stirring.

The Keeper carried her inside the house and eased her down to her feet, hands steadying her shoulders.

"Mooncussers," she murmured faintly.

The Keeper nodded, understanding. "False-light starters," she muttered. It made sense.

The wreckers, or mooncussers, as the woman called them, were false-light starters. They were salvage crews who had long been used to scavenging shipwrecks for usable cargo, scouring the coast at night for the hulks of great ships tipped on their sides during low tide. There was a window of time before high tide swept in and filled the tilted vessels, potentially sinking them entirely.

Mooncussers were not interested in saving any crew still aboard. Their interest was purely commercial. They kept an easy truce with harbormasters and captains, who saw them in the same light as carrion-feeders. Plainly, they were unpleasant, but they survived off of castoffs and didn't hurt anyone.

The relationship had fundamentally changed with the advent of the lighthouse, when their brisk business slowed to a trickle. It didn't take long before some of them began to imitate the signals of real lighthouses to create confusion and cause ships to founder and crash into shoals or reefs, giving up their contents once again.

"I can't abide wreckers," spat the Keeper.

She heard a pounding of footsteps outside and a cry of "Roo? Roo??" just as the Change came over her. The woman swayed a moment, and the Keeper reached a hand to steady her shoulder before stepping back. The Keeper felt herself departing the room as the door flew open and a dark-haired young man burst in, in a complete panic. He didn't notice the Keeper but rushed over to the young woman, who, without hesitation, threw herself into his arms. "Roo, I saw blood outside and I . . ." The Keeper felt herself held there a moment longer, immaterial, observing.

The man held the woman tightly and brushed her hair back from her forehead in a familiar manner. He murmured something to her, and she stood comfortably in the circle of his arms.

The Keeper averted her face from the clear affection between them and firmly tamped down the knifing longing it evoked in her. *I don't have that*, she thought, unable to think of a similar thing she did have. *Sorry, Wisdom,* she thought, *I can't think of anything.* She faded into the background, and before the woman lifted her head from her beloved's shoulder, the Keeper translated.

~: 8 :~

Suffering with a courageous spirit, O Lion, bear the unbearable.

HERODOTUS, *THE HISTORIES*

Gurnet Point, Plymouth Harbor, Massachusetts Bay Colony, American War for Independence, 1776

SHE LANDED DURING A HOWLING rainstorm, reverberating with thunder. She lifted her rain-soaked lashes and saw two steady beams from the powerful twin Lights above her. The Lights were about fifteen feet apart, separated by a dwelling in between. The wind ripped at her hair, loosening her braid, and she turned to squint out to sea to see if there was a ship in peril. *Beaufort score: 4,* she thought, and shivered.

Suddenly, one Light began to flicker above her. She'd taken two steps toward the tower when a little boy exploded from the base of the Light. "Johnny!" cried a woman behind him. "Quickly now, to the house, keep the lights doused!" The boy flew past her on stubby legs, not seeing her in the shadows, and the woman, presumably his mother, dashed out on his heels.

She was a stout middle-aged woman, her hair pulled back in a severe bun, her sodden skirts sweeping the hard-packed ground in a swirl around her ankles. She had a harried look about her, but when she saw the Keeper, she stopped with an involuntary scream, her hand flying to her heart. "Good heavens! Who are you?" She looked her over from head to toe. "How did you get out here? At this time of night!"

"I—I'm from the Company," stammered the Keeper. She rarely had to explain her presence to anyone, let alone the resident light-keeper. "I've been sent to see if there is anything I can do to help," she said in a rush.

"Why would they send *you*?" the woman said, not unkindly, but baffled nonetheless. "They sent a woman? In this miserable weather? However did you get here?" She frowned down at her, and then realizing they were both getting wet, she shook her head. "Never mind. We have to put the other Light out. They're scouring the coastline tonight and they've got cannons. They'll blow us to kingdom come." She looked back at her and shook her head. "You look like a ghost." The ground shook from the force of lightning striking not far from them. "I don't understand how—" She looked back up at the Light. It was flickering. "It's still lit—we have to snuff it out. Quickly now."

The Keeper had never in her life snuffed out a Light purposely on a dark night, and she wasn't entirely clear about why they were putting this one out, but she knew urgency in a voice when she heard it. She ran on the woman's heels to the other Light, twining up the staircase behind the older woman. *Older being relative, of course,* she thought.

They reached the top stair and the small platform that held the second of the twin lights. It burned whale oil, she could tell immediately, and it gave her a primitive, ill feeling in the pit of her stomach. Smoke filled the small space, and she automatically picked up a rag to start cleaning off the glass in the lantern, to make the Light more visible from the sea, before remembering they didn't want the Light to be visible from the sea. The woman worked quickly, extinguishing the flat-wicks of the spider lamp, working as fast as she could. The Keeper stood dumbfounded behind her for a moment, swaying on her feet, trying to figure out what her role in this could possibly be, and then reluctantly started to help the woman extinguish the Light.

Oh, how she hated the smell. She tried not to think of the poor whales killed for the spermaceti oil that was extracted from their heads. As wick after wick was extinguished and carefully trimmed, the small lantern room steadily filled with thick smoke. The oil was pressed to be as clean-burning as possible, but it always created smoke. The woman finished her task, and it was as though the whole world went dark around them, and she was a puppet whose strings were cut. She slumped against the rounded wall of the tower and slid slowly down to the floor.

The Keeper eyed her warily. She didn't seem like the slumping type. The woman looked up at her and shook her head briskly as if to wake herself. "Well then, ghost, that's that, isn't it?" She looked out to sea, and the Keeper had the distinct impression that she was waiting for someone to come home. *Which would be hard to do*, thought the Keeper, *since the Lights are out and the coast black as pitch*, but she didn't point it out.

"My name is Hannah Thomas," said the woman politely. No doubt she thought there was no use in being rude to a ghost, particularly a helpful one.

"I'm a Lightkeeper," replied the Keeper hesitantly. "I haven't a name. I'm here to help you for the moment. I shan't be here long." Perhaps Hannah was dying? What of the little boy, who had headed to the house below?

"How do you do?" asked the other woman. The Keeper inclined her head in acknowledgment. Strange, this gift of politeness in what clearly had to be a trying moment. That surely hadn't lasted into the future. *A shame, that,* thought the Keeper. There was something particularly valiant about being polite when one would rather lie silently slumped on the floor, awaiting possible death by cannon fire.

"My husband left for the war," said Hannah, bleakly. There was just enough moonlight for the Keeper to see the expression on her face. It was a post-bomb blankness, empty and exhausted. Her eyes kept being pulled to the glass overlooking the sea, despite the darkness. "I've been keeping the Lights in his absence. It's difficult some days, what with Johnny and Nate running underfoot and . . ." She trailed off and stopped pretending not to look outside. "Little Hannah tries to help as best she can," she continued. "It's difficult, with their father gone."

With the stench of whale oil filling her nostrils, the Lightkeeper listened while Hannah told her about her husband, her hopes for the future, her fears for her daughter and sons, and her worries over keeping the Lights. Perhaps the anonymity of speaking with a ghost had loosened her tongue, or perhaps it was loneliness. She wanted to hire someone to help her with the work, but the government paid her so little.

"The British vessels often scour the coast," explained Hannah. "The Light may shortly go off for the duration of the war." She paused and a sadness stole over her voice. "It's safer that way."

The Lightkeeper knew that sometimes the patriots would destroy their own lighthouses to goad the British, though it seemed to her like cutting off one's own nose. She watched Hannah in the wan moonlight. *She is so graceful*, thought the Keeper. Hannah had straightened her spine eventually, sitting up straighter against the side of the Light, while she spoke. *Would that I could be this graceful under fire*, she thought admiringly.

The Keeper wasn't sure she should be taking sides in wars— though, truth be told, she already knew the outcome of this one. She thought of the Woman, Wisdom, and how it had felt to swallow the small sun, which she could feel warm within her. *Oh, how I wish I'd had more time with the Woman! I have so many questions to ask her. I want to know why I'm here sitting with this Hannah Thomas in the dark of a snuffed-out Light. Am I here to listen? Perhaps all this woman needs is someone to listen. Is that enough? Is that what my life is for? To help? To go from Light to Light to help in some way?*

She listened to Hannah for a long time, and said nothing, and when the footsteps of one of the boys sounded downstairs as he headed to the base of the Light, she reached out to a startled Hannah, grasped her hand in both of her own and gave them a squeeze. *I have two strong hands to hold Hannah's with,* the Keeper thought. She translated before the child made it up the steps, though to her dying day, Hannah swore that the phantom Keeper had been real, and that her hands had been warm, despite the storm.

∾ 9 ∾

Great things are won by great dangers.

HERODOTUS, *THE HISTORIES*

Rake Point Light, 1908

THE HEAD KEEPER OF THE Rake Point Light was a fastidious man by the name of Ebenezer Wiggins. He kept a strong Light and a tidy cottage, and prided himself on the maintenance of both. He wasn't unlike many keepers in that, while he found great joy in the beam emitted by the Rake Point Light, he was rather less enthusiastic about the near-constant ringing of the fog bell.

He had taken his supper, tended to the Light, and wound the manual fog bell's new clockwork apparatus that, thankfully, had automated the bell ringing. It rang once every thirty seconds and would stay functional for about four days. He barely tolerated the sound of the bell, but there was nothing for it, and as any professional who did a repetitive task learned to do, he had grown insensible to the deafening ring of the bell marking the passage of time. He felt relaxed this evening and had already completed an entry in the log, his small scrawl taking up as little space as possible on the long page.

AUGUST 12, 1908

Light breeze, no ships sighted. Fog bell and Light in good working order. No visitors.

Below that, he had written his name, followed by "Head Keeper." He, in fact, felt so calm and at peace that he was sure something had to be wrong. He checked on the Light, feeling drowsy. Why was he so tired? And then, with the sort of cold-water clarity that came with catastrophe, he realized that it was silent outside and he could only hear the lapping of the waves far below. It was about half past two in the morning when he came to the heart-stopping realization that the fog bell was silent.

The Keeper translated to what looked like a small building adjacent to a lighthouse. She was on a tiny balcony-like precipice that protruded away from the cliff face, out toward the ocean. She took a quick glance up at the sky and could just make out the ring of the corona borealis; a small smile lifted her mouth. A cursory glance revealed that the building housed the fog bell. She wasn't sure what she hated more: whale oil or fog bells, but it was a close tie, in any case.

She thought the love she had for Ronan's cottage was in large part due to the lack of a fog signal at the Loon-Call Light. Perhaps it was an area that didn't have much fog, or perhaps there were other navigational aids, precluding the necessity for the fog signal. In any case, she quite detested them. They were insistently loud, repetitive, with a shrill cry that was obnoxious to her in every way. They rang from twice every fifteen seconds to once every thirty seconds, and she knew of keepers driven mad by the relentless noise. She made her peace with it when she had to work alongside one, but she never enjoyed it.

She was pulling her coat collar up to get the chill off the back of her neck when a deafening bell clanged—all around her, inside her skull, jarring her bones, and reverberating from the small platform out over the inky sea. *Beaufort 12*, she cursed. She looked around, to the right and left, trying to find a way off the platform. There was a door behind the massive bell that led into the small building, which housed the supplies for the upkeep of the fog bell, and she edged around the bell, intent on getting as far away from the automated signal as possible. She got through the door, into the building, and nearly to the outer door before it sounded again, and she paused in mid-step, her hands reflexively and uselessly flying to her ears, while the jarring sound echoed in her bones.

She estimated the bells had been about thirty seconds apart, and when she emerged from the building that held the fog bell she turned her face to the Light, where her real task likely lay. It was burning brightly, and as she gazed up, she saw a keeper come into view in the lantern room far above. He seemed to be in good health, and the Light seemed to be in working order. *Uh-oh*, she thought, glancing back at the fog bell. She noticed two things at once: a thick, insidious fog was rising above the ocean water, and the bell had gone mercifully silent. The stillness was foreboding, eerily calm, and the Keeper reluctantly faced the real reason she had translated to this Light. *Uh-oh*, she thought again.

She wanted the keeper in the Light to realize his fog bell had gone silent, but she couldn't afford to wait. Any ship out at sea could founder, and it only took minutes to make a deadly mistake this close to the shoreline. She quickly edged around the massive bell to inspect its automatic clockwork mechanism, and quickly determined that it wasn't functioning.

The Keeper rushed back into the storage room and rummaged hurriedly through the two drawers in the cabinet against the wall. Cleaning supplies, rags, polish. *Where was it?* The silence had already lasted at least a couple of minutes. She reached into the back of the second drawer until her hand closed on a small, heavy wooden object. *There.* She clutched the small wooden hammer in her hand and rushed to the side of the massive bell. She braced her feet widely, in a small crouch, and with both hands brought the wooden hammer as hard as she could against the side of the bell.

The bell gave a pathetic, dull burp, which resounded mostly in her body, moving up the handle of the hammer to her hands and arms, and rattling her teeth more than anything else. High above, in the Light, Ebenezer Wiggins heard this odd sound, and it roused him from his paralysis. *What in the world was that?*

She sighed, exasperated, and flung the hammer down. She rushed back into the storage room and rummaged around, looking for anything else she could use to ring the bell manually. She could feel the minutes slipping between her hands. She knew that any ears that had been following the sound of the fog bell would be straining to hear it and possibly edging closer to shore. She could imagine being on deck, fog rolling up on the ship from port, quite suddenly.

She thought of the crew, bobbing in the water, just able to make out the sound of the station bell, until it was cut off. Worrying about steering for the coastline and harbor, and in a word, blind. A ship's captain was blind without the Light and the fog signal. He could consult a star map, he could send down a lead line to see what came up in the tallow, but he relied on the Light. And when it was foggy as it was then, when the fog refracted the light so that it was unreliable, he relied on the signal. She hoped any ship relying on her had put down its anchor, but just in case, she decided she had to do the next best thing.

She squatted beside the massive bell, thinking it was likely over two tons, and reached beneath it for the clapper. It was uncomfortable, her crouch was precarious, and the huge iron clapper was heavy. She grasped it in both hands, pulled it to her, and gritting her teeth she let it swing, bracing for the sound. It didn't disappoint her. It was a full-bodied, painful gong that nearly deafened her, and she found herself thrown back from the momentum of the swing to land on her backside. She quickly shot up, and ducking out of the way of the barely swaying bell, she grasped the clapper again, silencing it. The gong had gone far out over the water and died to silence in the air, but the sound continued to reverberate in her head.

Twenty-eight, twenty-nine, thirty. She swung the clapper again, regaining her balance more quickly after the third attempt. This time she partially stood from her crouch for a moment before reaching back within the bell to silence the clapper. Her head was pounding from the sound of the bell. It echoed endlessly inside her, and her ears kept ringing long after each peal had ended.

She realized quickly that the keeper in the Light above wasn't coming. She was doing her job too well. Her choice was either to let the fog bell go silent again and retrieve the keeper, allowing perhaps a half hour to pass when any ship at sea would be without its aid, or continue to manually ring the bell, enduring the maddening sound. It was tempting to abandon this loud, painful thing she was doing, to go get someone else to do it, but she didn't want the bell to go silent for that length of time.

She soon fell into a mindless pattern with her work. Crouch, reach, pull, release, grit teeth, stand, crouch, silence, count. She counted to thirty over and over again, until the numbers meant nothing to her. She crouched so many times her thighs burned from the exertion. Her hands started to bruise and chap, and she had several sprained fingers from bending them back against the swinging clapper. She couldn't think about her head and her ears. Could her body be permanently damaged? She didn't know. Was there any ship out at sea that required her assistance? She wasn't sure. She didn't know if a ship out at sea could even hear her bell.

Her body became sore after the first hour, numb by the third, and painful beyond endurance by the fourth. Trapped in the lonely asceticism of hard manual labor, she had to send her mind elsewhere to survive and finish the task. With rising madness as the hours dragged on she thought *This. I hate this more than whale oil. Formally.* In her core she held the warm sun and cast about for a thought that might help keep her sane. Her thoughts caught the passing wing of a memory as it brushed by, that of three men fighting madness while tending a Light far to the north. She closed her eyes, caught the clapper, swung, and remembered.

Cape Sarichef Light, Unimak Island, Bering Sea, Alaska, 1912

She had translated into a small room with three men who, oddly enough, had their backs not only to her, but also to each other. Glancing out of the window she noticed that the Light was dim. There was little to see outside, other than a complete whiteout of snow, and she heard the wind screaming with a near-human voice that set her nerves on edge to listen to, even for a moment. It looked like an icy, angry blizzard and she was heartily glad she had translated inside rather than into that storm.

The room was warm, musty, and smelled like socks. The three men were disheveled, sitting in a loose triangular formation, and were all eating from separate cans of beans, each one staring off into a corner of the room. The room crackled with tension.

One of them seemed to think of something and rubbed the back of his head in a way that caught the attention of the man on his right. The Keeper was taken aback by the look of supreme irritation he leveled at the first man. He made a sound that seemed to annoy the first man, who shot him a look of pure hatred.

The third man was caught by the noise made by the first two men, and in keeping with the theme of the night, also looked monumentally put out. One thing led to another, it seemed, and before the Keeper could tell what had happened, the three of them had put down their cans and come to blows.

The first man took the second man by the scruff of his shirt, and the third man, instead of trying to get between them, sat back with an angry sound and put his head in his hands. The Keeper wasn't entirely sure what she was doing there, but she stepped forward to try to get their attention, thinking she might somehow stop the fight.

The three men started as if they'd seen a ghost.

"Holy Mother!" exclaimed the first one.

The second one said, "Wait, you see her too?"

The third one, lifting his head from his hands, gasped aloud and made the Sign over himself.

They stared at her openmouthed, then at each other, and then back at her. One of them tentatively reached out and touched her shoulder, then gasped.

Being so much more substantial than other humans did serve a purpose here, it seemed. There was no telling whether three half-crazed men in the middle of nowhere would deign to behave as gentlemen after being alone out here for however long they had been. Which seemed like a long time. The Keeper took another step forward and said "Hello."

The three of them jumped, obviously not having expected her to say anything, and looked at each other again. She took a careful look at them for the first time. All three of them were unshaven, dirty, and looked like they had a few bats loose in their attics.

No one said anything for a long moment, so she helped herself to a seat. She cleared her throat, and one of them quickly pulled the cap off his head.

Once they deduced that the ghost didn't mean them any harm, their story haltingly emerged. They informed her that this was a stag Light—unnecessarily, as she could tell there had never been a woman in the house at any time, past or present. The three of them had been stuck indoors together for nigh on four weeks, unable to go outside, and they were just about ready to kill one another because they were so fed up with each other. The Light was usually shut down completely in winter, given that the Bering Sea froze over, but their ride home had failed to arrive, and the fall storm had caught them unawares.

They had started out as the closest of friends and had applied for the position together, having previously enjoyed each other's company—this was related by the second man, who couldn't tamp down a sneer of disgust while saying this. In the last three to four weeks relations had deteriorated quite rapidly. They couldn't stand the sight of each other, and any sounds that the others made were not to be borne.

They no longer wanted to make food for each other, and the sounds of each other's voices had become so grating that they had imposed a rule of silence so as to avoid doing bodily harm to one another.

One of them even admitted that he had thought, just that morning, of throwing open the door and running out into the blizzard raging outside. The other two looked at him without surprise, having clearly had similar, if not more urgent, thoughts. As if a pressurized wound had been lanced, the three friends sat with the Keeper and talked through the night, relating their stories, telling her about their families and their fears of going mad in the lonely, existentially cold Alaskan wilderness.

The first man described a cold so deep that he felt the blood slow as it pumped through his heart. The third relayed how it burned to breathe it in should they venture out of doors.

She listened to the second man admit, gruffly, that there was a woman back home—her name was Mary—who might see him as a man now that he had worked here and made an income. He thought he might ask her to marry him, come spring. All three of them looked lost in thought at this pronouncement. The first man admitted he would not be returning. The other two nodded, as if admitting to a great failure.

"As soon as the storm passes and the ship comes," said the third. The other two nodded. The Keeper hoped they weren't trapped there for the winter and that the ship would indeed come before the sea-lanes closed for the frozen season.

Apparently, as far as the Keeper could discern, she had been sent there *to listen to the three men and help them hold onto sanity for a while longer. Sometime in the middle of the night the three men, each having sat down where he stood, passed around a bottle of gin they had saved for a special occasion. When they finally nodded off, the Keeper looked from one slumped figure to the next and sighed with the exhaustion and loneliness she had absorbed from their tales. She made the Sign over each of them, and as her fingers sketched it over the last form, she translated.*

The Keeper thought of those three men now. She thought of staving off madness, and how much courage it took to do so, as she stood during that long night and rang the fog bell. She thought how there always came a fork in a difficult journey, and to some extent, you had to *choose* sanity. She felt the sun within her blaze with warmth and life, as if in response to her thoughts. *Yes,* she thought. *You have to choose sanity and keep choosing it, and eat your beans cold out of a can while staring at a wall, even though it would be so much easier to run screaming into a blizzard and let the howling wind rip your voice out of your throat, and the cold steal your breath, and the madness take your life.*

Eat your cold beans, she told herself as she rang that bell faithfully and methodically every thirty seconds through the darkest hours of that night. Later she became convinced that if anything in her long life had aged her, it had been standing vigil over that fog bell.

Just as dawn was breaking on that interminable night, she glanced up at the sky above her and could no longer make out the constellations above. She continued her vigil through midmorning, when the sun had finally burned through the dark clouds above and dispersed the fog below. She stopped and took a long breath. The keeper in the Light above would come down to check on the bell when he noticed the absence of the ringing, but for now, it was no longer needed.

Trembling, she allowed herself finally to take stock of the effects of the night. Her ears still heard the sound of the bell, ringing with the din although it had ceased. Her legs burned from the repetitive motion of squatting for the clapper. Her hands, though, were by far the worst off. She couldn't bear to look at them. She registered pain but couldn't comprehend it yet. They had cramped into claws. She tried to make a loose fist with her right hand and cried out with the pain of it.

She took a deep breath. *Think,* she commanded herself. *What do I still have?* She continued to take stock. *Surely there's something left.* She cradled her hands against her middle, as if to protect them, and it came to her: *I have my sanity,* she thought. As she dropped to her knees in the bell tower, she felt herself translate.

~: 10 :~

I am bound to tell what I am told,
but not in every case to believe it.

HERODOTUS, *THE HISTORIES*

As her knees struck the sand, she felt lighter, despite the agony of pain in her hands. Wisdom sat on a small dune waiting for her, hands resting on her knees. The Keeper tripped to her feet and stumbled forward, her skirts catching a little, to stand beside the All-Keeper, who tilted her head up and smiled at her. She motioned to the spot next to her, and the Keeper gratefully sank down beside her.

Wisdom reached her right hand toward the Keeper's forehead and laid it gently against her clammy skin. Immediately, the ringing stilled. "You've been practicing," Wisdom said, her eyes kind. She regarded her for a moment, and then asked, "What may I do for you, daughter?"

Wordlessly, the Keeper held out her numb, clawed hands. Wisdom took them in her own warm and gentle hands, and the pain dulled. The Keeper sighed with relief.

"Why did you stand watch all night?" asked Wisdom. "You didn't have to, and I fear your hands will never be quite the same." They both looked down at the hands curled within Wisdom's.

"What else was I to do?"

Wisdom didn't reply, and they sat together, angled toward one another, the ocean before them.

The Keeper was prepared this time and planned to ask as many questions as she could before she translated away. *Unless I'm dreaming here.*

"It's not a dream," said Wisdom, though the Keeper had not spoken aloud.

The Keeper nodded, took a deep breath, and turning to Wisdom asked the most important question of all. "I don't understand. Why?" she entreated quietly, desperately. "Why am I ripped through time from Light to Light?"

Wisdom's eyes were filled with compassion as she watched the Keeper, cradling her hands in her own strong palms for so long the Keeper was sure she wouldn't answer. Then she finally spoke, softly, her lips barely moving, though the Keeper could hear her clearly in her mind. "For you, daughter," she said softly. "Your soul needed time. It's being perfected, as all souls are. And the King gives to each soul precisely what it needs."

The Keeper froze as the meaning of the words scalded through her numb thoughts. Then she yanked her hands from Wisdom's and stumbled to her feet. She could hardly think and felt her heart work its way up into her throat, until she could hardly breathe for the knot there.

For me? Being torn through time, being without home, possessions? Her throat worked, so dry. *Being without love? That was for me? To learn what?* She stood under the warmth of the sun, the sea ebbing and flowing against her ankles, and felt stricken. She gazed down at Wisdom still sitting on the sand dune. "For me?"

Her voice rose, more sob than words. "How?" she cried, anguished. Wisdom said nothing, but rose to her feet beside the Keeper. "How can this be for me?"

Wisdom watched her steadily, emanating calm, but the Keeper felt anger mounting within her. She curled her hands into fists and buried them in the folds of her dress. She felt her muscles tense, still tight and painful from the long night she had spent tending to the fog bell. *The fog bell! Was that for me too?* Her hands came up to frame her temples; she felt her head was going to swell and perhaps simply explode. She wanted to scream.

Wisdom continued to stand before her silently, and the Keeper felt that if the silence wasn't broken soon she would go mad. "Do you know," she began, in a voice not quite her own, a bubble of hysteria welling up inside of her. "I fished a man out of the sea last year. His body was bloated with water and his face—" She choked, suppressing a scream. "His face had been eaten off by fish. He was unrecognizable." The Keeper squeezed her temples with her fists hard enough to cause pain this time. "How—" She choked again, her heart firmly in her throat. "How can that be for me?"

Wisdom still said nothing, and the Keeper felt the tide of rage and hopelessness rise up in her. "No," she cried, and before she could think it through, she had thrown her body and her will at Wisdom, falling on her in a tangle of arms and legs.

The Keeper was momentarily stunned by the impact and give of the warm body beneath hers, her right shoulder colliding with Wisdom's middle, toppling both of them into the sand. All thought fled. She heard Wisdom's grunt as she knocked the wind out of her. The momentum of her lunge sent the two of them skidding down the small dune to the seashore below.

The Keeper came up fighting, and found both of her wrists manacled above her head in a strong grip, sure and calm. Wisdom stood opposite her, both of their hands locked above their heads, their bodies straining toward one another. Wisdom's face was composed, and she regarded her evenly. The Keeper shrieked at her, inches from her face, infuriated by her calm. *For me?!* she screamed internally. *For me?!* She found herself screaming again, her wrists becoming sore from Wisdom's strong grip.

The sand beneath their feet was wet, the waves lapping at their ankles, and as the Keeper strained her body angrily toward Wisdom's, she felt her feet squelching in the sand and being sucked down.

The Keeper twisted her wrists down hard and broke Wisdom's grip, throwing her body at her again. The Keeper felt the pull of the wet sand beneath her feet, her gown heavy with seawater. Wisdom caught her and gently turned her body away. The Keeper screamed in frustration at this deflection and threw herself at her again, grabbing her around the middle and dragging her to the ground.

Their bodies fell together to the wet sand, their gowns drawing up the salty seawater, and both soaked, they struggled together by the seashore. The Keeper clung to Wisdom, trying to pin her arms to the shore, but the Woman managed to twist her hands out of her grasp. She took the Keeper by the wrists again and, surging up, flipped her onto her back. Again and again the Keeper would gain the upper hand, pin Wisdom to the sand, then find herself pinned in the next moment. Wisdom was warm and alive beneath her, and the Keeper felt herself come alive wrestling with her.

They struggled for what seemed like days but might have been minutes. They wrestled in the sand until the Keeper felt her breaths come in long gasps. Her legs burned, and she could feel her body near complete exhaustion. She panted, both of her wrists grasped in Wisdom's, held at a painful angle above her head, her body bowed back in the other Woman's arms as though they were dancing on the seashore.

She attacked the All-Keeper with all of her remaining rage. She found that she had accumulated quite a lot of it over the years. She had picked it up in her moments of helplessness and in every grim realization that she had no choice. She had also unknowingly picked it up on behalf of others, when she felt that life had been unfair or unnecessarily painful to them. Every keeper she had buried planted a seed in her heart, and she found, while she wrestled in the sand with Wisdom, that they had bloomed into a garden of bitter herbs and poisons. *You are unfair,* she seethed. *You are unkind. All the pain I've seen: was it necessary to do it?*

Wisdom made no answer, but her eyes, normally so kind, were now full of sadness, and somehow, this seemed to break through the haze of righteous anger in which the Keeper had cloaked herself. She had never seen sadness in the face of the All-Keeper, and it stilled her wildness long enough that she could breathe for a moment, and *think.*

Oh, she thought suddenly. *You too?*

The Keeper took in Wisdom's sandy gown plastered to her skin, her disheveled hair and torn hem. Wisdom met her gaze, and the Keeper saw the sheen of tears she hadn't noticed.

"Of course," replied Wisdom, her grip tightening painfully for a moment on the Keeper's wrists. "Did you think you were the only one who sees?"

Sees, feels, understands. The only one who knew the pain of humanity, knew it in her body, assumed it into her spirit.

Yes, thought the Keeper. *I thought I was the only one.*

The anger drained away, leaving a vacuum of emptiness in its wake. She knew the moment the anger was gone, because her body went limp, as though the anger had been the only thing animating her. She felt a tightening at her wrists and saw that Wisdom held her up by them. *Not the only thing,* she thought. A profound sense of sadness settled in her to echo what she saw in Wisdom's face.

Without the false courage of anger, she felt a swift shame in her gut and, wrists still held, she bowed her head before Wisdom. *My Lady,* she began haltingly. *Forgi—*

"No," said Wisdom aloud. "There is no need. Not for this."

The Keeper looked up at her again, at the strong, beautiful Woman before her. She climbed to her feet, taking her weight from Wisdom's grasp. *You allowed this*, she thought with a pang.

"Yes," replied Wisdom. "You needed it."

"It was for me," said the Keeper numbly. It struck her. *It's all for me.*

"Yes," said Wisdom. She slowly brought down the Keeper's hands, until she was holding them cradled between their two bodies. The ache of the long night the Keeper had spent ringing the fog bell had settled into her body, and the wrestling hadn't helped, but her hands, safe within Wisdom's, were free of pain.

"It's all for me," murmured the Keeper, flexing her hands experimentally.

She suddenly felt tired, so tired. It would take her a lifetime to sort out what this meant. What it meant to have a life over which she had no control, no power. And that her life—*if I can even call it that*—was that way for her own sake. She wanted to close her eyes and sleep for an eternity.

Wisdom's eyes sharpened, and her grip tightened momentarily. "You may, if you wish," she said, her tone unreadable. The foam at their feet stilled, and the wind seemed to draw in a breath and hold it.

Pay attention, the Keeper said to herself sternly, shaking her head through her exhaustion. "A moment longer, please," she begged.

She stood, the sun warming her back and beginning to dry her sodden gown. The sun she had swallowed warmed her from within. The sea stilled, and Wisdom, patient as time itself, stood clasping her hands.

Think, she commanded herself. *I am meant to understand.* She thought of the little girl who had given her the necklace of wildflowers. Of the copy of *Moby Dick* and the tiny whale that had flashed on her instep. She thought of the farthest back she had traveled, of the fires burning on ancient hills. She thought of her home, the cottage, and how she was not allowed to keep anything. She thought of the tasks she was given, and of how solid and unbreakable her body was, for one who felt so brittle within that a strong northeast wind should rightfully be able to scatter her. She thought of the things she desperately wanted: a home, a family, to be loved, known, and remembered. She thought of her friend Claire, and felt a pang of loneliness. *Think*, she told herself. *Practice again. What do I have?* She took a deep breath and blew it out through her teeth.

Is there anything I have? She tried to remember what she had thought of since last seeing Wisdom. *I have sanity. I have two strong hands. I have life, and this solid body. I have time . . .* Her heart stilled. *Time. I have time.*

I have had nothing to call my own, except . . . "All the time in the world," she whispered aloud. The foam seemed to exhale at her feet. Wisdom's hands tightened again on hers before gently releasing them.

"I have been given absolutely nothing but all the time in the world." Her voice rang with conviction.

"Yes," agreed Wisdom, "for now."

PART II

*Whatever our souls are made of,
his and mine are the same.*

EMILY BRONTË, *WUTHERING HEIGHTS*

～: 11 :～

What cannot be said will be wept.

SAPPHO

Loon-Call Light, Maine, April 1910

THE KEEPER KNEW SOMETHING WAS different from the beginning. The translation had been hazier than usual, and she arrived in broad daylight, her eyesight cloudy, with a ringing in her ears that had nothing to do with the echo of the abominable fog bell. She squinted ahead, her feet stumbling forward clumsily. A man rose before her, approaching her slowly, as if through water. The insistent ringing in her ears grew louder, and the last thing she knew before pitching forward was his hand reaching out, slipping between her face and the ground. This hand was no bird-boned thing; it was warm, broad, and made of whatever she was.

She woke with the sun's rays against her eyelids and reveled in the luxury of waking midday in a warm bed. Her mouth curved in a smile and she pulled the blanket up to her face, burrowing down deeper into the bed. She took a deep breath and stilled. Two things occurred to her at the same moment: the scent of the place was familiar, and she was not alone in the room.

She lowered the covers from her face and opened her eyes to find, folded into an armchair beneath the window, a still, broad-shouldered man in a stock navy blue lightkeeper's uniform. His dark hair and beard were thick but neat, and he held a cup of something steaming lazily in one hand. A book was propped open on his crossed knee. He was not looking at the book, but regarding her with an open, steady gaze that neither frightened nor invited. He looked solid and balanced; that was her first impression of him.

"Good afternoon," he said, in a deep baritone.

She nodded, pulled herself to a sitting position, and propped herself against the headboard. She felt muddled, confused, and her mouth full of cotton. "I've been here before," she said carefully, taking in the bed, the room, the kitchen. There was a warm, familiar feel to the room, but something remained just beyond her grasp, something important. Her head was pounding and so uncomfortable, and she wanted the ringing to stop more than anything. She shook her head, while he continued to sit quietly, regarding her evenly. She had the feeling that he was a still one, and that he would sit there interminably until she spoke again. She leaned her head back against the headboard, purposefully bouncing her head lightly off the wood, trying to knock some sense into herself.

She closed her eyes momentarily and took a deep breath. The scent was unmistakable. Her eyes flew open and she turned back to him. She took in his size, his shape, and his hands. The color of his eyes. She'd seen those eyes—like the sea in midwinter—before. *Oh.* Her gaze fell on the book in his hand. She squinted. Herodotus. "Oh." A gasp escaped her lips and her heart clenched within her.

"No." She shook her head, drew back the covers, and swung her legs over the side of the bed. Her eyes swept the small space and she stumbled to her feet. Her head swam with the effort, and she reached out a hand to steady herself. "My cottage," she murmured, shaking her head in denial. The curtains over the kitchen window were missing, the dining table looked newer, there were fewer books scattered about, and the keeper . . . *Ronan*, she thought. Her eyes flew up to meet his. "No," she cried more forcefully, and brought a hand up to cover her mouth. She stumbled forward, and he put down his cup, instantly rising to his feet, alert.

"What—" He stepped toward her, one hand outstretched.

"No," she cried again, and threw herself toward the door.

He found her beneath the small apple tree he had planted, somewhat self-consciously, three years before. The salt in the sea-air made it difficult to grow fruit trees, and anyhow, he lived in Maine, and the growing season was not known for its generosity. He'd known it was unlikely to survive, but the tree was scrappy and seemed to be holding on to the soil.

Several lifetimes' worth of tears were trapped inside her. All the times she felt as though she would burst, the sorrow she carried in her helplessness, and the inexplicable way this man's death affected her all rose up in her. The Keeper found that she could weep, after all. Between his sea-colored eyes and Herodotus, the dam inside her had cracked, and when she recalled his name, the walls washed away like sand against a determined sea. The tears, having had nowhere to go for so long, found at last the soil under the apple tree. She wept them all up there. It felt like lancing a wound under pressure, and the pain that opened up the dam was followed by relief as deep as the ocean.

He found her prostrate, her head on her arms, her body outstretched in the soft spring earth. She was weeping, and he heard bitter, ugly, gasping sobs from her small form. They seeped into the ground beneath her cheek, which was becoming muddy.

Ronan wasn't scared of weeping women, per se, but he liked to know why they were crying, so as to try to make it stop, and he could see no reason why this one was weeping. Were her sensibilities offended? Perhaps he oughtn't have put her in his bed. Some women were funny about that sort of thing. But she had fainted dead away, and when he had taken her up in his arms he had only thought of her comfort. He sensed that she wasn't the type to fly into hysterics, though. She had taken a long, measured look around the room when she first awoke. She had noticed something, had said she had been there before, and then had flown out of the house like she was trying to outrun a tornado.

Overhead, the sky was darkening, and he thought vaguely that he should check on the Light soon, after whatever storm was brewing here subsided. Ronan knelt beside her.

She turned her dirt-stained face toward him. "What year is it?" she breathed. She had a strong, clear voice, despite the weeping.

He told her. Her cries stilled. She put her face down over her arms in the dirt and a shudder went through her. It went through him as well, and it was somehow worse than the sobs.

She slowly got to her hands and knees in the dirt, wiped an arm across her eyes, and sat back, her knees tucked beneath her. He wanted to reach out and wipe the smudge she had left across her cheek and place a hand beneath her elbow to help her up, but he crouched next to her under the small apple tree and waited patiently.

Spring was just beginning, the sea grass out over the dunes registering the impossibly young green that stole over them after the starkness of winter. The migratory birds were starting to appear from the south, the days were lengthening, and life was slowly shaking off the long sleep of winter. Ronan felt sluggish, like a great bear waking after a long winter, clumsy, awkward, and slow on his feet next to this woman who was having a crisis in the shade of his apple tree.

She glanced at the copy of Herodotus still in his hand, closed, though one finger was wedged in to hold his place. He hadn't realized he'd brought it. Her eyes trained on the book and then welled with tears, silent this time. *She is an odd one*, he thought. *Perhaps she hates Herodotus.* She continued to look at him, intent, sorrowful, and then her gaze dropped to the soil. She laboriously rose to her feet, shaking her head at his quickly proffered hand and dusting her hands together.

The weeping had helped a little. She had a feeling she would be weeping constantly now that she had learned how. Some deaths arrowed past the gaps in her armor in that fatal, Achillean way that was no less terminally painful for being familiar. She was well acquainted with the feeling and didn't question it; some deaths were just this way. She straightened to her full height. It wasn't much, but she seemed to look down on him from a high place.

She glanced at the little apple tree and the thought occurred to her that perhaps her torrent of hot, grief-filled tears had kept it alive for all those years, scrappy as it looked now. She finally addressed him.

"I've been here before," she said, her tone nearly even. *This is my home; this is the only home I ever had.* "Forgive me, please. It was a bit of a shock—" She paused. *I know you. I closed your eyes. I buried you beneath this apple tree in winter. The ground was cold and hard. Your body was heavy.* "I, uh, have been unwell." *I will never be well again.* She had a hard time meeting his gaze. "I won't trouble you longer. Please excuse me." *I cannot stay here.*

He stood near her, within reach, but he might have been a thousand miles or thirty years away, for all it mattered. *You're dead*, she told him silently. *You died.* He shook his head slowly and cleared his throat. "The nearest village is an hour's walk, and I wouldn't feel right sending you alone."

She felt the sadness of the foghorn rise up within her again. She felt the confusion of the day and the disorientation of being back in this place, with this man, at this different time. *What do I have?* She asked herself. She raised a hand to her face without thinking, and caught the incongruous smile before it could slip free. He might think her mad, after all. *I have tears,* she thought, and her heart lightened a little.

Ronan looked over his shoulder. "I have to tend the—"

"Light," she finished. "Of course. I can help you." He eyed her warily but didn't question her. He nodded and she followed him, as though she had not wept up her soul into the soil of his apple tree.

They worked side by side in the waning early spring light, Orion's Belt visible above them, until the Light was strong and sure, a beacon against the approaching night. He didn't question why she knew where he kept his supplies, or why she knew how to expertly clean the lens, donning apron and gloves before he could open his mouth to say anything. He didn't question her, but a sense of foreboding rose steadily within him.

This is not the type of woman to throw a hysterical fit, he thought, eyeing her. Whatever her story was, he had a feeling he wouldn't like it.

When they were finished, he brewed a pot of strong tea, poured two cups, and sat across from her at the scarred kitchen table. And waited.

~: 12 :~

Men trust their ears less than their eyes.

HERODOTUS, *THE HISTORIES*

THE STORY THAT EMERGED FROM the strange woman across from Ronan was the stuff of grief-deranged dreams. First of all, she knew his name. When he lifted an eyebrow at this she pointed to the book, sitting now on the edge of the table. "It's on the inside cover." He checked and shook his head. "No? Not yet, then," she said quietly. Another shudder swept down his back.

"I have been tending Lights as long as I can remember," she started. He said nothing. "I tend Lights in different places."

So perhaps she works for the Company, he thought dubiously.

"And in different times," she added.

Or not, he amended.

She shook her head, as if to clear it, and then in a rush: "I usually arrive for a short period of time. I usually find a task to be completed. Either a Light is about to go out, or has just gone out, or a person is drowning in the ocean. Or a keeper is asleep. Or ill." She looked down at her hands. "Or dead." The hair rose on the back of his neck. She lifted her eyes back up to his.

She had the grace to hold his gaze then. She couldn't do it without tears, though his eyes were dry, and his throat drier still. He felt exposed, though he couldn't understand why.

"Go on," he ground out, roughly.

"It was a cold day in midwinter. The sky was storm-filled and—" He was shaking his head. She stopped. "I put you under the apple tree," she said softly, and bravely met his eyes.

He stilled, as though caught in crosshairs. There wasn't time to grapple with her words, but he knew he would later. He was like saturated soil, the water just sitting on top, pooling. She knew the exact moment when her words seeped slowly in, because his eyes hardened.

At first he didn't understand her, or his mind refused the information she offered. Was she trying to tell him that she traveled through time? Doing what the devil, exactly? Tending lighthouses? If anything made less sense than that, he couldn't think of it. What comprehensive absurdity was she claiming? Was she trying to assert that she had buried him? *Under my own blooming apple tree?*

In his mind, he got up abruptly and said something unspeakably rude to her. Lashed out angrily, though he was a soft-spoken man. Asked her if she was a selkie, a witch. Swept his copy of Herodotus—*his* copy!—from the table and left the room without a backward glance. Or upturned the end table on his way out. He wanted to turn her out of the house—*his* house—into the cold night. He wanted to break something with his hands. Something that was either costly or beautiful or weak.

He did none of these things.

He flexed his right hand into a fist. He had strong, capable hands. How dare she come into his home and make him feel the— what was it? The impotence. The *shame* of death. Like he'd done something to be ashamed of by dying, sometime in the future. Who knew how long in the future? And then he paused in his musings. She hadn't moved.

Her eyes were lowered to her lap, back slumped. *I put you under the apple tree*, she'd said, almost apologetically. Like it was the best she could do. Like she had done her best.

The Keeper sat at the kitchen table, and as it had done so many times in her life, the river of time seemed to cease its flow. Over the course of time beyond her memory, she had become intimately acquainted with the ebbs and flows of the river, stepping in and out of it in different places as she did. Sometimes it flowed past in a rush, as when she went ahead and things seemed to speed past her. Other times, like the night of the fog bell, it slowed to a trickle so that each moment was interminable. Now, as she sat in an eddy, the water circling around her, waiting for Ronan of the Light to pass his sentence, the river slowed. *Surely he can hear my heart beating.*

She thought of what she did, moving through space and time, tending Lights, and the impersonal way she had buried him, and the tears rose up again inside of her. Her tears were developing an ebb and flow as well, like the river of time, and like the sea, and she felt she was going to be learning their rhythm quite well now that she knew how to weep.

I did the best I could, she thought desperately. *I always—almost always do!* Shame and anguish consumed her as he sat across from her at the table, face thunderstruck, his eyebrows an angry slash.

How could Wisdom mean this? That this is all for me? How could I have buried this man for me? She hadn't had time to process what the All-Keeper had told her, but she felt horror and revulsion rise up inside her on a tide of tears, and she thought she might be sick. *How do I ever dare?* she asked herself. *How can I lay hands on another human being, thinking I am helping?* She worked herself deeper and deeper into her own misery, so that she startled and looked up when Ronan cleared his throat.

His mouth opened, but no words came out. He sat still for a long time, anger warring with fear and grief within him. And maybe a little hatred, truth be told. At her? Probably not. He didn't know her, after all. But he had to get out, to think about what she'd said. She was either completely raving mad, or she had some explaining to do. But he'd had all he could take for one day.

She sat immobile, as though she were particularly good at it, though every emotion she felt seemed to cross her face. He felt nearly sorry for her. Nearly.

She outsat him while he worked out everything and nothing in his mind. Finally he opened his mouth again, and to her surprise he said gruffly, "I need to check on the Light. Do I at least live the night?"

She started, then said hesitantly, "You were an elderly man, back when—" she paused— "when last I saw you." He nodded once, briskly, and was gone into the night.

ᴄ: 13 ᴄ

Very few things happen at the right time, and the rest do not happen at all.

HERODOTUS, *THE HISTORIES*

He was absent the whole next day, but in the evening he made an appearance, looking haggard and saying little. The Keeper sat in the house and watched the Light's beam come to life while she was apart from it, removed as it were, by his choice. Though he knew her to be capable from the previous night, he clearly didn't want her help. It hurt. *He's hurting*, she thought. *I hurt him.* She, who was so unused to waiting for anyone, listened to the mournful cries of the loons by the riverbend as she waited for him.

After he had tarried in tending the Light as long as was humanly possible, he dragged himself with heavy steps into the house. He barely glanced at her, but did say a polite "good evening" and made a pot of tea. The Keeper had not presumed to cook anything in his kitchen, feeling like an interloper the whole day, so she sat at the fire, trying to control her edginess and uncertainty. To her surprise he brought a low stool and positioned it next to her by the fire. He went back into the kitchen and lifted the teapot from the stove. She got up to help him and he held up a hand. "I have it," he said gruffly.

The Keeper restlessly sat back down, burying her hands in the folds of her skirt. They were not used to being idle. He brought the teapot, and to her relief there were two chipped teacups in his other hand.

Ronan suddenly realized he didn't know her name. It seemed an awkward time to ask, but it surely wouldn't become less so the longer he waited. She knew his name. He shuddered involuntarily at that. "I don't know your name," he began, his voice rough, meeting her eyes as he sat beside her. He handed her a teacup.

She started, as though not asked her name often. She shook her head as she accepted the cup and thanked him. "I don't know that I have one," she replied apologetically. "If I had one, I don't remember it," she added, drawing the cup of tea between her hands and relaxing into her chair as soon as the warmth reached her fingers. He watched her as she was almost transported, keeping her face above the steaming cup, closing her eyes a moment and nearly sighing out loud. He shifted on the stool and glanced away.

"Well," he said briskly, "we'll have to come up with one then. I can't call you 'Light Lass' as it stands." He quickly changed the subject and asked her to continue her tale from the previous night. Her hands tightened on the cup and she took a deep breath.

"It was a cold day in early winter and I arrived in late afternoon, around the time the Light needed to be lit for the night. You were there, at the Light, slumped forward on your arm at the desk. You were gone, and your spirit had left your body not long before I arrived, I think, for your eyes were still open and your skin warm. You had eyes like the sea, which I closed." She swallowed against the bile in her throat.

"You expect me to believe that?" he asked tightly. He shifted on the stool and set the cup of tea down on the floor, untouched. His face was in profile to her, and she could see his clenched jaw by the firelight.

She said nothing for a long moment, and when he made to stand, to burn off some nervous energy and walk out into the darkening twilight, she finally spoke quietly. "No."

He turned then to really look at her. She had a strong, unadorned face and eyes that reminded him of the evergreens that made long winters bearable. Her hair was dark brown and curled in a generous profusion. He had always liked curly hair on a woman. It both disturbed and angered him that he found her attractive. It disturbed him even more that she didn't look anything but sane. Her eyes were intelligent, bright, and held a spark of humor perhaps, but not madness.

"Then why do you say it?" he asked, hearing the desperation in his own voice.

"Because it's true," she replied simply.

"I cannot believe it," he told her, his heart in his throat. "You're telling me you came here at the end of my life and buried me, and yet here we are." He held out a hand between them, and the Keeper saw his strong palm and the calluses he had acquired from tending the Light. She remembered that hand well. She had moved that hand from where it rested on the keeper's log and taken the small wooden comb from his fist.

Her eyes filled with tears again, and this time they seemed to upset him. He turned away from her as they leaked down her face.

I don't normally do this! she wanted to cry. *I have never done this before, in fact. I only learned how yesterday!* But she said nothing, and finding the hole in the dam within, she stuck a finger in it to stop it up for the moment so she could deal with the crisis at hand.

"Excuse me," she said stiffly. "I just remembered something. I'm fine now." She found that it was much harder to will herself to stop weeping than it had been to begin.

He was unmoved by both her tears and her speech, and the lines of his body spoke hurt and disbelief. *Well,* she thought. *I'm done here. I haven't the strength to stay and spar with this man.*

She thought of the seafoam on the shore with Wisdom, and how it had felt like it was waiting for her decision when she wanted to lie down and sleep forever in the sand, after she had wrestled with the All-Keeper. She felt like that, like she could just lie down and sleep forever.

Whatever the task is, it must remain undone, she thought. She suddenly recalled the hundred and twenty-seven she'd left to drown and tasted the tang of fear that the thing she would leave undone here would somehow be even more tragic than that. She took another glance at Ronan, eyed the stiff lines of his body, and felt that it must be so. She set down her teacup, also untasted, and stood.

Ronan looked up at her with a bleak expression on his face. The moment she had stood, he knew. He knew she was not fabricating a story, nor was she just garden-variety crazy, as much as he wished it so. He knew she was telling the truth with the neat click of the teacup against the side table and the decisive way she had stood to her height beside him.

Her cheeks were still wet with tears, and he had the sudden fleeting thought that she perhaps didn't weep often, and felt remorse for turning away from her moments before. He saw her gather her dignity around her like a garment and grudgingly admired her for it.

In the moment before she could muster up the strength to say goodbye, Ronan stood beside her. She waited while a muscle worked in his clenched jaw. He said nothing for a long moment, and then he bent over to pick up her teacup and held it back out to her. It looked out of place in his large hand, but the Keeper reached for it, and mind made up, she took it in her hand.

He motioned her back to her seat, and she gingerly eased into it. They said nothing for a while, and then Ronan, voice rough, said, "I don't take you for the running type, Light Lass. If I upset you again, you should say so, and stay to fight." They were hard words to say, and harder still to hear, but he said them, and she heard them.

"Go on, then, if you please," he said, his voice still uneven, his hands braced on his knees as he sat hunched on the small stool. He looked a little green around the gills, but he was listening to her.

She took a deep breath, remembering. "You were white-haired, your hands were spotted with age but appeared strong. I remember thinking you were so large, broad-shouldered and unstooped by age. Most remarkably, you were solid."

"What do you mean?" he asked quickly.

She shrugged. "You feel differently to me than the other humans."

He gave a tight, nervous laugh. "So you're not human."

She looked taken aback. "Of course I'm human," she retorted, sounding nearly offended. "Whatever else would I be?"

He let out another strangled laugh. "You tell me, lass."

"I'm human," she said definitively. "I just don't age." She refused to look over to see his response to that and continued instead. "Others feel insubstantial to me, like small animals or birds. But not you." She looked at him then, her eyes wide. "You feel like me," she said, a hint of wonder creeping into her voice. She shook her head. "It made it very difficult to bury you."

His back stiffened and he tried to sit still but couldn't. He came to his feet, pacing before the fire. She had stopped speaking, so he impatiently waved a hand at her to continue.

"I'm listening," he said gruffly. "I can't take my own death sitting down, lass."

She spoke more quickly then, more purposefully, and he got the impression that she was pinching her nose to swallow something distasteful.

"I had to ruin your bedsheet to drag you to the apple tree—I'm sorry," she said ridiculously. He didn't even know where to begin, so he said nothing and squatted back onto the stool.

"The ground was hard, and I found a pickaxe and a shovel." She fisted both her hands as if in imagined pain. "It took most of the night to make a hole deep enough and long enough. I couldn't feel my hands. I prayed the entire time—I was terrified I would be called away—I prayed that I would be allowed to bury you. I prayed over you. I kissed your face. I had to roll you into the hole."

She paused for breath. Ronan had no words, but he listened. "And I made you a grave marker, based on the name I found in the book; it took me a few months. I didn't know your age," she added, apologetic again, and he realized she had finished her absurd narrative.

There was a lengthy silence, drawn out like a long, unpunctuated sentence, unbroken by sound or thought or movement.

They both sat back, spent, gazing into the fire. He felt he should offer her a cigar. He didn't know if he should thank her for burying him or comfort her in her obvious grief. Or if he should comfort himself. Or apologize for dying. He was fairly certain of only one thing: she was telling the truth as she knew it.

Finally, three decades of good breeding won out and he spoke up. "Well, it spoils the ending a little, though not by much," he said, trying for lightness.

She glanced over at him, and the warmth in her eyes spoke appreciation of his effort.

"We all die in the end. You've just startled me with the ending, is all," he added lightly, and ran out of words.

They sat there for what seemed like ages, and then he reached across the space that separated them and placed his warm, solid hand over hers where it rested on the arm of the chair. Hers turned over in an instant and clasped his with an otherworldly strength, holding on as if for her life, his life, and the life of the world.

They parted to sleep for the night as two who had met at the funeral of a close friend, thrown into premature familiarity, but having a common acquaintance that told them enough of one another to form the most basic trust. There was no more talk of her leaving, and neither mentioned it again. There seemed to be no point. They had shared a death, after all, which is the closest of intimacies.

The Keeper knew she would live to be grateful that Ronan had stood to make her stay and fight when he did. She had the feeling that had he not, she would have walked out, and translated, and that the course of her life would have been forever altered. She didn't know why she was there, but she felt it was of vital importance.

The telling and the tears seemed to snip all of her strings at once. The next morning she took a chair outside to the garden and slumped into it, spent, all the words wrung out of her. Ronan greeted her politely, but formally, his true personality beginning to shine back through the trial of the last two days. He was a mild-mannered man, impeccably polite to all, including animals, and it was not in his nature to be gruff.

Normally, the tears that leaked unheeded down her cheeks would have been enough to undo Ronan—they were, truth be told, but she needn't know that. He felt that those tears were the product of desolation, and though he had an idea of what had caused them, he had no notion of how to fix it. He couldn't undie, as it were.

So he merely handed her a bowl with a polite word and left her in the strengthening spring sun. She sat with the cool stoneware bowl of tart yogurt cupped in her hands and watched the waves clapping themselves against the cliffs below. She listened for every third wave and could just make out the musical sound of a cascade of seashells tinkling as they were dragged in the undertow of each receding wave. She looked up at the flapping of wings and saw Canada geese in formation above her.

Her eye caught on an early monarch butterfly investigating the area by the doorstep. It flitted, seemingly helplessly, from one scent to the next. She had become so used to thinking of herself as a particle of time-flotsam, and now she was cast up on a shore, unsure of what, why, or for how long. *This is somehow for me*, she thought. *What could Wisdom have meant?*

As much as she'd wanted to come back to her cottage, she couldn't have imagined coming back to it while *he* still occupied it. She thought of how much she wanted to sleep for days and months and years. It was as though her whole life's burdens had caught up with her when she explained to Ronan that she had already buried him. She thought about time and how wretchedly impersonal it was and how terrible it all was and how unfair. And how much like a petulant child she felt, for a woman of uncertain age who had met and wrestled with the Keeper of All Lights.

She couldn't imagine how she was supposed to coexist with this man whom she had already buried. His death had leveled her.

There were many things she could do, and do well. She knew how to light just about any navigational aid, ancient or modern. She knew that when pulling a drowning person into a skiff you pulled them over the stern so you didn't capsize the boat. She knew how to keep a fog signal blasting. Ronan of the Light was another story. She understood neither him nor why she was there with him.

Does he need something? The Light was as strong as its keeper. *Why am I here? Is there anything I can offer beyond the finality of a burial service?*

Am I here for him? Her mind couldn't come up with any possibilities that made any sense. She thought of Claire of the hearth with a bittersweet pang of happiness. Was it somehow for her friend that she'd returned?

She felt tired enough that she thought no amount of sleep would ever erase the fatigue. It had settled within like the cold of midwinter, heavy upon the bone. It mocked her efforts and the progress she had made. She remembered, a seeming eternity ago in Claire's kitchen, that something was about to perfect her. The thought came to her: *This is it.* She didn't know how, but she knew Ronan of the Light had something to do with it. She still felt the warmth of the sun she'd swallowed, but it was faint, and once again she felt she could never sleep enough and never be dry enough, ever again.

She thought about how remarkably tedious it could be to heal a human heart and mend a human spirit. How she was tired of being tired, and tired of the betraying way her body felt as weak as a wet newborn kitten. And how her healing was going to outlast her patience.

Ronan watched her surreptitiously while carrying out the tasks of his day. He checked on her between feeding the chickens and collecting the eggs, and again while he prepared the midday meal, which she barely touched. He checked on her after pulling weeds to prepare the garden for planting, and glanced at her as he went to trim the wicks in the Light.

He didn't speak to her, but left her to her own devices, because he had been in mourning before and recognized the signs. Besides, he felt that he was in mourning himself. He knew that tears such as she had watered his apple tree with only flowed from deep grief, and that if needed, it was best to grieve properly and at length.

He left her in the chair overlooking the sea so that the earth and the sun and the sea might heal her. He knew it could take days or weeks or months; he didn't think of forever, because he knew they surely didn't have that. He knew he didn't, at the least. He swallowed the lump in his throat at the thought. There was no use in thinking of it. He watched her out of the corner of his eye as she curled her hands around the steaming cup of tea he passed to her in the afternoon, holding it until it cooled, not taking a sip. He replaced it later in the day and tucked a blanket tightly around her slight frame. She sat there for most of the day, her eyes now blank, now filled with tears, now bright with anger. The anger reassured him, a little.

He slept on a pallet in the base of the lighthouse, and she slept in the bed. There had been her soft protestations, his firm, unequivocal negation, and he'd gotten his way in the end. "Ye'll let me be a gentleman in my own home, lass," he'd said shortly, an extra blanket tucked under his arm. "I need to be close to the Light anyway," he'd added, glancing over his shoulder at it.

The next day and the one after were the same. On the afternoon of the third day she lifted her wet eyes to him, and he felt the plea in them, though he didn't know the question.

He tucked a small bowl with an egg and bread into her hands. "Listen," he said, not bothering to keep the urgency out of his voice. The line of his back was tense, and his left hand was curled into a fist.

"I don't know what causes you to weep," he told her, his right hand extended palm up. "Or how to ease your suffering. But you have a safe place here while you weep. For as long as you need to weep," he finished. His face was flushed, but he held her gaze.

Somehow the offer of a place to weep, which she had taken because she needed it rather than because it was explicitly offered, stopped her tears. She hadn't said anything in a couple of days, but his kindness loosened her tongue. "You've been nothing but kind, Mister—"

He shook his head, as if to shake off her thanks. "Ronan," he said firmly. "Everyone calls me Ronan. Or Ronan of the Light."

"Of course," she said, and felt a small smile work its way to her lips. *This can be done,* she thought. *This human interaction, with this man.*

The Keeper gazed at him a moment longer, until he turned away, squinting at the Light beyond the house, the wrinkles at the corners of his eyes creasing easily into the familiar pattern. She didn't know how he understood her pain, just that he somehow did through bitter experience. *What happened to you, Ronan of the Light?* she wondered, watching his averted face.

Ronan looked back at her. She was somehow still dignified, while she sat bundled in the chair overlooking the garden and the sea. He watched the procession of emotions cross her face. *She was telling the truth*, he thought. *Everything she said was true.* Which made her life a cataclysmically tragic tale, much worse than hearing about one's own distant death from a stranger, however incredible that might be. *Except*, he thought, *she doesn't feel much like a stranger, does she?* He had the uncomfortable feeling that he could trace his life's arc from her, and that there was a sense of inevitability about the whole matter.

At the end of several long days, in and out of the chair for necessities and sleep overnight, when Ronan had lit his Light and come around to check on her, he found her asleep in the deep chair, curled upon herself like a question, her face erased of tension while she slept. *There's nothing for it*, he thought. He was a man of humble means, and if the sun and the sea couldn't heal her, he had nothing else to offer. For now, the sea and sun would have to take his place and thaw her by degrees, and bring her slowly back, until he could be brave.

∽ 14 ∾

The sea-bird wheeling round it, with the din
Of wings and winds and solitary cries,
Blinded and maddened by the light within,
Dashes himself against the glare, and dies.

HENRY WADSWORTH LONGFELLOW, "THE LIGHTHOUSE"

S HE SLEPT UNEASILY THOSE FIRST few nights, dreams of the
hundred and twenty-seven replaying in her mind. She heard
the fog bell, the incessant ringing, and felt the cold night air and the
cramping in her hands from that turbulent struggle, until she woke
with the memory of her hands cradled in Wisdom's on that far, calm
shore. She hurriedly completed her ablutions and swung the bedroom door open, glancing around for signs that Ronan had had his
breakfast.

She discovered that she enjoyed eating with Ronan of the Light,
though there was tension between them. The stove was cold and
there was no smell of coffee in the air.

She turned the doorknob and pushed out into the brisk April
morning, gasping at the cold and quickly turning back for her coat

against the deceptive spring sun. She found that she did not need to sit in the chair this morning. She felt vibrant and itching to move. Bundled against the chill, she came around the side of the house to head to the Light, when the sight before her stilled her steps.

She had seen this sort of thing before. It typically happened in fall or spring, during migratory times. Birds were drawn to the Light and were either confused or blinded by it. Ronan stood at the base of the Light, gathering bodies, his movements slow and heavy. He looked up when she reached him, face stark and wind-chapped. It pulled at her, and she didn't want to think about why, because there was nothing to be done about it. She glanced at the ground, which was littered with the bodies and bloody feathers of about a dozen birds. Ronan looked tired, and his face spoke the sadness she felt as he piled up the bodies.

She knelt slowly to pick up the bird nearest her feet, gently lifting its broken heft into her hands, trying to avoid the blood-matted feathers. "Did any of them survive?" He looked up at her, and she noticed that his eyes were red-rimmed.

He cleared his throat. "Not this time."

So he had done this before too. She cleared her throat as well, and helped him silently.

When they finished, she glanced up at the Light. She could make out bits of blood and feathers against the glass. "Was the lens damaged?"

He shook his head. "Just the birds."

The Keeper looked around her. The birds looked like a small flock of Canada geese. They had likely been flying north before they encountered the Light. Now what remained was broken breastbones and snapped necks. The sun was rising and Ronan stood beside her, swaying a little on his feet.

She turned to him. "Have you slept, Ronan?" she asked, trying to keep her voice brisk and free of concern.

He shook his head. "They struck the Light as I was drifting off to sleep. I'll rest once I've cleaned this up."

"May I?"

He blinked heavily. "May you what?"

"May I take over here, while you go rest?"

Something in her tone must have conveyed the spirit in which it was asked, and he began to nod, exhaustion overcoming him. Then he forcefully shook his head, as if trying to wake from a trance, and exclaimed, "What, you mean clean up after the birds?"

"I've done it before," she replied quickly.

"Done *this* before?"

"Yes. More than once, unfortunately. I can take care of this. Please, Ronan." There was something about hearing the combination of a plea and his given name that made all protest die on his lips. He came to the sudden and rather dismaying realization that if she asked in that way he might be helpless to deny her anything.

It was absurd, really. One did not go lie down and leave a lady to clean up dead birds. He knew that as well as anyone. But what was it about her that persuaded him to be led up the path? She led him not to the Light, where his pallet lay, but to the recently vacated bed in the house, which was so warm and comforting.

She left him at the door and closed it softly behind her, assuring him she would wake him if she needed him for anything. He kicked off his boots and made quick work of shucking his clothes to the wooden floor. His last thought after the bliss of crawling between the sheets and pulling them up to his face was that the capable woman outside would likely never need him for anything.

The Keeper filled a large pot with water and set it to boil in the kitchen. She pushed back out into the chilly morning and inspected the damage done to the birds. A few had hit the Light at such an angle that their bones were no doubt crushed; they would not be edible. These she would pluck before burying. She chose one to cook for their supper, and then went to find a sack, which she filled with the rest.

She paused outside the bedroom, but there was no sound or stir, so she made her way to town with the remaining birds, where she asked the butcher if he had use for several Canada geese. He showed some skepticism about her finding them, but he gave her a reasonable price and she pocketed the coins, refolding her sack. Before she headed home—*home*, she thought—she stopped by Dahlia's bakery and asked about Claire, but the saleswoman gave her a blank look and offered to sell her a pastry. She bought a loaf of nondescript bread instead and walked quickly home, smiling when she rounded the bend and saw the house, with the Light behind.

Ronan was still thankfully asleep, and she made quick work of plucking feathers and dressing the bird she had chosen for their supper. She slid it into the oven and slung the towel over her shoulder, surveying her kitchen. *It's yours now, is it?*

While the goose roasted she went back outside to clean the side of the Light and dig a grave for the remaining few birds in the garden, where they could nourish her plants come summer. *Your plants, is it?*

She was about to check on the roasting bird when Ronan's sleep-dented head appeared at the front door. Her mouth softened at the sight of his hair sticking up on one side and the look of confusion on his face. It made her feel lighter, inexplicably, but perhaps that was the result of a productive afternoon well spent.

She smiled slightly and slipped past him into the kitchen to pull the goose from the oven, filling the house with the delicious smell, while Ronan trailed back in. He watched her as one would watch a strangely behaving new species of waterfowl: curiously but not without a wise amount of caution.

He poured a glass of water from the spout and drank it at the sink where he stood. The Keeper watched him tip his head back, the long column of his throat working to swallow. *I could watch him for hours,* came the unbidden thought. Suddenly she felt crowded in the small kitchen.

"Are you hungry?" she asked a little too brightly.

He looked over at her, dazed. "Is that one of the geese from—"

"Yes."

His eyebrows rose. He looked at her for a long moment. "You're a resourceful one, aren't you?" he asked, not expecting an answer, but trying to be polite. He felt the rising panic of two nights before re-emerge in his chest.

"Yes, typically," she answered truthfully. "I also sold most of them to the butcher. He gave me a decent price for them, too. I haggled with him for a few minutes, but it was worth it in the end. I used some of your coin when I was here last . . ." She trailed off, and seeing his expression, her own fell.

Ronan had been keeping his composure for the last two days, his mind still grappling with her truths, but when she talked of things like replacing coins she had used in the *future*—

She tried again. "I didn't think you'd want to eat goose for so many days in a row, and I wanted someone to be able to use them before they spoiled," she explained, setting the table quickly and efficiently.

Ronan watched her as though a thick veil separated them. She was so normal, so undisturbed. "Excuse me," he said and stood abruptly. He had to go outside, had to get air.

He felt anxiety well up inside of him again. *Who is this woman? What is she doing in my life, for God's sake?* A cursory glance showed him what she had been doing the last few hours. He looked up and saw the clean Light. She had sorted, buried, sold, and roasted the birds. Replaced coins she hadn't used yet. Traveled through time. Buried him. His mind couldn't process the traveling-through-time bit, so had suspended disbelief there, but the cold efficiency with which she had disposed of the birds was a hard stopping point. He found his feet taking him several paces away from the door, up the path.

The Keeper opened the front door timidly behind him, unsure of what she'd said to put that look in his eyes. He was bent over, hands on his knees, his broad back to her. He heard the door open and looked over his shoulder at her. She felt his hard gaze on her, and it stung her, even at a distance. He turned away from her and was violently sick in the middle of the path.

She sighed as she watched him retch. *Stay,* she told herself. *Stay and fight. There's a reason I'm here.* His back still to her, he walked to the outdoor pump and rinsed his mouth for several long moments. For good measure, he doused his whole head with cold water.

She went back inside and washed her hands at the sink, preparing to put away the food. She smiled to herself ruefully. *The first meal I ever cook for a man, and he takes one look at it and loses the contents of his stomach in the road.*

As she dried her hands, she heard Ronan stomping the dirt off of his feet at the door. Wordlessly, he came inside and returned to his side of the table. The tips of his eyelashes were wet, star-tipped. She gave him a tentative smile, which he couldn't return, but he picked up the knife and began carefully to carve the goose.

She leaned on her elbows across from him as he worked, and watched. He carved the same way he wrote in the keeper's log: neatly, precisely, and methodically.

She told him so, and saw a faint blush steal across his cheeks. She bit her lip. *Stop,* she chided herself. She hadn't meant to embarrass him. "I felt that I would have liked you, based on your handwriting," she told him, unthinkingly.

She saw him swallow, thickly, and other than a slight hitch in his movements, he continued to carve the goose. He held out a piece to her plate and she took it, grateful that he hadn't made for the door again.

They said nothing for several minutes, then he quietly said, "You said this morning that you'd done this before. When did you last bury birds?" He didn't meet her gaze, but became suddenly interested in the contents of his plate, though she doubted he tasted anything he was eating.

She eyed him speculatively. "You won't lose your supper?"

A hint of a smile moved under the beard. "I make no promises," he said lightly.

"All right," she said, and rolled her shoulders.

"I remember one time quite well, though it happens from time to time," she started, hesitantly, feeling surprisingly vulnerable and watching for his reaction. "I found myself at a Light along the mid-Atlantic coast in the late 1870s."

I was a child, thought Ronan. *She was doing this when I was a child.* He felt the same sort of vertigo he had felt before, as though the room sat on a floating axis, but he fought through the nausea to hear her out.

"It was a fixed white Light during the fall migration—the fixed Lights seem to attract them—and the keeper was asleep, as it was about the middle of the night. The night was calm and dark. They often are when this happens, in my experience."

In her experience, he thought. It struck him as a singularly confident statement, and he couldn't think of another woman who had uttered it in his presence.

"The Light was strong, the keeper was asleep, and the foghorn was in good working order. I had no sooner started looking to see if anyone was in the water, or if a ship up the beach was in distress, when I heard them above."

So she rescues drowning seamen? he thought. *By God. And how efficient she must be at it all.* He imagined her arriving in her prim attire, at odds with her wild hair, arranging the Light, its keeper, and anyone who tried to drown, then sitting beside the fire with a book.

She was watching him carefully. "I don't always get to ships in time, or sailors, for that matter."

Lucky guess, he thought, but he began to see the fraying edges that she had been showing him with her tears in the last few days.

She shrugged. "The Light had been a tall one, one hundred and four steps." She paused.

Has she counted the steps of my Light?

"Forty-two," she said, her eyes suddenly bright through the weariness he had detected.

"Stop that," he insisted, his lips curving in an involuntary smile.

"I heard the sound above as I stood at the foot of the Light," she continued, and sobered, remembering. "It's a singular sound. I remember the dull crunching, and then there was a flurry above, and I heard it again and again and again." She had a stunned, faraway look on her face. "I stood there, paralyzed, for several minutes while bloody feathers rained down on me. I remember one of the birds glancing off my shoulder on the way down, and that it hurt." She brought a hand up to rub absently at her right shoulder.

He found himself frowning, wincing, and hanging on to her every word. "Do you feel pain?" he asked. The words dropped into the space between them, and into her gut.

"Nothing breaks my skin," she began slowly, "but I do feel pain." *Do I feel anything else?* She thought of her practice again. *I have pain,* she thought. *It's a mercy at least to feel that.*

He nodded, unaware of her internal struggle, and she continued. "The lantern room was badly damaged, and it took the keeper and me hours to deal with it."

He could imagine her, working alongside some faceless keeper, and he frowned a little at the image. "Do you do that often?" he asked, his tone unreadable. "Work alongside other keepers?"

She shook her head. "Not often, no. I usually work in their absence. This keeper woke while I was sorting through the birds." A wan smile passed over her face. "I think he took me for a concerned citizen from town, visiting the Light."

Ronan said nothing, but continued to listen. "It wasn't all one type of bird, as it was this morning," she continued. "There were different kinds of warblers, sparrows, thrushes. I even thought I saw a robin among them." Her voice held a hollow mournfulness. "Over a hundred birds in all."

"A hundred!" he exclaimed, shaking his head.

"Yes," she replied, "it was awful. I had dreams of bloody feathers raining down on me for days after that."

She shivered, and he felt a sudden pity for her. Capable as she was, that did sound awful.

"I've probably buried more birds than most people see in a lifetime," she added. There was not a hint of pride in her voice, Ronan noticed. She was simply stating a fact, though that didn't make it less unsettling. His supper stayed down, mercifully, and they got through the meal in peace.

∻ 15 ∻

SHE WOKE IN THE MIDDLE of the night gasping, the sheets twisted around her legs. She brought a hand to her heart and felt it pounding beneath her palm. *Will I never be able to sleep peacefully again?* She made loose fists with her hands then wriggled her fingers, willing away the imagined pain. She looked around the darkened room, so familiar and yet still different, still masculine. *When does it change?*

She pulled on his coat and slipped into her shoes. She stepped out into the cold night and crossed over to the Light, watching as its rays stretched far over the water. It was a good, strong Light, like its keeper. She and Ronan were developing a tentative coexistence after the last several days. There was honesty between them, at the least. *It doesn't get much more honest than losing the contents of his stomach in the yard over me,* she thought, gathering the coat tightly around her.

Ronan was a young man, likely in his middle thirties, and solidly built. *He's handsome, too,* she thought clinically. What was he doing in such an isolated place, without the love of a wife or little ones climbing his legs? She could see his kind eyes taking in a family and his shoulders being a support and comfort.

She shook her head. *You're just thinking those things because you're lonely,* she told herself sternly. *You're not thinking of him at all. Selfish. And don't you dare look to him for any of it. You know better than that.* Her conscience was right, and she knew it. There would be no fairness in seeking any comfort—or providing any—here. *But,* she told herself in a new, calmer voice, *there's no harm in being his friend. I'm here, and I don't know when I'll go. Plus, I'm older than the pyramids, and he knows it.* With that thought she pushed open the metal door at the base of the Light.

She climbed the stairs and found him leaning out over the railing, watching the ocean below. He had his log in one hand, a finger holding his place, and a pencil tucked behind his right ear. He turned at the sound of her steps, a small welcoming smile softening his face. He glanced at his coat on her and said nothing. *Are you sure,* she asked herself, *that there can be no comfort here?* She smiled back and stepped in next to him.

"Can't sleep?" he asked.

She shook her head, her hair whipping in the cold wind. "Bad dreams," she replied shortly.

He turned to look at her and nodded knowingly. "You should forgive yourself, then," he said, turning to look back out to sea.

She swayed back on her heels a bit. *Well, then,* she thought, *that's that. There's nothing to say to that.*

He was the best kind of companion, the type who could hold his peace, who didn't need to fill silence with mindless talk, and he emanated warmth. She pulled the coat tightly around herself and inched closer to him, careful not to touch him. She could see his face dimly in profile, the crow's feet at his eyes, doubtless from many hours spent squinting out to sea or under the sun's rays.

"I failed someone once." He stopped to clear the gravel of sorrow from his voice. "I still work to forgive myself." She waited patiently. She could out-wait, out-sit, out-stand anybody, and if there was a fitting friend for a solitary man on an outcropping of land with none but the seabirds for company, it was surely she.

The Keeper kept her eyes trained forward to the sea, but she sensed him take a steadying breath beside her. Out of the corner of her eye she could see that his head was bowed against the wind and his broad shoulders were stiff, his hands gripping the railing with pale knuckles. She gave up pretending and turned to look openly at him. His eyebrows were a dark, angry slash, and his jaw looked wired together so forcefully that if it became even a hint tenser, a fissure might open across his cheek.

He looked tightly wound enough that he might spring up and vault over the railing to attack whatever it was that had put such a fierce expression on his face. It was incongruous to think of this type of coiled energy in such a gentle man. He noticed her watching, and carefully, as if he were extracting them from a death-choke, his hands loosened from the railing, his jaw unlocked, and his eyes cleared, until there was just grief.

There were no words for this kind of pain, and she didn't offer any, she who was well acquainted with sorrow. She subtly tugged the sleeve of the coat down over her palm and placed it carefully over his shoulder. They stood there for a long time, watching for ships, the strong beacon periodically slicing across the dark sea above them. A schooner passed them, flashing a lantern light in gratitude. She counted the larger crash of every third wave over and over and over again, her heart calmed by the sound. Gradually, the rise and fall of his shoulder became less tempestuous and more like the sea beneath them, full of a nervous energy, but the surface more or less still enough to reflect the moonlight. *Light air, ripples at the surface,* she thought. *Beaufort score: 1.*

She hoped vaguely that if she translated, the rules would mercifully not apply to a thing that was separated from her by layers of clothing. She liked him enough that she preferred to leave him standing there whole, rather than have him as a picture of himself on her body. Or whatever would happen. She had never tried trans-lating with a person before. *Best not to find out,* she thought. *I'm not intending to keep him,* she prayed fervently, hoping that if she thought it hard enough, perhaps it would be true.

He didn't move, except for the warm rise and fall of his breath. They stood there for a portion of the night, during which the silence cemented their tenuous friendship. The waves lapped up the shore below, the loon-calls were familial and comforting in the distance, and his breath beside her was soothing.

At last he turned to look at her. "You're a steady one," he said, appreciatively. "I don't usually lose either staring or silence contests." He chuckled, shaking his head, and she removed her sleeved hand from where it rested on his shoulder.

She let him draw the smile out of her. "Remind me to tell you about the time I lost my ability to make a proper fist," she said mys-teriously. She waited to see if he would crack right away, but he only smiled back, amused.

"Do you see anything in the moon?" he asked her suddenly, jut-ting his chin out at the full moon over the water. It spilled light in an unrolled carpet from where it hung suspended over the water.

"Sometimes I see a woman in it," replied the Keeper, gazing up.

"I see a warrior," he told her. "He's slaying a dragon. Do you see his outline there? He's on a horse."

"Saint George, then."

"Yes, that's it," he told her. "That's who I see." She looked over at him and smiled, glad to be normal with someone. She had a feeling Ronan was about as normal as a person could be, which made him rather extraordinary.

"I like to look for constellations," she told him. "Do you have a spyglass?"

He nodded and, reaching into the front of his uniform, pulled out a small spyglass to hand to her.

As she took it she thought of the night she had buried him, and how she had looked up and seen the Dippers. She lifted the spyglass to her eyes and looked for them. The night sky leapt up in front of her, large and clear enough to reach. She jumped and laughed a little in wonder at the sight. There was a contented smile on her face when she handed the spyglass back to him. He was watching her with an even sobriety, and she ducked her head under his scrutiny.

"I think I can sleep now," she murmured. "Thank you." He nodded, pensive, and she felt him slip back into his memories as she turned from the railing and made her way back to the cottage, tucked herself under the warm covers, and fell into a dreamless sleep.

The middle-of-the-night meeting had loosened a knot she didn't know had been tied in her middle. The next morning Ronan found her kneeling in the garden, wearing one of his old shirts over her dress. His eyes rested on her in his shirt and lingered for a moment. She was yanking up weeds by their deepest roots, as though her frustrations were buried in the earth and she could banish them as easily as shallow-rooted weeds. *That's a lass*, he thought. *The earth can take it.* By midmorning she was dirty and exhausted, but not a single weed had escaped to cast a shadow in the small garden plot. He passed by, hauling driftwood he had found to patch the chicken coop.

She sat back, surveying her work, a pleased look on her dirt-smudged face, and as he passed by she glanced up, saw him, and flashed him an unguarded smile. Ronan of the Light stopped in his tracks, held fast by the sight. Her smile arrowed across the small space between them and skewered him where he stood. He could only manage a nod and a gruff word in return before ducking his head into the driftwood to hide the rising flush beneath his beard.

Over their midday meal, she asked him, hesitantly, if he knew her friend Claire. He frowned, thought it over, and shook his head. "I don't think there's a Claire in town," he said, and then seemed to think better of it. "Well, there's one Claire, but it couldn't be who you're speaking of. She's nothing like you describe." The Keeper left it at that.

~: 16 :~

IT WAS MID-SPRING. THEY DIDN'T speak about whether she would be pulled away again to another time, but they both lived in anticipation of it. There was nothing to be done about it. She knew that at some point she had to have left, in order to have come back to bury him. It could have been a day from now, or a year, or the remainder of his life. She grieved his death that second season in Ronan's cottage, as she had not known to do the first season.

They fell into a comfortable routine of waking in early afternoon and tending the small garden, seeing to the chickens, preparing an evening meal, and tending the hundred small tasks of a Light-station together. She couldn't pinpoint exactly when he had allowed her to tend the Light with him, but it had been early on. Once he had tentatively asked her if she wanted to help with the Light, she knew he had begun to accept her story, her presence, and in turn, her.

Some nights she stayed up with him to keep the Light, but sleep was a luxury she had gone long without and she found herself tucked, many nights, under the warm covers with her nose in a book. The keeper had a magnificent library, and she was steadily working her way through a section of it.

"What are you reading tonight?" he asked her one night in late spring while he was preparing their evening meal.

She paused in her perusal of the bookshelf and looked over her shoulder at him. "Pardon?"

Bemused, a smile tugging his lips, he asked his question again.

"Oh, I, uh . . ." she was midway through a sentence, and she had nearly settled on a book. "This one, I think," she said, flipping the book closed for a moment.

"It's all right," he said, a smile in his voice.

"What?"

"Nothing. Nothing at all." He smiled down at the potato he was slicing.

"What?"

He laughed outright, but she didn't hear him. She had gathered the book in one hand and tucked her legs beneath her in the armchair. She was lost to the world, sinking into the book as she had sunk into the chair, her attention rapt. He finished preparing the evening meal and glanced at her now and then. She was transported. He had learned by now that there was no speaking with her when she was like this.

An hour later she stretched a crick in her neck and realized she'd forgotten herself. She looked up, startled to find Ronan gone, and hurriedly marked her place in the book before heading outside to look for him.

She found him tending the Light and apologized sheepishly for being absent. He looked up and smiled good-naturedly at her. "Lass, you're lost to the world when you read," he laughed. He had continued to call her "Lass" or "Light Lass" and hadn't brought up the idea of giving her a name after the first mention. She hadn't brought it up either because it seemed too intimate, and she didn't mind answering to "Light Lass" because secretly, it sounded like an endearment.

She nodded and bent to help him. "Reading has always been a comfort to me," she told him. "Wherever I've traveled books have been some of my few companions." *I have books,* she thought, practicing. *I can read. That's a mercy.*

He nodded. "I know how it is." They worked companionably side by side. "What do you like to read?"

"Oh, everything," she told him, her eyes widening, and he couldn't contain his answering laugh.

"Recently I've reread the poems in *Gitanjali* by Tagore." She seemed to suddenly remember something and muttered under her breath.

"It's all right, lass."

She looked up at him apologetically. "Give it a few years. In 1913, I think."

"Don't trouble yourself," he reassured her. They worked in silence for a few minutes until he looked up to ask her, humbly, "Do you know any of his poems? I don't recall the name . . ." He trailed off.

"Oh, Tagore!" she said, eyes bright. "Yes, yes of course." She thought for a moment, remembering.

My song has put off her adornments. She has no pride of dress and decoration. Ornaments would mar our union; they would come between thee and me; their jingling would drown thy whispers.

My poet's vanity dies in shame before thy sight. O master poet, I have sat down at thy feet. Only let me make my life simple and straight, like a flute of reed for thee to fill with music.

Her voice was strong and sure, and it seemed to resonate in the small space. Ronan eyed her with surprise, as though seeing her for the first time.

"The workers in the field sang—will sing—his poems like songs. They're prayers in my mind, in any case."

"Tagore," said Ronan, trying the name out on his tongue.

"He's one of my favorite poets. I can share some others," she said. He assumed she meant others who hadn't yet written their work. Her brow knit in hesitation.

Beside her, he chuckled. "Don't worry," he said lightly. "I live on an outcropping in the middle of God-forgot-Maine, lass. I'll not be stealing another's work."

She nodded, smiling, and then something else occurred to her. "How do you know?" she asked, her voice serious.

In all seriousness he turned to her. "Your face is an open book. Sometimes, at least." They headed back down toward the house for supper, she a few steps ahead of him on the narrow path.

"Have you read Conrad?" she asked, as they turned into the warmth of the kitchen.

"*The Heart of Darkness?*"

"Yes, that one."

"I finished it a few weeks ago," he said over his shoulder as he set out a loaf of bread.

"What did you think of it?"

He took the knife to the end of the bread and began to meticulously slice the loaf. "Chilling, I thought," he said, brows meeting in concentration. "Do you remember the part when they're drifting down the river, and Marlow realizes that the cannibals are all slowly starving to death, but haven't made a move to eat him or his companions?"

He waited until she placed the scene in her mind and nodded, sitting across from him. He continued to slice the loaf, the knife neatly sawing thick slabs.

"'Why in the name of all the gnawing devils of hunger didn't they go for us—they were thirty to five—and have a good tuck-in for once,'" his strong voice quoted.

"Yes, yes," she exclaimed, delighted. "I'd nearly forgotten. That is a brilliant bit there."

He finished slicing the bread and slipped a piece onto her outstretched plate. "And then he hopes, in a rather vain way, that it's not because he's unappetizing. Imagine!"

"Yes," she said, smiling at his obvious pleasure in the recollection.

They began their meal in companionable silence for a while until he said, "I've been meaning to ask: what is it about Herodotus?" He had seen her try to pilfer his copy on more than one occasion.

She thought for a moment, her head tipped slightly to one side in a way he was beginning to expect. "He defies categorization, for one," she said finally.

He looked at her incredulously for a moment. "Mercy's sake, woman, it's called *The Histories*, as you well know!" he burst out, laughing. He took a generous bite of his bread and leaning forward, propped his elbows on the table.

Her eyes danced with laughter. "Herodotus," she began primly, her hands folded in front of her, trying to keep a straight face, "was a moralist, a comedian, a teacher, and . . ." She fumbled for a moment.

"A historian?" he supplied helpfully, his voice solemn.

They stared at each other across the table, each trying to hold out longer, until they both lost the battle and gave in to laughter.

"Bless you," he said finally. "It feels good to have a laugh." She bowed from the waist as much as she was able to while seated at the table.

They said nothing for a while, the silence as comforting as the soup they were sharing. "You know," she said, "book genres begin to blur." She did a little wave with her hand. It was the same sort of hand wave one would use to say "and so on and so forth," except with her, it meant "in the future."

"Do they?"

"Yes. You still have many of the same ones as you do now, but they expand and change, some unrecognizably." He nodded encouragingly. "You still have histories." She ignored his smirk. "You have biographies, fiction, nonfiction. Things start to degenerate in the middle of the twenty-first century, though. There will be books designed to make you feel cold again as the climate of the earth heats up." He paused, the spoon partway to his mouth. She continued, "Then there's a whole genre of books about post-apocalyptic happenings. We become single-mindedly preoccupied with our demise as a species."

He eyed her warily for a moment, as if gauging whether she was being humorous or not. Deciding on the latter, he put the spoon to his lips and continued eating. To lighten the mood a little the Keeper said, "And of course you have the classics, though that broadens from the Greek classics to include literature over a hundred years old in general. Arthur Conan Doyle, for instance . . ." She trailed off suggestively.

He stopped eating entirely and put his spoon down. "You blaspheme," he said aghast, eyes dancing.

She nearly snorted her soup, shaking her head in denial. "It's true! All the English works that survive into the twenty-first century are more or less considered 'classics.'"

He smiled broadly at her and then shook his head. "The way you say 'the twenty-first century,'" he said, attempting nonchalance.

She sobered quickly, eyeing him across the table. "Does it bother you?"

He thought for a moment, the silence between them no longer entirely comfortable.

"*Bother* is not quite the word," he said carefully. "It makes my hair stand on end a bit. It's difficult to explain." And then he shook his head, forcing a small smile. "Sherlock Holmes a classic! Imagine!"

They lingered over their dinner, quoting aloud from various books, and she couldn't remember what they ate, but she got up from the table satisfied.

The next night they were working side by side at the Light when he asked her suddenly, "Is it difficult, traveling alone? As a woman, I mean." His mouth quirked and a flush rose on his neck, but he didn't take the question back.

She straightened to her full height and tipped her head back to look up at him. "What do you mean?"

"Well, is it safe for you, when you travel alone? No one bothers you or tries to insult your person?" She continued to look at him blankly. "You're a woman alone. No one tries to take advantage of you?" His face was flaming red.

She knew he was asking out of concern, but an imp of mischief in her was annoyed that he felt he should be concerned. She furrowed her brow and tilted her head to the side, her face a clear question mark. He looked more closely and saw that she was holding back mirth and her eyes were laughing at him. He shook his head and turned away, not sure why he was bothered by her reaction. She briefly touched his shoulder.

"Ronan," she said, chastened, "I thank you for your concern. But no. No one has taken advantage of me or abused me in any way." He still didn't look back at her but busied himself cleaning the lens. She continued to explain. "Humans feel insubstantial to me," she reminded him. "And times change quite dramatically for women, you know." That captured his attention.

"It won't be too long now, actually," she remembered out loud. "In just a few years women will begin to vote." His eyebrows rose, and she grinned. "You might as well side with the suffragettes." He eyed her warily, as though he knew she was about to say some more unexpected things, and she didn't disappoint. "They become scientists, barristers, captains, pilots, doctors, professors." His eyebrows were frozen, high on his forehead. "Presidents and prime ministers," she added. The eyebrows seemed to disappear under his thatch of hair. "Astronauts," she said, her eyes widening in sympathy with his.

He cleared his throat. "I'm unfamiliar with that word."

"They travel into space." She pointed up, and his eyes helplessly followed her finger. The sky was a deep blue above them, the sun shining down as it had on any other day, and yet, she knew, she had perhaps said too much at once. Her feminine pride had been stung by his implication that she needed protecting, and she had lashed out at him in the most unsubtle way. It was a little like killing a beetle with a blunt shovel: pitiless and with unnecessary force. He stood pinned to the ground, face tilted up to the sky, seemingly lost in time.

He finally looked back down at her, and she mourned the new knowledge in his eyes. *I did this*, she said to herself mercilessly. *I put that world-weary look in his eyes because my pride was stung. And because I hate being the only one who knows.*

He gave her a long, unreadable look and simply said, "It must be difficult for you, knowing what you know, to be here, in this time."

Contrite, she shook her head before her mind could formulate a denial. "No—that is, no. Not at all." He looked at her with open disbelief. "Well, some things are difficult. The lack of access to information is difficult." She was definitely going to save the long conversation about the internet for another day. "There are difficult things about freedom and equality as well," she offered, unsure of how to explain. "The rules of relationships change such that women are often trapped between obligations in the home and their place of employment. Child-rearing becomes almost a luxury." He stared at her as though she had sprouted a second head.

"Oh, and in your time, women lightkeepers have equal pay for equal work!" she finished, trying for lightness. "That's rather progressive—it doesn't happen in some other professions for at least another hundred years." *That's quite enough*, she reprimanded herself, not meeting his gaze. "Suffice it to say," she finished, "I like this time well enough." She looked up at him and gave him a warm smile he could feel was genuine, and a peace offering. "It has much to recommend it."

The bewildered look on his face relaxed somewhat and he nodded down at her. He was quiet for a time and then finally said, "I'd like to hear more about this later." She nodded up at him, and they finished tending the Light together.

Later that night, when they sat in armchairs by the fire, Ronan set aside *The Red Badge of Courage* and angled his body toward her. She smiled at him and set aside her own book.

"Do you often go into the future?" he asked her, without preamble.

The Keeper hesitated for a moment.

"Of course you don't have to answer."

"Oh, it's all right," she replied hastily. "I don't mind talking about it. I just don't know that it helps. Do you think it would bother you to know what is going to happen before it does?"

"What kinds of things?" he asked, settling back more deeply into the chair.

"Oh, the big things," began the Keeper slowly. "Wars, natural disasters." She trailed off for a moment. "Deaths," she added, looking up to meet his gaze.

He had wondered on several occasions if she remembered the exact date of his death. He didn't think about it overlong, as he was wiser than to request knowledge that would doubtless cause grief, both in the telling and the hearing, but he had naturally wondered.

The Keeper watched him with her request in her eyes. *Please, Ronan*, she pleaded silently. *Please, please, please. Please don't ask it of me.*

He sighed. "What about the little things?" he asked.

She saw the resignation and acceptance in his face, and saw what it cost him to stay his tongue. How could he sit with her, knowing what she knew, and keep his peace? *This man's spirit towers*, she thought.

She forced a small smile. "Of course. I can talk about the little things." She thought for a moment. "Have you ever been to New York City?"

"I was there years ago. I was young when my family traveled from Scotland," he said, some hesitation in his answer.

"I figured," she began, smiling, and then realized that to him it amounted to an admission of some inferiority. *A conversation for another day*, she thought. "Well," she began, "I don't often go Ahead, as I think of it. Everything after lighthouse use declines—" She paused. Automation toward the latter half of the twentieth century had all but replaced lightkeepers entirely. Being replaced by a light bulb surely qualified as a big thing, didn't it?

He hadn't missed the pause. "Whyever would lighthouse use decline?" he asked with polite indignation.

"I didn't say they stop being used, Ronan, but they are relied upon less. It has to do with the light bulb and electricity." She could feel the tension in him as he sat next to her. "Are you certain you want to hear about these things?"

He was quiet for a moment, during which he no doubt deliberated the merits of hearing her out, and then replied in the affirmative.

"The first time I saw New York City was from the torch of Lady Liberty," she began.

"My God." He brought the cup to his mouth and took a deliberate swallow.

"Yes, well," she said, mildly embarrassed by his look of open admiration. "As you know, she functioned as a Light briefly, from 1886 to 1902, before it was decided that the Light was too expensive to maintain and not quite bright enough to merit the effort." He nodded dumbly.

He sat staring at her over his teacup until she looked away. "It wasn't much, Ronan, really. The Light had dimmed and I sent up a signal that night. Who knows whether it helped anyone anywhere. It wasn't much." *Stop apologizing! Stop talking!* she thought.

He eyed her speculatively, and she had the sudden feeling that she had been found out, and worse, by something she herself had said. He seemed to need something to do with his hands, because he cleared his throat, broke eye contact, and stood for a moment to retrieve his whittling from the mantel, and then hunkered back down.

She continued. "I remember gripping the torch with my left hand and leaning out as far as I could to the right, to see the city. The second time I saw New York was Ahead, from the Little Red Lighthouse under the George Washington Bridge."

He leaned forward and began to carefully trim a rough piece of wood, and the Keeper watched as a long curlicue of wood shaving lengthened under his focused attention. It made her happy to watch him whittle, though she knew not why. She wrapped herself into her memories and began to recount what she remembered.

Little Red Lighthouse, Hudson River, New York City, 2010

She didn't often get to go Ahead, as she thought of it, after the decline of lighthouse use, but she found she liked it. By the end of the twentieth century there was little need for her services unless both the new technology and the backup failed, which wasn't often. Sometimes she was there for a local fisherman who had capsized his boat, or for a swimmer too far out to sea. In either case, she served the person who needed her and quickly went into the nearest city to snatch up the nearest newspaper. She devoured all the books at hand, the newest she could find, reading frantically and learning all she could before being called away.

Her second time in New York City, she had spent one frantic week in a library, her heart racing as she sped through everything she could read, chewing down her fingernails, pausing periodically to cover her face with her hands in horror at the news, or sighing in relief that an outcome had been better than she had expected.

The Keeper had arrived in trousers—those she remembered fondly—topped by an odd, abbreviated cotton shirt. She found herself at the edge of the Hudson River by the Little Red Lighthouse beneath the George Washington Bridge. She had read about the lighthouse in a children's story once, and she could see tourists milling about. The wind whipped her hair against her face as she remembered, "Once upon a time a little lighthouse was built on a sharp point of the shore by the Hudson River." It certainly is a sharp point, isn't it? She couldn't remember the next line, but then came something about it being "fat and jolly and red." Yes, that was it. "And proud," or something like that. Well, it was certainly fat and jolly and red. Like a Santa Clause lighthouse, she thought, glancing over her shoulder at it.

That's when the woman above her jumped off the George Washington Bridge and fell with a sick splat into the water before her.

God, she prayed, and in a trice broke into a run and dove into the river.

Some humans valued their lives little until they were threatened with death, as she herself had done. She thought often of that day in the ocean, and of the change of heart she'd had as the foghorn sounded in her ears while they filled with water. The woman she pulled wide-eyed and sputtering from the murk of the Hudson was not one of those humans. She rounded on the Keeper, filled with spitting rage.

The woman screamed something unintelligible and tried to drag them both down. "Let me go!" she screamed again. It was a high, horrible sound that robbed the Keeper of breath with its anguish. The woman struck out at her, connected with her face, and the Keeper reeled from the stinging pain.

The woman screamed again and tried to slip out of her arms, raising them above her head. The Keeper had the brief impression of a child who, not wanting to be picked up, put her arms straight over her head to slide out of her mother's grip. And suddenly they were surrounded. A pair of strong arms gently relieved the Keeper of her burden, and another two pairs contained the furious woman.

The woman was sobbing by then, bobbing in the water between two rescue workers. She gave the Keeper a look of pure loathing that stung her more with its violence than the blow across her cheek. "I hate you!" the woman screamed. "Who asked you to save me?" She tilted her face to the sky and shrieked her fury as she was drawn away from the Keeper.

The Keeper found herself also in strong arms, her body frozen in shock as her senses slowly recovered. She felt the cold water, saw the traffic stopped above on the bridge, people peering down in morbid curiosity or concern. Or both. She tasted the sludge of the river, briny like olives on her lips, and winced at the pain on her cheekbone. She smelled the man who held her, spicy and sweet at the same time. She looked up into his face. He was dark-skinned and handsome. "Don't worry about her," he said, his voice a deep rumble in his chest. "She didn't mean it." The Keeper closed her eyes for a long moment, and unable to help herself, she tucked her face against him.

She remembered his heart beating beneath her ear as he held her in the cold water of the Hudson. She didn't often get this close to others, and it felt better than anything, to be held against a human heart this way and told not to worry, though he couldn't know what she truly worried about. Certainly not that the woman hadn't meant it. Of course she meant it. She understood both the woman's pain and the intolerable sting of a thwarted will. She had been held against her own will her entire life, after all.

Oh, why didn't I just let her drown? she thought. *The moment lengthened, the river of time slowing to a pond around her. Why not let her have what I cannot? But she didn't want to be dead just then. She was quite enjoying being held, hearing a human heart against her ear, being alive and cold and wet, with a painful cheekbone and the foul river water in her mouth. Perhaps we all need someone to choose life for us at one time or another, she thought, though the thought didn't fully satisfy. She thought of the woman screaming and spitting, furious at being rescued, and was not sure she had done the right thing.*

She continued to think of it as she was gently helped to shore and given a blanket to dry off and warm up with, and later, after she'd been predictably forgotten and had slipped away to think under the bridge. She sat there for a few minutes, watching the flashing lights and the journalists getting the story from the three rescue workers. The one who had briefly held her in the water thought, as he recounted the tale, that there was something important he was forgetting, but for the life of him he couldn't remember.

The Keeper sat and thought for a while, and then, realizing she couldn't answer this question readily, decided she would make the best of the time she had left while she was Ahead. She laid the blanket out to dry next to a man sleeping huddled under the bridge, and with one last glance at the fat, jolly, red Light, she walked out onto the main road.

She thought a little longer, lost in the memory. She had gone on to live an entire glorious week in the New York City Public Library, until she translated to the next assignment, but the thought of the young woman had stayed with her the entire time.

How would it have been different had she known what Wisdom later told her? If she had known she was there for herself rather than for the woman who had jumped off the bridge? *I would still have gone in after her,* she thought. *I must have been there for her. Perhaps,* the thought came to her, *I was there for both of us? Both her and me? Is every assignment that way? Is it for me and for them?*

Aloud, she continued her tale to Ronan. "I realized later that I hadn't thanked the rescue worker," she said regretfully.

Ronan regarded her and then quietly asked, "Do you not think he knew that you were grateful?"

The Keeper shrugged. "I'm not often on the receiving end." He nodded, still watching her closely. *Why does he look at me like I'm giving every secret away?*

"In any case, I certainly felt thankful, and I hope he knew how grateful I was for his kindness. I've thought of him many times," she added more slowly. "Who am I to receive comfort from one such as he? His life is so brief, and it cost me nothing to jump in after the woman in the river. People like him risk themselves daily for others. There is no risk to me."

"It doesn't mean your time or sentiment matters less."

She wasn't sure that was true, but didn't say so. Instead she said, "I wonder how others feel when I offer them an anonymous service. I wonder if it leaves the same impression of kindness, or if it smacks of charity?" She shook her head. "*I* don't like it, in any case," she said, uncomfortably.

"What don't you like?"

"I don't like to receive. I like to give."

He nodded again, and she had the distinctly uncomfortable sensation that he now somehow knew all there was to know about her.

There was a long silence. "Well," he said finally, his tone mild, "there's nothing wrong in receiving." He looked over at her, and she had the impression that he was telling her something about himself now. "I received much kindness once," he explained without elaborating.

She thought back to the night he had told her to forgive herself. *What happened to you?* she wondered.

"I've had too much time on my hands to think it over," he continued, almost sheepishly, "but it seems to me that it is easier to give than to receive. It requires a great deal of humility to accept a meal offered in kindness. The pride in me would rather I starve to death, you understand?"

I understand, she thought. And on the heels of that came a second thought: *It would be the easiest thing I've ever done to let myself care for this man.*

He gave her a small smile. "In any case, I learned to accept help. It makes people feel good to give it, and sometimes a body needs it. And there's a grace in accepting it, as you know."

Had I known? she thought. She did now.

~: 17 :~

RONAN WOKE ONE AFTERNOON ABOUT six weeks after her arrival to find the house empty and the Keeper gone. He walked to the bed and found it unmade, which was unlike her. She didn't normally leave the house in the morning with an unmade bed in her wake. He tried to breathe through the pounding of his heart—he had no right to have a pounding heart where she was concerned. She had to leave at some point, right? So where did the feeling of near-betrayal come from? He certainly couldn't expect a goodbye based on what she'd explained of the process of translating. Nor could he hope for anything from the girl. *Woman,* he corrected. *She's probably older than the Medicis.*

He searched for her, though he told himself that wasn't what he was actually doing, and dragged his feet to tend the Light, waiting until the sun was waning and he could no longer delay. He could hear himself eating when he sat to his nightly meal. He chewed, swallowed, and drank some water. Why did it sound so loud? He hated to hear himself eat. Why had he never noticed that before? That evening he automatically brewed two cups of tea and brought them to the table. He glanced down at the extra cup in his hand, shook his head, and economically drank them both. Then he finally admitted it: he missed her.

Well, it's to be expected, he thought logically. *I've not had company in a while. It was comfortable having her here. She was an interesting woman. Told good stories. It was bracing to have another body around, for the company and the noise.* Then he thought *It's too quiet,* and his mind immediately rebelled at the thought. When had life become too quiet?

I miss her, specifically, he thought, and the thought iced the blood in his veins, because, well, where in the world was she? Her *specifically* was a problem, because if there was ever a woman who would have trouble giving her hand to a man, this would be the one. She left in the night and—God in heaven—*she's already buried me in the hard winter ground, for mercy's sake.* He ran a hand through his hair and found that the hand shook.

Well, she's not here, is she? he told himself harshly. *Whether or not you miss her or want to talk to her over supper, there's nothing in it. There's nothing to be done except get back to work.* And with a heavy heart, he did.

Reykjanesviti, Baejarfell Hill, Reykjanes Peninsula, Iceland, 1912

It was a cold, clear night with a sky of endless ink above her and a million stars to steal her breath. The cold frosted her eyelashes, burned down into her lungs with each breath, and settled in her bones for what was sure to be a long night's vigil. She missed home. *When had it become home?*

I'll probably never go back there again. Surely my work there is done. The thought felt wrong, and she felt in her heart that it was a betrayal of home. Of *him.* She hadn't done anything for him yet, and she still didn't know what her assignment for Ronan of the Light had been. *What it still is,* she thought. *I have to go back. Please.* She didn't know where the thought came from, but she didn't fight it.

There was no ignoring the ache in her heart. It was so new, to have emerging feelings for another human somewhere and be known by him. To know that he perhaps missed her as well? It felt soft and hard and warm and cold at the same time. Well, nothing felt warm at the moment. She could imagine him whittling beside her. *Am I so starved for companionship?* But no, it wasn't just that. *Please let him remember me,* she prayed. It would feel so much worse to be forgotten by Ronan of the Light than by the nameless faces before him. She couldn't think on it just then. She had a task to do.

The Light rose up behind her, whitewashed with a slash of red up top, burning brightly in a single beam out over the plains around it and toward the dark sea. The night was bitterly cold, and she snuggled down into the thick coat and layers of flannel she had translated into.

She cast her eyes above to the stars winking down at her, wondering which had died long ago, leaving only their light behind. Did it make them any less beautiful, that they were no longer really there? Or was it enough that their light glinted down on her? She thought with a brief pang of Ronan, who had died so long ago, and yet was so real to her and had become so essential.

She reluctantly drew her gaze from the sky and headed to the base of the Light to check on the keeper and find her task. She wound her way up the staircase and found neither anything amiss, nor a keeper. She looked out from the tower and noticed the keeper's lodgings a small distance away. Gazing out to sea from the lighthouse perched high atop Baejarfell Hill, she couldn't make out any sign of a ship.

Her brow furrowed and she climbed back down the stairs to make her way quietly to the cottage nearby. She eased the door open, and it slid back on well-oiled hinges. There was likely no need to keep a door locked in such a place as this. She wandered around the keeper's cottage, but there was no one home.

It happened once in a while, though she wasn't sure what to make of it. There was a need here, but she couldn't see it. It disturbed her when she arrived and nothing was amiss. She was left to linger for a time, short or long, without a clear reason. Perhaps she was to keep the Light for someone far at sea whom she could not see but who could just make out the beam from the Light.

Perhaps. Or perhaps her presence somehow allowed the keeper a night off. She chuckled to herself. Or maybe the shadow she cast caused a butterfly's wings to beat a quarter of an inch to the right and that somehow kept the Earth on its axis. She shook her head at her thoughts. She didn't like these assignments at all.

Though I can imagine this assignment being for me. Not all of them, but this one. Would she be here months as she had been in Ronan's home? *Home*, she thought, her heart rising in her throat. She picked her way around the cottage and found the supplies in the kitchen scant. She tucked her hands into her pockets. She didn't need to eat. If the keeper was coming back he would need what little remained. She braced herself against the wind and made her way back to the Light and up the steep stairs. Perhaps she would just stay in the Light, waiting through this long night. Perhaps someone would need her out at sea, though she didn't know how she would get there, so far away. She stepped out onto the ledge of the Light far above the ground and gazed out at the plains between herself and the sea. Nothing. There was nothing obvious. She walked around the back of the narrow Light and bent her head into her gloved hands to warm them.

Something caught the edge of her vision and she lifted her head. Far away from the sea, back beyond the cold wind, on the dark side of the lighthouse, was an undulating warm light that seemed to link the earth and the heavens. Green, red, yellow, it swelled and sang with silent music, connecting the sky with the earth and rippling in the air like the waves of the sea. She stopped in her tracks, hands cupped against her mouth, breath a frosty puff between her fingers, eyes as wide as she could make them, and tried to drink in the sight before her.

It was like watching ocean waves mirrored into the sky, in brilliant color. She didn't know how long she stood there at the back of the wind, on the dark side of the Light, her breath burning in her lungs, her eyes pressed down into her head from the stillness and silence around her, looking out at the lights dancing in the cold, clear night sky. There were no thoughts to think, gazing at a sight like that, for what thought could she have that was worthy? It appeared her only task was to stand and drink with her eyes, and fill what had seemed a bottomless chasm within her.

It might have been minutes or hours, but her body stilled and her mind blanked, and she just stood and stared away the year of darkness that had weighed her down between the Burial, as she'd come to call it in her mind, and the Return. The lights played on her eyes, a riot of color against the night sky, and she let her shoulders lift under the dropped weight of that dark time. *I have these lights for this moment,* she thought. It was a good day in a world where lights like these existed.

If you asked him later—and she did—he could have sworn she arrived on a gust of cold wind smelling of the icy North. He didn't see her return, precisely, but he felt the cold air and rushed out of the house, his heart racing, to find her making her way, calm as you please, up the walkway, her hands tucked into a light coat, her cheeks pinked by an unseen chill, and her hair decidedly windblown. She had a small, secret smile on her face, and he stood in the doorway, his eyes warm on her, as she made her way to the house.

It felt like home, and she looked like home as she tilted her head back to smile up at him when she neared the doorway. He smiled back slightly and moved out of her way so she could enter.

"Welcome back," he said, his voice rusty from disuse. *Welcome home*, he thought.

Her smile brightened. "It's good to be back." *It's good to be home.*
"How long was I gone?" she asked, less brightly, but her voice steady.

His smile flattened a little but he answered her in his easy manner, "A week or so." He paused, and she saw something vulnerable in
his gaze that was immediately shuttered. He let out a small laugh.
"Lass, it's been just about nine days and seven hours, if you'd really
like to know," he told her. She did want to know. It told her all she
needed to know, and more besides.

He ushered her inside, taking her coat and shutting the door
against the night chill. "I've tended the Light and had supper. Are
you hungry?"

"Ravenous," she replied, and he laughed, leading her in and rustling around in the kitchen while she settled at the table.

"Something has lifted that melancholy."

"Yes," she said. He set bread and cheese across from her and sat
at the table with her. "I'm not certain why I was there," she began,
"and I'm not certain where exactly I was, but the lights in the night
sky were . . ." She opened her hands, her palms meant to show that
she had no words to describe what she'd seen. He listened with rapt
attention.

She dug into the cheese and bread, and between bites she tried
haltingly to explain what she'd seen. He listened, his eyes drinking in
through her words what he could not—and, she realized with a sinking feeling, what he would likely never—see. He noticed the exact
moment her tone changed, and his eyes gentled on her.

"Lass, almost no one in this age has seen the aurora," he said
lightly.

"The what?"

"The aurora borealis. Galileo described the northern lights as such
in the sixteen-hundreds," he explained. "That's likely what you saw."
Her eyes widened at him. "What?" he said in mock indignation. "Just

because you're older than the Titans doesn't mean you know every-thing!" Her burst of laughter seemed to startle her more than him, and he smiled as her shoulders relaxed, her body free of tension in the seat across from him.

They sat in companionable silence while she finished her meal. He watched, drinking in her happiness. She found herself smiling crookedly across the table at her friend, happy to be alive, and happy to be home.

❧ 18 ☙

H E DIDN'T CONSIDER HIMSELF AN unobservant man, but it took him another week to realize that, other than the brief handclasp the first night at the kitchen table, she avoided touching him directly. After the second nearly spilled plate of rolls that week, when she did some strange finger-dance in midair to avoid his touch, he eyed her oddly and slid the plate over to her. She kept her head bowed over her plate, silent for a moment.

"So," he said shortly, "you don't prefer to be touched?"

Her head came up quickly, startled. She took a roll in two fingers and began to fiddle with it over her plate. "It's not that at all," she said, shaking her head decisively.

"Just me, then," he said, trying to hide a twinkle in his eye.

"Oh no, of course not." She had reduced the roll to crumbs, realized what she had done, and sheepishly scooped them into her soup. She hated to waste food, war or no war, and she knew one was on the horizon.

"Really. It's not you at all." Her fingers paused in reaching across the table to touch him. She folded them instead, and explained what happened when she translated with something she intended to keep. She drew the neck of her gown to the side to show him the smudged circlet of flowers around her neck. Her gaze was earnest as she explained all this.

By God, but she has a direct gaze, he thought, almost regretting having teased her. "I'm just teasing you, lass," he said softly. He did, however, wish she hadn't pulled back that small, work-roughened hand at the last moment.

She nodded slowly. "I'm starting to understand you," she said, tilting her head to one side, her curls falling over one shoulder.

He watched her, mesmerized as a small smile bloomed over her face. *Would you look at that,* he thought wonderingly.

Her face became stern. "You know," she began, and he had the rising suspicion she had the same bit of the devil in her that he had. "You should have more respect for your elders." She arched her left eyebrow.

It was the same arch his grade school teacher, Mrs. O'Connor, had moments before she'd whisked him up by his ear and given him an exceptional paddling for pinning Mary Ellen's single red braid to his desk. He had been speechless: couldn't they tell that he loved Mary Ellen and this had been the only way—really the only way—he could think to show her? He had singled her out!

He was rather more adept at expressing himself these days, and what this woman sitting across from him surely needed was a bit of flirting, or he didn't know his own name. "What?" he exclaimed in mock outrage. "A little bit of a thing like you, with all that hair?"

Her burst of laughter was like a benediction. It was joyous, she didn't try to stifle it, and her shoulders shook as her laughter rained down over the both of them, drawing an involuntary smile from him. A man could get used to laboring to draw that kind of reaction from her.

They ate in companionable silence, broken now and again by an observation he had made during the day or an idea that had occurred to her. They gathered up the dishes together, and he soaped and she rinsed, side by side at the sink. They didn't touch, and he was care-ful—after realizing that he would run out of dishes at the rate they were breaking them—to keep his long fingers out of her way. She didn't mention it again, but he understood that there was a reason for her distance, and he was nothing if not a patient man. Then, as was becoming habit, one of them put on the kettle for tea while the other checked on the Light.

He knew that she was a Lightkeeper. He understood that she was out of time, in a sense, and that she had traveled to his Light at the end of his own life, though the details were unclear. He wondered, some nights, in the distant way that elders sometimes look at their lives, at his ready acceptance of all this. It was otherworldly, and he wasn't certain he wanted to think about it much more than that. Though it did seem improper, her staying in his home, with him a bachelor and—he stopped short. *Not that again. You know she's older than the Enlightenment.* He had a feeling she might be older than that, or had at least traveled much farther back than that. He tried not to dwell on it so as not to lose his supper. She was obviously only with him temporarily, and calling the authorities to do something about her not only would be inviting trouble to his remote home, but he found he did not want to share her with anyone quite yet. He enjoyed her company; she was the best companion he'd had in years. *Since Margaret,* he thought, and tamped down the surge of sadness.

At night, while she told him a story from her long life, he would either carve something or write some thoughts down. He had recently taken up whittling to while away the hours, and though his work was pitiful in his opinion, it was slowly improving. She had leaned over to inspect a small peg he had started that week and smiled approvingly, the clean, human scent of her hair lingering a moment after she drew away. He had backed away from her quickly. *Best not to complicate things,* he thought.

She asked him about his writing one night, and he showed her his small, handbound notebook. "I'm just writing down some of your stories, lass," he said, a smile in his eyes. "You'll want to read them one day, perhaps."

She wanted to tell him that no, she hadn't seen that particular notebook when she'd been there before, that she had dragged Herodotus around with her everywhere, but the look in his eyes stopped her short.

∾ 19 ∾

"WHAT WAS YOUR FAVORITE ASSIGNMENT?" he asked, little curlicues of wood settling around his stocking-clad feet as he worked on a peg.

She leaned back in her seat, hands wrapped around her cup of tea, and thought. "The Sumiyoshi Toudai," she replied definitively.

Sumiyoshi Toudai, Ogaki, Japan, 1742

Somewhere along the Narrow Road leading to the Deep North along which Matsuo Basho was said to have found enlightenment, surrounded by an almost embarrassingly generous profusion of cherry blossoms in full bloom, stood the short, squat, dark Light. It sat, already lit, its light illuminating the blossoms, and the Keeper stood on the shore of the Suimon River and wondered what could possibly be amiss in a place this peaceful. She didn't often find herself inland, and she rubbed her arms through her wide sleeves, enjoying the warmth of spring by the river.

She gathered the unfamiliar silk brocade enough to walk comfortably and, circling around to the small building adjacent to the Light, found the door slightly ajar. She removed her shoes and placed them next to a larger pair, padding along in her white toe-socks. The house smelled faintly of the rapeseed flower oil she knew they used to fuel the Light.

She headed toward the back of the house and found, kneeling on the ground before a tea service, a dark-haired man, his straight back to her. She waited, patiently, for him to sense her presence. She let her sleeves fall down to her wrists and straightened her shoulders.

He took a sip of his tea, his hand steady. He set the small bowl down and looked over his left shoulder at her. His dark gaze was as steady as his hands, though it seemed a little unfocused.

"Forgive me for starting without you. I wasn't sure if you'd come tonight," he told her, his voice somewhat unsteady. He turned around and extended his hand to the space across from him. "I've just begun."

The Keeper kept her footfalls light and gave him a wide berth as she stepped over to the place he indicated.

He waited for her to settle her skirts and tuck herself into the space across from him, and then reached across the small space for her hand. She gave it to him. His hand felt like all of theirs. Small, bird-boned, almost made of light. She wondered if hers felt like lead to him.

"I've missed you, dear one," he said quietly. She carefully squeezed his hand, for lack of a reply. Am I mother, lover, child? she wondered. He certainly doesn't know I'm really here. He thinks he's dreaming, but it is important to him that I'm here nevertheless.

He released her fingers, and she watched closely as his hand searched for her bowl. His fingers skimmed the top of it and he gracefully brought it to himself, his other hand drifting to the teapot. He kept the tip of one finger on the lip of her bowl and carefully, reverently, poured the fragrant green-gold liquid until he could feel the warmth below the tip of his finger.

She glanced up and saw the scroll hanging from the wall behind him. She followed the script: harmony, respect, purity, and tranquility. She closed her eyes, smelling the grassy, sea-salty sencha as the Keeper finished pouring.

He carefully set aside the teapot and offered the tea to her. She looked directly into his unseeing eyes and bowed.

He waited while she rolled the mildly sweet, grassy flavor over her tongue.

"It has been three years today," he told her quietly. She said nothing. His eyes filled with tears that he tried to swallow back initially, then with a firm shake of his head, lifted to show her, as though she were worthy of them. Her own eyes wanted to fill with tears as well, but couldn't, and she could feel them back up inside of her. His eyes were earth brown, and she felt as though she was looking into his deep soul to see its state, though he could not see so much as her face.

"It was like an amputation," he told her, his voice full of tears, his eyes burning her where she sat, immobilized. And finally, "I didn't tell you enough, beloved. The loss of you is worse than the loss of my eyes." He reached again for her hand, and she gave it to him wordlessly.

She sat folded in her silk brocade, the smell of sencha rising between them, the warmth of the hearth at her back, the Sumiyoshi watching over both them and the river, and held onto the blind keeper's hand while he silently paid tribute with his tears in a wakeful dream to the one he'd loved more than his eyes.

She'd been haunted for a long time by that keeper's words. *It was like an amputation,* he'd said. That was what it felt like to lose his beloved. She looked over at Ronan, who was eyeing her evenly, several questions in his eyes.

"So he was asleep?"

"No, he was awake, but I think he thought it was a dream. It was a ritual he performed yearly, from what I could tell. I never had to do anything to the Light. I was called there for him."

Ronan nodded. "So his need—for a hand to hold his own during the most difficult night of the year—that need was the most dire need in the world at that time? And there was no one else available in time to hold his hand but you?"

She looked up at him, startled. She had never thought of her assignments that way. Then she slowly nodded, her face pensive. "Perhaps."

He sat beside her in companionable silence. "It's good work you do, lass," he said finally.

An incredulous laugh escaped before she could stop it.

"No, really. It's work like any other, and some days are worse than others, aye? There are days when I don't want to get out of bed to face the day or nights too cold for God or man to be about, but I have to tend the Light. Everyone has days at work that are best left unspoken-of."

She eyed him across her left shoulder and didn't say anything for a while. Finally, she unfolded her legs from beneath her and shifted in the armchair. "A job, then, is it?" She smiled broadly at him. "The impertinence!"

He laughed outright at that. "Well, it is. You are a lady lightkeeper. You just work at different Lights is all." She lifted an eyebrow in that effective way she had. "You keep Lights in different times as well, but what of it?"

Her other eyebrow lifted to join the first. "You forgot to mention that I'm older than the plague," she said dryly.

"Lass, my mother would have liked you," he laughed aloud. "Cheeky and a little spitfire, with too much hair to boot!" He set his mug down and smiled widely at her.

She smiled back and they sat companionably for a while until she offered: "You know, I don't often end up in the same place and time repeatedly. I've been drawn back here for some reason." She trailed off as if something had just occurred to her. He glanced up and realized her cheeks were flushed.

He hadn't been so long out of the world he couldn't recognize a damsel in distress when he saw one. "Oh? And where else have you been drawn back?"

"There were a few places. But there was a place in Italy I went back to that makes me laugh." She flashed him a smile, which he hadn't had forewarning to brace himself against, and it caught him squarely, like an unsporting punch in the gut, of which fact she seemed entirely oblivious. "It satisfied my sense of justice, anyway," she went on, unhindered.

"Do tell," he prompted, finding his voice.

Lanterna, Genoa, within sight of the Sampierdarena fishing village, 1163

It was always cold, this close to the sea, though here, at the top of the hill of St. Benigno, it was colder still. The Light was built on an outcropping that jutted impudently out into the Mediterranean Sea. The water was an impossible blue and she stood still witnessing it. It was difficult to tell where the rocks ended and where the Light began, they were so intimately connected.

She could hear the din of market, amplified out over the water to her from the far right, where the village lay, tucked into the elbow of the inlet. It's not a bad place to be, for a time, she thought, though there was hardly much to read, Europe still largely in the grip of the Dark Ages. A bad time, that, she thought. Or this, rather, she sighed, looking around her.

She turned her attention to the Light. It was a marvel, for its time. It was hewn into the rock below it, made of three towers, crenellated, the wood-burning light at the crown. They burned juniper wood, and she liked that best of all in this place.

She looked down from her elevated perch and realized that she had been there before. It had been about 1450 or thereabouts. Ah yes, she thought, grimacing. Antonio Columbo. The uncle of that upstart, Christopher, who had terrorized the New World with his exploration. She crossed her arms against the cold. The keeper uncle hadn't been a bad *sort, but the nephew was an oblivious lad who had trampled around, heedless to the damage and disease he left in his wake. The only satisfying part of that particular story, she thought, glancing at it, though it would not be built for a long time: a statue of Christopher Columbus, in all his glory, that would be placed near enough the Light that when lightning should strike, it would unintentionally strike him, so that the Light would be spared. She smiled at the poetic justice of it, turning back to the fire, the smell of juniper in the air.*

He eyed her with open surprise. "They built a statue of Columbus there and it would take the lightning strikes?"

"A lucky accident," she said, a wicked little smile on her face.

"Why do you say that?" he asked, genuinely interested.

"He infected, killed, and conquered a nation that was running along just fine." Her gaze blanked and he noticed the procession of emotions cross her face.

He saw the slight hesitation in her hand as she set down her mug with a neat click and leaned deliberately back against the seat, not meeting his eyes. She was no longer with him, remembering. It sent a chill of foreboding down his back to look at her. She looked up at him with eyes that begged him not to ask, and then she turned away from him.

He asked suddenly, "Humans don't change, do they, then?"

She shivered. "Humans don't change, Ronan," she answered. "They just get more creative with the ways they hurt each other."

He glanced over at her. A single tear cut a valley down her smooth cheek, and he watched it as it trailed down to her chin and hung there.

He waited for her to come back to herself. "Lass, are you all right?"

She nodded slowly, not meeting his gaze. "As Herodotus said, fathers will keep burying their sons. Mad men will keep warring against each other to the end of time, Ronan. At least as far Ahead as I've traveled." The look she gave him asked him not to ask, and he didn't. But he remembered her words later, when the Great War began.

~: 20 :~

THE FIRST LOAF OF BREAD she made was as flat as a doorstopper and harder than tack.

He watched discreetly as she rifled through his mother's old recipe box, her fingers dancing over the cards, until she stopped on one she liked. Her fingers hovered, hesitating, then reached to pull it from the stack. She cleared a workspace on the table and began bustling about, gathering supplies.

An hour later, after measuring and mixing, her brow furrowed in concentration, she emerged triumphantly from a cloud of flour with a small round of dough, which she nonchalantly placed in a clear bowl by the window and covered with a damp towel. He looked away quickly as she turned from the window, hiding his amusement behind *Sherlock Holmes*. "Bread's rising," she said in a studiously offhand manner.

He looked up from his book and smiled at her. "That's grand."

They went about their day, and twice she went to the window, lovingly rolled her dough about, and set it back to rise. She seemed almost reluctant to put it in the oven when the time came, but she mustered up the fortitude and did it, anxiously lingering near the oven while it baked, and keeping his pocket watch, which he had lent her, close at hand. On the hour, she handed the watch back and used the end of her apron to pull the bread pan out.

He had given up pretending not to watch her, and walked up behind her at the kitchen table while she set it down on a towel. He could tell by the slump of her shoulders before he had even seen the loaf. Nevertheless, she straightened her back and looked down on the pan. "Well," she said, defiantly, "are you ready for supper?"

He almost took a step back, but quickly nodded and said, "Of course. I'll bring out the soup."

They set the table silently. She handed him the serrated bread knife to slice the bread, then slipped across the table from him. He looked from the knife in his hand, to the lump of bread in front of him, to the woman looking challengingly up at him. He felt the mirth trying to bubble up inside of him and tamped it down hard. She'd worked for hours on this lump of bread!

He palmed the loaf, which was rock-hard, and slid the knife against it. There was a sawing noise, but the bread didn't budge. He gripped it harder and put more pressure on it, while trying to make sure it didn't look like he was struggling. He couldn't look at her. He wanted to pick the bread up, knock it against the table to see how hard it truly was. A bead of sweat formed on his forehead. He struggled for an interminable minute before glancing hesitantly down at her.

Her head tilted to one side, she smiled up at him. "As a matter of academic interest, how long were you going to struggle there to make sure my feelings weren't hurt?" He let out a wheezing laugh and set the knife down.

She reached out and did exactly what he'd been wanting to do: she picked up the loaf and banged it a couple of times on the cutting board. It was indeed as hard as a rock. She shook her head. "I did exactly what the instructions said," she insisted.

She looked up at him and realized that his eyes on her were soft. Not pitying, but gentle. "No matter," she said quickly. "We'll just have to eat the soup without bread." She stood and swept the board with the bread on it into the kitchen.

Ronan watched her go, unsure why a woman who had lived so many different lives and traveled the world would feel so invested in the outcome of a loaf of bread, but there it was. He followed her into the kitchen, plucked the recipe card from where she had propped it against the cream jug, and brought it with him to the table.

She spooned the soup into the bowls and eyed him as he perused the recipe. He slid the card between them so they could both read it. "Lass, did you sift the flour when you measured it?"

She shook her head, lifting a spoonful of soup to her mouth. "I patted it down, to get more flour into each cup."

He nodded gravely. "Well, here, where it says to measure the flour: if you sift the flour as you're measuring it you get a more accurate amount, and a—" he hesitated. "A lighter loaf."

"All right," she nodded, motioning for him to continue.

"So then you measured your flour and water. What about the yeast?"

"Yes," she said, as though reciting a lesson. "I measured the yeast and added the boiling water."

The look on his face must have stopped her. He tried. He tried, but he couldn't keep the smile from splitting his face. "And after you killed the yeast with boiling water, what happened?"

She tilted her head to one side and nodded slowly. "Ah, I see."

He nodded.

"So that fizzling sound . . ."

"Screaming yeast, yes." A bark of laughter escaped.

"Well," she said with mock indignation, "and I suppose here, where it says to 'fold' the dough . . ."

"My mother was a gentle creature, for all that she was a spitfire. She actually meant to 'pound' the dough."

"I see." Her eyes were alight with laughter. "Well."

"Yes," he said. "We can't have you making bread that . . ." He trailed off.

"Is fit to choke a man?" she supplied helpfully, and they both gave in to their suppressed laughter.

They ate in silence for a few minutes, and then something seemed to occur to Ronan. "You know, it's nearly June," he started hesitantly. She nodded, attentive.

"The next lighthouse inspection is in June," he explained, sobering.

"By the commission?"

"Yes. It's a great to-do. Being a fastidious man, the inspector starts in June with the top of the coast and works his way down until he reaches Florida. He likes to do things in order."

She nodded, encouragingly.

"He comes ashore in his lighthouse tender and goes over the house and the Light. With white gloves."

"The house? Whatever for?" she asked indignantly.

"To make sure I'm tidy, clean, and sober."

"But your home is private!"

"No," he told her evenly. "It isn't. It's government property and they want to make sure I'm fit to keep the Light."

"Well," she huffed. "There's nothing here for him to see, in any case."

"I'm not so sure about that," he hinted gently.

"Oh! Me?" she said, flushing. "But surely they would understand that I'm just—"

He said nothing, and her face flamed more brightly. "But I'm just—"

He stepped in. "Just a beautiful, unmarried woman who lives here and helps me tend the Light?" His voice was gentle, but he didn't meet her eyes. There was no need to discuss how it sounded. "I'm not certain he'll believe that."

Her cheeks burned ever redder. "What would happen if they found me here?"

166

"I don't know," he answered honestly.

"Would you lose the lighthouse commission?"

He shrugged his large shoulders. "I might. It's difficult to predict how he'll react. It wouldn't be seen as proper, you understand." He didn't look at her when he said it, and she saw that his cheeks were flushed as well.

"I— I have to leave," she said haltingly. He shook his head as she was speaking.

"No," he said, his voice firm. "Not that. We'll think of something."

"I could go into town," she said, thinking aloud. "If only I could find Claire. Is there anyone I could stay with?"

"I have no family left," he began slowly. "There's a boardinghouse, but we would have to explain you somehow." He looked uncomfortable, unsure of himself. She didn't like it.

"I'll find another place to stay," she said. "I'm not certain how much longer I'll be here in any case. This is the longest I've stayed anywhere without a clear assignment," she finished, feeling bruised but unable to articulate why.

"Lass," he said carefully, "I want you here." She looked up and met his warm gaze. "You belong here." He looked like he had more to say, but not the words to explain it. "Do you understand?" She smiled faintly.

"In any case," he said, "we have a few weeks to think things through." She nodded, responding to his earnestness. She would have to think of something soon.

There was a barrier between them, for all the easy camaraderie they had developed. She had buried him, after all. It was too intimate, and yet it was an unfordable river between them. She supposed at some point it would be freeing, though her soul didn't yet reach that depth. Nevertheless, she was happier than she had ever been in her life, there, at the height of her uncertainty. *It's the house*, she told herself firmly, even while gazing at him over their steaming nightly tea, telling him of her travels while he listened attentively. *It's not the—it's just the house, that's all. I've never had a home.*

She knelt on the front doorstep, planting seedlings in small containers to tide them over to true spring inside the kitchen. *I might as well, metaphysics be damned. I did enjoy that tomato, in any case.* It was in the garden that she had first known that something uncomfortable was about to perfect her.

She jammed her third finger on a small rock in the soil and winced, pulling her hand back. She watched the small drop of blood well up, fascinated. *What am I, in this place?* So she wasn't allowed to drown in Cornwall, but here, in the place where she wanted to live forever, she could cry and bleed red like the rest of them? She sat back on the balls of her feet and watched the blood seep out of her finger. She lifted it to her mouth and tasted the surprising metallic tang on her tongue.

He found her there, frozen, staring at a smudge of blood on her finger. He put a hand to her shoulder and she jerked under his touch, moving away quickly. She held her finger up to him, lips pursed in agitation.

"You don't seem like the type of lass to cry over a little blood like that," he teased, pulling a handkerchief from his pocket and pressing it to her finger, her hand cradled in his.

Her mouth opened and closed, no words emerging. His smile faded as she swallowed thickly. "I'm the type of lass that doesn't bleed at all," she reminded him. His grip on her hand unintentionally tightened.

He squatted next to her. "At all?" he echoed, voice hollow. She shook her head slowly, fingers numb from the force of his grip. She gently disentangled herself from his grasp and wobbled to her feet, dusting her skirt. Her eyes teared up from the force of the brisk wind. *This is going to hurt,* she thought bitterly.

She was given enough time to put her seeds in the earth. It was during the daytime, and Ronan had been tired from several nights of poor sleep. She urged him to take the bed, assuring him that she wasn't tired, though that was not entirely, existentially true. She was always tired, and it was perhaps more accurate to say that she wasn't any more tired than usual. She moved quietly around the cottage, careful not to wake him. She was drying a plate, her eyes wandering to the window, to the garden now slumbering in the moist May soil, when she translated.

~: 21 :~

Of all men's miseries the bitterest is this: to know so much and to have control over nothing.

HERODOTUS, *THE HISTORIES*

H E WOKE TO THE SOUND of a shattering plate, and a smile stole over his face. "Lass, soon we won't have a single plate left," he teased drowsily. He waited for a sassy retort, but there was only an unnatural silence. He opened one eye sleepily toward the kitchen and sat up slowly in bed, heart sinking. He drew back the covers and swung his legs to the side of the bed. He aged in the moments it took to gather his courage, haul himself up, and walk calmly to where the dish had been dropped, where the hands that held it had vanished. He unthinkingly stepped on a shard of ceramic as he stooped to scoop up her fallen wrap. The pain only made sense, truth be told.

He mechanically gathered up all the shards of the plate, including the one that had made its way into his foot, and put them in a bowl to fix later. He fisted the wrap she'd left behind in his right hand, and then as though he was hurting her, murmured "sorry." He shook his head. At least no one was around to witness him losing his mind. He crossed the room and laid the wrap down on the bed.

It was not comparable to the last time she had gone. Before, she had been nearly a stranger. And now, he thought, after only a handful of weeks, *how do I bear this?* How did the strangest wisp of a woman, whom he had known for such a short time, who barely took up any space, leave such a vast chasm in his life? He turned a slow circle to look around him at the cottage. *So empty,* he thought desolately. *When had she filled it so completely?*

Later, through the long night, when he startled at the slightest sound, smiling preemptively in case it was her rounding the nearest corner, when every sound reminded him of her moving about the house, when the food tasted like ash in his mouth, he realized that the joy of keeping the Light had become a burden for the first time in many long years, since *that* night. He retrieved the peg he had been whittling, and while he manned the Light that night, his strong hands finished the peg while he thought of all he would tell her when she returned home. When his thoughts became unbearable, he resolutely pulled out his log and refined a few entries. When his heart ached so much he didn't think he could bear it, he looked up to realize that the dawn was mercifully breaking.

He tended the Light, palmed the smooth but imperfect peg, and went inside his home. Except it didn't feel like home anymore. *Damn her.* She had drawn the light out with her, pulling it from every crevice. He took out his tools and indulged in some much-needed hammering to attach the peg to the wall, next to the one that held his winter coat. He hoped she had at least gone somewhere warm, where she would not need the wrap. He scooped it up from the bed as he would have lifted up a lover and reverently hung it on the peg, running his rough hands down its soft length.

~: 22 :~

*Some men give up their designs when they have almost reached the
goal; while others, on the contrary, obtain a victory by exerting, at
the last moment, more vigorous efforts than ever before.*

HERODOTUS, THE HISTORIES

Colossus, Rhodes, Greece, 226 BC

THERE WAS NO TIME FOR grief, and she had to think quickly,
for she found both of her hands wrapped tightly on metal
rungs of what appeared to be an endless ladder, her feet supported
by a rung beneath her. She looked hesitantly down and realized that
she was a dizzying height above the ground, a storm was raging all
around her, and she was clinging to the side of what appeared to
be a giant statue of a man looking out to sea. She was somewhere
around his right shoulder, a considerable distance from the ground.
Although, as she peered down, there was no ground to be seen now.
A large wave hit below, the spray reaching the statue's knees.

Where in creation was she? She gazed out to the bruise-colored
sea, churned by furious wind and waves. *Beaufort score: 8,* she
thought automatically. *Confound it.* She could see lightning in the

distance. She counted to determine how far off the lightning had struck by how many seconds passed between the light and the thunder. She held her breath. *One-one thousand, two-one thousand, three*— the thunder nearly loosened her grip on the rung she clung to. That hadn't struck far off at all, and if she wasn't mistaken, she was clinging to the tallest thing around.

She squinted her eyes at what lay beneath her hands and nearly let go entirely. "Blast," she said shortly, tightening her slippery grip. Not only was she clinging to the tallest thing around, but it appeared to be made almost entirely of bronze. She had to get off before it was struck by lightning and she was roasted to a crisp.

The thought caught her off guard, and she paused mid-step between the rung she was on and the one directly below her foot. Her eyes stung with unshed tears. It had been many long years since she had taken a direct step to save her own life. *It's not the house,* she thought, with almost physical relief. *Ronan,* she thought with a wrench in her gut. *Ronan, Ronan, Ronan.* She looked below her at the rung, thinking *I have to get home to Ronan,* and then she heard the sound of a man's voice far above her.

She looked up to see a young, dark-haired man emerging hurriedly from the neck of the statue. He quickly clambered down several rungs toward her, slipping painfully once, knocking his head against the bronze, his arms wrenched to one side. She watched, transfixed, as he slipped and slid down rungs, getting closer and closer to her.

Was he her task? Was she supposed to save his life? She didn't even know if she could save her own. He was a few rungs above her when he noticed her, and he was so startled that he let out a yelp and nearly lost his grip entirely.

"What in the name of Helios are you doing here, maiden? Do you not know you could be killed?" She ducked her head in time to compose her face, and that was when she saw it. Behind her, straight out to sea and far above the churning waves, way out on the statue's outstretched arm, was a Light. It was already lit in the palm of the statue's hand, and she suddenly knew her task.

The man was nearly upon her. He awkwardly reached below him and grasped her arm, meaning no doubt to be firm but gentle. "Do not move! I will save you. Do not move!" His hand felt insubstantial on her arm and she slipped out of his grasp, carefully, so as to not unbalance him.

"I've been sent by—" She wracked her brain. "By the God of the Sun." *In a manner of speaking,* she thought. "To keep the Light while you proceed to safety," she told him quickly, moving another rung out of his reach. *Argos,* his name came to her. "Argos," she added out loud, to strengthen her case.

It was a tricky thing to twist in midair, glance over one's shoulder, look befuddled but reverent, all the while managing not to plunge to one's death, but he somehow managed it. Astonishment gave way to relief. *This sort of thing must happen at least with some regularity,* she thought wryly at his quick acceptance. *Or perhaps they more readily believe in what they cannot see.*

He looked out toward the roiling sea and then turned back to her. It was an awkward thing, but he managed a brief bow. "Blessings of Helios be upon you, priestess. Do you require any assistance?"

"No," she said, and he looped his arm through a rung to untie a pouch knotted to his belt. He reached out and passed it to her, and she quickly strung it around her neck for safekeeping. She realized as another large wave crashed hard against the statue that he was waiting to be dismissed.

She made the Sign over him, said a word for his safety, placed her hand on his head for a brief moment, then said, in a voice that brooked no argument, "Now go, faithful keeper, and get yourself to safety. I'll wait here for the will of God." His dark brown eyes met hers, strong and respectful and a little fearful, and then he turned and started scrambling down.

She wasted no time. She did not know what would happen if she fell from this height, but she did not particularly want to find out, in light of having bled for the first time just prior, back home. *No, she* thought. *Focus. No thinking of home.*

She could see, far off in the water, the ship that was heading toward the harbor. She knelt, now at the muscles of the statue's great arm, which was outstretched to sea. She crawled on hands and knees until a walkway opened beneath her, and she eased to her feet. The arm was as wide as a bridge, and she could have lain the long way three times and still had plenty of space, but the statue was slick with moisture and she was rather uninterested in falling off, so she stayed safely in its center where the walkway was and walked as quickly as she dared.

Halfway there, at the slight bend of the elbow, she looked behind her briefly and caught her breath. The statue wore the serene face of Alexander the Great, looking calmly out to sea. She doubted the real Alexander had often worn that particular look. Determinedly, she turned her face back into the lacerating wind, which tore at her hair and clothes, and scrambled onward. She dared not chance a look down.

As she passed over the knotted bronze veins of the Emperor's wrist, she wished faintly that she had time to admire this craftsmanship, and clambered up into the curve of his palm. It was a small slide down. The fire in the giant's hand was enclosed in a large glass bauble of sorts that was perforated to allow for smoke to escape vigorously in dark plumes. She pulled her scarf up around her mouth and nose, and leaning as far away from the glass as possible, and without pitching too far forward, she crept around the base of the glass-enclosed fire toward the giant's thumb.

Panting a little, she leaned forward against the slick bronze base of the thumb and found that both of her arms couldn't wrap around it. She held on with both arms, her heart pounding, and craned her neck to look out between the thumb and first finger to sea.

The scene stopped her heart. The sea was stirred to an angry boil far below, where the giant's feet stood steadily on a platform made of what seemed like marble. The base was now and again visible between huge waves that swept and crashed against the ankles of the giant, sending spray upward of his knees. Her heart thudded again.

Argos, she thought, despairing that she had sent him to his death, and craned her neck toward the body of the giant to see if the young man was still climbing to safety. Perhaps it would have been safer for him to stay enclosed in the head of the giant than to attempt to get down to the platform during this storm, but it was too late for second thoughts.

She suddenly spotted him. He was a much faster climber than she was and had made it all the way down past the giant's hip. He was moving quickly, one hand over the other, his strong legs flying down the rungs. She silently urged him on, her eyes locked on him as he made the steep descent on the wave-swept statue. He would have to time his descent carefully with the waves below so as not to be swept off the platform. She turned back to sea and saw the ship that had been farther out ease into the harbor.

She looked behind her at the Light, burning soot-thick but bright. She knew enough about the time she seemed to be in to know that they tried to keep this Light burning continually. If it went out they would likely have to bring burning embers from a hearth-fire and lug it all the way up the statue to relight the beacon. *Well, it won't go out on this watch*, she thought. There was likely a body up in this precarious spot at all times of the day and night, tending the Light so that it would not need to be relit, and she was apparently that body right now. *Priestess of the Sun God indeed. Wait until I tell Ronan*, she thought, and quickly turned her thoughts away. She needed her wits about her.

There was a brief calm in the storm, which she wasn't ever

particularly trusting of, but she was glad that it afforded Argos time enough to scramble down the leg of the giant and away to the marble base below. *Now, get far away,* she prayed. The ship had docked, and people began pouring out as though from a disturbed anthill as soon as it had moored. *You too,* she thought.

Am I here for the people on the ship? For Argos? Was that the task? It felt too simple somehow, though there hadn't been anything particularly easy about the assignment thus far. She was thinking *Perhaps now I can get off this lightning rod,* when she felt it.

There came a deep rumbling down in the core of the earth. *Of course,* she remembered. *The Colossus of Rhodes only lasted a few decades, after all.* She just hadn't realized it had been used as a Light as well. She thunked her forehead against the base of the giant's thumb a little harder than she intended to and winced. *I'm here for me,* she recalled. *These assignments are for me.* What was about to follow would undoubtedly be quite the spectacle, and she was unfortunately about to have the best seat in the house for it.

The earthquake started not too far from where she clung, but she kept her grip, both of her arms wrapped as tightly as possible around the thumb. There was a loud crack and the world shifted all around her. She turned her neck to see that the giant had cracked at the knees. She was, regrettably, above the knees. The stormy sky tilted, and she felt a moment of panic. *I'm here for me,* she repeated. *This is for me.* She remembered walking beside Wisdom, and in the split-second it took to think of her, she understood what Wisdom had meant.

The realization was followed by an emerging peace, though Ronan's face and the Loon-Call Light flashed before her eyes. She sighed, chest tight. It was out of her hands.

Either I'm about to have that long conversation I've been dying to have with Wisdom, in which I will finally have a full explanation for—well, all of this, or this is about to be the most spectacular translation of my life, she thought, her heart pounding in her throat. She swallowed thickly. *Either way, this is for me.*

As the Colossus tipped forward, crumbling, the force of its massive body carrying her toward the tempestuous sea, the massive hand, with the Light still lit, led the plunge. The earth continued to shake far below, but she could no longer feel it. A moment before she lost contact with the statue, lightning struck the hand she stood on. She could feel the electric spear of energy knife through her, and pain like fire seared from her right hand to her left foot. She lifted her face to the storm clouds, the gasp of pain passing into the statue below her. With a last prayer that she wouldn't crush anyone below, she lost her grip on the thumb. Her toes pointed, holding on, and then she lost her hold on the statue completely. She ascended into the receiving sky and felt the hand of Alexander the Great, and all the world, fall out from beneath her. She was lightly cast up for a moment, as weightless as a dancer mid-pirouette. There was a moment of pure peace within the pain of the lightning strike, and time arrested as she was poised for a heartbeat, accepting her fate. *I have a heartbeat,* she thought, and translated.

❦ 23 ❧

Loon-Call Light, Maine, 1910

SHE'D BEEN GONE FOR WEEKS. His beard was untrimmed and his uniform unpressed. He was glad it wasn't yet June, at least. *This wasn't what I had planned for the yearly inspection,* he thought. *There was no need to make her disappear entirely!*

He felt his age, every year piling up atop the others, throughout the month of May, and it took more courage than he had to wake up to the empty house and the empty Light. How had he hesitated in telling her when she was sitting across the table from him? How had he kept silent, adding the sum of his pride into an equation that should have held nothing but cherished companionship and time slipping through his fingers?

By the end of the month, the void she had left behind wasn't so much an absence as a presence that woke with him, walked with him, sat to table with him, and pressed down on him most acutely when he tended the Light. The prisms of the lens, so beautiful and clear, the panes he meticulously cleaned, all reminded him of her. He thought of her while he carried out those tasks and tried to imagine what panes she was cleaning, what Light she was tending, out in the eternity of time and space.

It was not a new feeling for him, to fear for someone, but it was new to have his heart beating somewhere else, far away, where he couldn't protect it, and he did fear for her, though he knew she was a capable woman.

He spent the last day of the month scouring the house and Light, cleaning every last curve and corner, banishing the dust that had settled in her absence. He didn't mind the cleaning, but he missed her even then, for the company. She would have loved to make the Light beautiful with him.

When the inspector came on the second day of June, his lighthouse tender bumping into dock, Ronan went out to meet him, his face cleanly shaven, his uniform pressed, and a mask of grim determination on his face.

Walter Sturtevant, the chief inspector for the region, wore a neatly tailored black suit, his necktie fastidiously knotted over a crisp white shirt, his coattails brushing the backs of his knees. He wore a top hat of medium elevation, and his mustache was neatly combed and trimmed. He did not go in for long sideburns, which Ronan respected him for, and his boots were clean enough to eat pudding off of. He never smelled overwhelmingly of cologne, like many of his compatriots, and he took his job as seriously as the plague. Most inspectors did, for one of two reasons, Ronan had concluded. Either they delighted in being Napoleon over someone else, or they actually cared about the safety of mariners and their cargo. Chief Inspector Sturtevant, mercifully, was in the latter category.

If the inspector noticed the blood from a few nicks Ronan had acquired in trimming his beard that morning, or the woman's coat that hung next to Ronan's on the peg in the house, he said nothing. After all, there was no other visible trace of her. *How can there be no trace of her*, thought Ronan, following the man as he respectfully but thoroughly examined the contents of his home. *She fills the place, don't you see?*

He almost wanted the inspector to say something, to question him, but the older gentleman merely ran a gloved finger over the stovetop. *She made a loaf of terrible bread in that oven,* he wanted to say. *I stood like a fool, trying to saw into it to spare her feelings.* He felt he would go mad, presently, but the inspector thankfully asked him to lead the way to the lighthouse, and the air outside helped clear his head.

The lantern room of the lighthouse rivaled the inspector's boots for cleanliness. It was even more difficult there to pretend she didn't exist. Ronan could practically smell her, catch a glimpse of her wild hair out of the corner of his eye. *The place is haunted,* he thought.

Inspector Sturtevant glanced at Ronan as he ran his white-gloved fingers over the outermost curve of the lens. His eyes were compassionate. "So you're still determined to stay out here alone?" he asked.

Ronan forced a smile. "It's always been a stag Light, Inspector." He stood straight-backed against the glass wall of the lantern room, the knuckles of his right hand resting on the small desk that crowded his hip.

"I've known you for a few years, Ronan. Even after Margaret died, you were never this . . ." He paused, shook his head. "Do you want an assistant? I can place a request with the Commission, though . . ." They both knew there wasn't money in the budget for an assistant, but it was kind of the inspector to offer.

"Please, sir," said Ronan quickly. "There's no need. I'm content without one." It was mostly true. "I thank you," he added sincerely.

"You don't want a holiday?" pressed the inspector, peeling off his white gloves.

"This is my home," replied Ronan. "I will stay here. If you find my work satisfactory," he added deferentially.

The Inspector shook his head. "You know you keep a meticulous Light, son. That's not the issue." He said nothing else for a moment, and Ronan followed him down the narrow spiral of the staircase.

Ronan walked him back to his waiting boat and stood beside it while the inspector made a few notes in a black book. He glanced up and told Ronan his score, which didn't surprise him. He tended to do well on these visits. It was usually a source of pride for him, but there was a hollow note in his voice when he thanked the inspector that didn't escape the older man's notice.

"What's her name, lad?" he asked abruptly, but not unkindly.

Ronan, taken aback, shook his head. "She has no name, sir," he replied truthfully. *She has no name*, he thought. *I have to give her a name when she comes back.* He felt the conviction of that thought and stood a little straighter.

The man looked unconvinced but said nothing to contradict him. "Well, I respect your choice, Ronan. If there is a Mrs. Ronan of the Light sometime this year, do write to the Commission and let me know, will you?"

Ronan found a slight smile lifting his mouth. "I will, sir."

"Good. Well, I'd best be off. I want to make it down the river a ways before nightfall. It's only June yet," said the inspector with energy. Ronan's smile spread a little more as he watched the inspector's boat pull out from the dock.

He walked slowly back to the Light, his footfalls heavy as he climbed the forty-two steps, counting them silently as she counted them to herself. He missed her. Damn her, but he missed her.

~: 24 :~

The destiny of a man is in his own soul.

HERODOTUS, *THE HISTORIES*

WISDOM WAS WAITING FOR HER by the sea, and the Keeper found that she had spoken all her words of anger with her body the last time they had met. There was neither anger nor shame. At least none directed at Wisdom.

The Keeper still felt the lift of weightlessness as she had hung for a heartbeat above the crumbling Colossus, and her body still burned with the memory of lightning coursing through her skin and bones. Thoughts came to her in a jumble. The weight of Ronan's hand, warm on her cheek, and the drop of blood welling up on her finger while gardening. Without preamble she cried, "It's for me! These translations are for me."

Wisdom waited patiently.

The Keeper continued, "You said I had been given nothing but time, for now."

Wisdom nodded.

Heart racing, the Keeper thought of the tears she had been able to cry, and of the metallic taste of her own blood. "But not anymore."

"You were given a taste of what might be," said Wisdom. The foam at the seashore swirled around the Keeper's ankles.

"My time has run out," she said faintly. All the fragmented notions that had occurred to her came together into one coherent thought. *Ronan*, she cried soundlessly.

"Your souls have both been a long time arriving to each other," said Wisdom. "But you haven't been waiting for him. You were right that this has all been for you." She paused. "It's time to make a choice, daughter."

The Keeper was certain, in the same way she had been when she knew something was about to perfect her, that this choice would be difficult, painful. Compassion radiated to her from Wisdom, from the sea and from the warmth of the sun. She took a deep breath and lifted her eyes to Wisdom.

Wisdom's face was stillness itself, and the Keeper's fluttering heart slowed just looking at her. Somehow, she knew that had she lain down in the sand before, she would not have been given a choice today. She understood that because she had wrestled with and then stood in the presence of Wisdom, somehow all would come right in the end.

"What must I do?" she asked, standing up straight and pushing her shoulders back.

The Woman's eyes on her were kind. "You have to choose. You can continue as you are, untouched by age or time, tending Lights."

The Keeper drew in a deep breath. *Here it comes.*

"Or," continued Wisdom, "you can become fully human, and let time touch you, and age, and live your life, and grow old. And die."

The Keeper took a sharp breath, stunned. *That's it?* She felt joy well up in her, but it was tempered by the look on Wisdom's face.

"Peace, Little Light," she said gently. "There's more. The great gift and burden humanity carries is free will. If you put down your immunity to time, you will pick up this burden you have never before carried."

It seemed too impossibly good to be true. "Do you mean to say that I would have a choice? A choice over where and when I translate?" The Keeper's voice rose in excitement, and she clasped her hands together to keep from flinging herself at Wisdom, this time in joy.

"Yes," said Wisdom. "You will learn, as all humans learn, the gift and burden of time. You will begin to understand the rapidity of its passage, its ravages, and the pain of choosing how best to spend it, on whom and what. If you choose to enter into time, and age, you will still continue your work of tending Lights, but you will have a choice whether to go when there is a need and do what you can—for you *will* grow cold, take ill, break bones, and fall to your death. And you will miss spending that time elsewhere, for this is the burden of choice and limited time."

The silence that followed was deep and wide, and the Keeper could hear all of her own heartbeats. She pressed the heel of her hand over her chest to keep her heart from pounding away. She thought of the Colossus of Rhodes, the smell of her hands sweaty from the metal rungs, and the precarious hold she'd had on the statue. *So far above solid ground*, she thought, and swallowed.

She thought of the rescue worker who had held her in the Hudson. To be like him. To be able to die. The costs were so much higher than she had ever paid. *But to be able to choose whether to pay them*, she thought exultantly.

"So I would keep helping, both the Keepers and tending their Lights," she said, not in the way of a question, but thinking aloud.

Wisdom's gaze sharpened on her. "Help them? Is that what you think you do?"

The Keeper's open-palmed hands lifted, her shoulders mid-shrug, confusion evident on her face.

185

"My child, you have taken as much as you have given. You can't help someone else. Not if you don't know them, and not in the way you think."

The Keeper thought then of her conversation with Ronan about giving and receiving, and anonymous good deeds, and knew she would be processing this bewildering thought for years to come. *If I have years to come.*

"Lastly," said Wisdom, and the Keeper braced herself for more. "I cannot guarantee Ronan."

"What do you mean?"

"I mean he's a man and must make his own decision about whether the uncertainty of your life is a burden worth bearing. This is what all humans must decide when they choose to love."

The Keeper's stricken expression did not mask her thoughts from Wisdom. *Will he want me? What if I'm not enough? What if the uncertainty is too much?* Her heart raced while her mind flitted from one dizzying thought to another.

I'm probably too much. She let that thought sit for a while, because it carried so much weight and worry. *Perhaps,* she thought, but her last thought was unequivocal: *With or without Ronan, I want a choice.*

Wisdom eyed the Keeper's set shoulders, the look of determination on her face, and smiled slightly. "If he chooses you, he will be your home and the place to which you return between your travels, should you choose to embark on them."

A home, thought the Keeper. *A home. A home with Ronan of the Light!* She felt tears well up in her eyes. *I have a choice,* she thought, her throat tight with mingled joy and tears.

Wisdom smiled down at her and, leaning forward, kissed the top of her head. "Do you want time to think about it?" she asked.

The Keeper looked up and shook her head, unable to contain her grin. *To be able to choose! To begin to age, to be susceptible to* disease, injury, death. It was all too much to take in. But to have a chance to live with Ronan of the Light, even for a short while, was happiness unimaginable. *Life*, she thought. *I choose Ronan, and life.*

She looked up into the All-Keeper's face and saw a Light rise up behind her, faint and seeming to sway in a far-off breeze. It was dark, looked like it had come directly out of Middle Earth, and the Light was unlit with some clearly foul weather afoot. She had never seen a translation before stepping into it, and she saw it now as a sort of suggestion, a path down which she could choose to walk. She felt her heart race with the excitement of it. "I, I uh, I have to go, don't I?" she asked hurriedly, not stopping to wonder if the All-Keeper knew of what she was speaking.

The All-Keeper shook her head, her face unreadable. "You must decide for yourself, daughter."

Completely unused to the heady power of choice, the Keeper stepped forward, past Wisdom, and felt the breeze of the translation sweep back her hair.

Alligator Reef Light, Florida Keys, 1876

The octagonal Light with the concrete frame stood on skeletal metallic legs, meant to keep it from succumbing to hurricane-force winds. The tower was topped with a dark lantern room. The Keeper found herself on the ledge outside the lantern room, not a soul in sight, and went inside to make quick work of lighting the beacon before descending the stairs to the quarters below.

She had barely rolled into the blanket on the narrow bed for a doze in early morning when she was lifted out of her bed on a tide of icy-cold, seaweed-laden water. She woke sputtering, barely registering the fact that she was gasping cold water. It took her but a moment to realize that the sudden storm was not only raging like a monster outside but had shattered the glass and burst into the keeper's quarters.

Gasping for breath and bewildered, she looked all around her. There were about two feet of standing water in the keeper's cottage. She glanced through the now-missing window and sensed the anger of the sea. The Light was being pummeled by waves, some rising to the height of the keeper's dwelling. *Beaufort score: 10*, she thought with a sinking heart, *and I a mere human.* Her heart lurched, and she fought down a rising tide of pure panic.

She scrambled off the floor, slid, stepping on a fish, and ran to frantically shove boots onto her feet to protect them from shattered glass and debris. She jammed the door to the keeper's cottage closed and threw herself headlong up the spiral staircase that led to the lantern room.

She spared a glance behind her at the sparse dwelling and was momentarily grateful to own nothing. That bed, those chipped plates, the blue jug sitting on the table. Though just objects, they meant something to some absent someone. They were all part of the fabric of that someone's daily life, and they were about to be swept out to sea.

She was relieved to see that the glass of the lantern room still held and the Light shone brightly. Wave after wave walled up outside the glass, one after the other. She looked below her at the keeper's quarters, which were being washed by successive waves. Every seventh wave was even larger, reaching up to the lantern room, so that there was only glass between her and a mountain of water. It happened over and over again, and she pressed her face against the glass as the tower was repeatedly engulfed.

Her clothes clung to her skin, frozen, and she tried not to think of pneumonia, or hypothermia, or whether she would survive to get home. She shivered in her sodden clothes. It was still unfamiliar to think of her life and whether or not she wanted to die right now, and the answer was unequivocally *no*.

She didn't want the cold to claim her or a wave to break the lantern glass and pull her and the lens out into the dark, churning sea. She wanted to go home. She had a home. She had a person. He knew her, and he was waiting for her.

Please be waiting for me, she pleaded silently. *I will be so much more careful next time. I will think of you, of our Light, of my life, when I decide what to do with my limited time. I will consider the danger, and the lives that are at sea, but I will also think of you, and of me.*

She, who had played fast and loose with time all her life, now wanted every last ordinary moment with Ronan of the Light. She pressed her palms against the glass, pushing back against the walls of waves. The tower that had at first seemed like such a massive, solid beacon, so sturdy and unshakeable, now seemed as if it could be tossed into the waves like a matchstick.

She was glad the keeper was not there, that she was the only one there to tend the Light, that the lens behind her was intact and the glass in front of her unshattered. She was also glad, joyously so, that she was afraid of death but still alive. *I want to go home,* she thought. *I have a home.*

She tentacled her will to that Light, through the dark hours while the tower was washed by the storm and into the small hours of morning, when the weather let up and she could make sure that the Light was well lit. The thought of home sustained her until she loosened her will and translated there.

PART III

~: 25 :~

It is better by noble boldness to run the risk of being subject to half
the evils we anticipate than to remain in cowardly listlessness
for fear of what might happen.

HERODOTUS, THE HISTORIES

Loon-Call Light, Maine, 1910

SHE ARRIVED IN THE GLOOM of early morning by the seashore, utterly full of buoyant and overwhelming gratitude. She felt no different outwardly. A quick swipe of her hand across her face revealed features in the same order.

I survived, she thought, body stiff and sore, as though the storm's fist still pummeled her within that Light. *I survived and I have a choice*, she thought. *With a word and a thought, I can choose! I have a human body.* She looked around. *I have a home.* On the heels of that thought came another, more sobering one. *I have so little time*, and she knelt where she stood to kiss the ground. She straightened, brushing the salty sand from her lips, and glanced up at the sound of raucous gulls overhead.

She experimentally approached the shallow breakers at the

shoreline and, squatting low, reached one hand to touch the ocean water as it ebbed and flowed. The cold nearly burned her hand, sharp as nettles. She yelped and pulled her hand back, jumping to her feet and scooting away from the shoreline lest any other part of her also touch the cold water. *Well*, she thought, *it's not entirely new.* She knew what cold felt like; she'd felt it before, but it had never felt this ill-intentioned, as though out for her life. *It is out for my life*, she thought. *Everything is.*

She found a patch near the hem of her skirt and dried her hand, which was starting to lose all feeling. She found that a few strands of eelgrass had wrapped themselves in a circlet around her right ankle, and reached down to work them loose. Her hand tingled from wrist to fingertips, and she tucked it into the pocket of her coat. It didn't ease the sensation, so she stuck it down the front of her bodice, yelping a little from the shock of frozen fingers against warm flesh. *There,* she thought. *Bliss and abject misery in the same breath.* Was *that* what being fully human felt like?

She turned her face toward home. Ronan would be asleep at this time of morning, but she couldn't wait to greet him, and her skirt wrapped around her legs tightly as she lurched in the direction of the house, her heels kicking up sand. She hurried up the path to the side of the house and peered in through the window, hair whipped by the wind, cheeks flushed and beginning to ache from the grin that threatened to split her open. She paused by the open window and peered in.

Her grin froze. He was awake when he should have been asleep, sitting at the dining table, his head in his hands. She stood transfixed in the window, watching him with growing concern. His beard was untrimmed, his hair disheveled. He took a deep breath and rubbed his face with his broad palms. He stood with less than his usual grace, and she couldn't help but think that he'd aged. What had done this?

Her heart raced and she turned away from the window to slowly flatten herself against the wall of the cottage. She waited several long minutes, the joy of her arrival dimmed. What was eating at him, this beloved man? Surely not her absence? She hoped he had missed her, but she hadn't counted on such disquiet.

She heard some rustling and realized he must be trying to go back to sleep before the long night. She waited by the window, heart worriedly attending him, until she felt that a long enough time had passed. She made her way over to the apple tree and gazed at her garden. Small green shoots were beginning to peek up from the moist soil, and she could imagine the green riot about to unfold in the small space in the coming weeks. Ronan had fashioned a crude wooden slab against the curve of the trunk to act as a small seat, and she sat there, at the base of the tree, head leaning against the trunk.

It was a beautiful, warm day. *I have to think about the cold now,* she thought. *I can get frostbite and pneumonia. I can get sick and die.* She snuggled down more cozily into her light coat.

A fearful voice within her wanted her to go, hurry, wake the man, greet him as she wanted to, lest her time with him be cut short before he awoke, but a larger part of her, the part that had not let her lie down on the shore before Wisdom, now bade her let him rest, and wait until the time was right.

Despite the bark at her back and her cramped position, exhaustion overcame her. The combination of warm sun overhead, mild wind coming in offshore, and the sweet joy of waiting made her glad and drowsy. She wrapped the happiness and anticipation of the day close and fell into a light sleep.

Ronan woke from troubled dreams of a woman. It wasn't the usual nightmare of a drowned woman and a selkie pulling him back from death. No, this had been a soft-smelling woman, and she had been made of light, and she vanished when he tried to draw her to himself. He knew exactly who she was.

In one dream she was drying dishes. In another she was watching a thunderstorm roll in, her shape framed in the door. He approached her repeatedly, wanting to draw her into his arms. He had good, strong arms from tending the Light, and he wanted to fill them with her. He ached with the need to hold this woman, and he woke frustrated, his arms empty again, as they had been the previous day.

He had been optimistic after the inspector's visit, but this week it was more difficult to hope that she would return while he was alive. She hadn't been gone this long the last time, and he was beginning to understand the desolation of a life lived without her. He washed his face at the sink, letting the cold water wake him, and drank a glass of water. He looked out the kitchen window at her garden and decided to weed it for her. He would shave his beard, and he would do better in her absence, so that home would be familiar to her when she came back. *She has to come back*, he thought, and then his eyes caught the trailing edge of her dress under the apple tree.

He leaned forward, and there she was, her small form slumped back against the apple tree in the unmistakable shape of slumber. The world shifted, righted itself, and his feet skimmed the ground as he raced to her sleeping form. He bent down beside her, his hands reaching of their own volition, soft on her hair that he had no business touching. *I will make it my business*, he thought.

She woke slowly, a small smile curving her lips, and it filled him with joy. He braced for the blow of it, and she didn't disappoint him. When she realized it was him, the smile bloomed across her face. "Ronan!" she exclaimed.

God in heaven, is there a sweeter sound? he thought, and she surged up into his embrace at the same time that he reached down to pull her into it, and it was so perfect he could hardly breathe. Her small, beloved form, home safely in his arms. *Where she belongs,* he thought defiantly. *This is where she belongs, do you hear me?*

All of a sudden they both remembered themselves and drew shyly back, untangling themselves one from the other, though reluctant to completely disengage. She found her hand held so warmly and securely in his that her heart swelled with the rightness of it.

He couldn't contain his smile, and she laughed and gripped his hand more tightly, and before they knew how it had started, they were drawing each other into a second tight embrace. She could feel his arms around her, so warm and solid and secure. His breath was against her hair, and he breathed what felt like a kiss to the top of her head. It was so unlike any feeling in her long life that she felt her heart was too small to contain the happiness of it. There was nothing to do but hold on and laugh aloud against him.

When she began to loosen her hold, he tightened his almost reflexively, and she caught her breath and understood the pain he had experienced in her absence. She would have to remember this reflex, always.

"I had hoped," he said softly, loosening his hold. She stepped back and saw the flush across his cheeks, his head bowed down to her own. She could see his hair curling at the nape of his neck. He held her hand loosely, the pad of his thumb running back and forth along the back of her hand, the sight thrilling her with its indescribable rightness.

A lump formed in her throat and she looked up into his face. She swallowed first and then asked him weakly, "How long?"

He sobered, his tall body swaying slightly away from her, as though her words hurt. Then he purposely stepped closer. "About six weeks," he replied gruffly. There was a world he didn't say, and there was no apology or expectation of one, but only shared pain.

She who had never been free with her touch, who had no one to belong to or who belonged to her, hesitantly reached her hand up to touch the untrimmed beard over his cheek. The coarse, springy hair was unfamiliar, but somehow like coming home. He took in a quick breath and she moved to take her hand away, but he caught it against his own, and pressed it back against his cheek. He closed his eyes and she felt his mouth beneath the beard curve into a slight smile.

He took a deep breath and opened his eyes. "Where?" he asked, eyes alight with curiosity.

It took her a moment to understand what he meant, because every nerve in her body was in her fingertips. She looked at him blankly, and he released the hand cupping his cheek.

She finally understood and shook her head, smiling at him. "Well. Do I have a story for you!"

"I expect no less," he said, the fiendish glint back in his tired gaze.

He glanced over her shoulder, then back at her, his gaze hesitant to leave her. She noticed and resolved to shield him from uncertainty as much as possible. "I have to care for the Light," he said.

"Let's go," she said, smiling up at him.

He seemed to remember something. "I have something for you." She regarded him expectantly, as if she'd already accepted his gift.

He took a deep breath. "*Aine*," he said, warmly.

"*Aine?*" she asked, eyebrows arched. Where had she heard that before?

"Yes," he declared. "I'll tell you over supper." Heart light, she tucked her hand in his, and he drew her with him. "Come tend the Light with me."

~: 26 :~

OVER THEIR EVENING MEAL, DURING which he could barely take his eyes from hers and whatever they ate was the best meal they'd ever had, he kept partially reaching across the table, though he didn't touch her again, as if to reassure himself that she was really there. The lines of his face were relaxed, and his smile reached his eyes. Her face was wide open in wonder, as if taking in the whole world—a world made new—all at once. It was over their meal that he gave her his gift.

With the remnants of their meal between them, he leaned forward, features somber, his strong hands folded on the table. "Will you let me give you a name?" he asked gravely.

She zeroed in on his left hand, the strong, blunt fingers and the dark hair on the backs of his knuckles. She could sense that he had thought long and hard about his words. Her heart raced with the knowledge that they were alive, that he was alive, and that he was here, with her.

"What did you have in mind?"

"*Aine*," he said softly, and his mouth curled over the two syllables, the "ayn" and the "ya" like two hands curling over her shoulders. Her shoulders hunched, and he watched her closely. She said nothing, but her right hand reached over to rub her left arm through her sleeve.

"After the goddess of the bright summer sun." He waited. She didn't meet his eyes, but he could feel her hanging on his every word. A smile stole into his voice. "It means joy and radiance," he finished gently, and he might as well have touched her bare skin. Her face was ablaze. He coughed to conceal a soft laugh, and pushed back from the table. She reached out blindly and connected with his warm arm.

She looked up and caught the full force of his smile on her. *There it is*, she thought. *That's how he feels. And he's not one bit shy about it.* "Thank you," she managed, her voice nearly abandoning her. He nodded once, his hand briefly covering hers, then headed to the sink with the dishes.

She took several deep breaths and tried to sit up, but it felt as though her insides were made of butter, and he had just heated her up past her melting point. She sat and melted at the table while he sorted the dishes and made a comfortable commotion in the kitchen. She took a few deep breaths, put her hands to her middle to hold her insides in, and stood shakily to her feet. She opened her mouth and ate up a few more breaths, the scents of soup and the wood fire filling her to the brim so that a few more deep breaths of the smell of home and she might start leaking tears onto the table.

When she had recovered enough to walk, she wordlessly joined him to rinse the soapy dishes. There was an almost painful pleasure in standing and rinsing dishes beside him, their fingers occasionally brushing. She could have stood there for ages and it not become tedious.

They were drying and stacking the dishes when something caught his eye and he started. He reached for her hand, and she glanced down. Beginning at the tip of her middle finger and running up her arm to disappear under her sleeve was a thin, red, branching—burn, scar? They had been so preoccupied she hadn't noticed it before. She pulled her sleeve up and they both followed it with their eyes, transfixed. She got as far as her shoulder and realized that it disappeared under her dress. Unthinkingly, she pulled the fabric away from her chest and peered down the bodice. "It continues," she said, baffled.

She quickly bent down and pulled off her stockings. There it was: the same ferning pattern, on her left foot. She guessed her right hand had been wrapped up higher than her head on the statue of the Colossus and had been struck first. The lightning had traveled down her arm, then her body, and out through the opposite foot.

There it was, etched into her skin, the branching, ferning shape she had seen in the sky innumerable times during lightning storms and for the instant after, when she closed her eyes and saw the same pattern burned on the insides of her eyelids. She was about to lift her skirt to examine her left leg more closely when she heard a strangled sound from Ronan.

"Are you all right, Ronan?" she asked quickly, glancing at him.

He seemed midway between hilarity and a heart attack. He looked at her, eyes determinedly on her face. "I'll be fine," he said, "but I'd better head off to the Light. You'll be all right in here?"

"Well, yes, of course," said Aine, confused at his manner. "Is everything all right?"

He had already started to turn away, but something in her tone of voice made him pause. She sounded unsure, and she looked lost standing there, stockings in hand. He didn't know if he should laugh or turn and flee.

"I think it's from the lightning strike," she was saying.

And now she's talking about lightning, for mercy's sake. He zeroed in on her mouth and realized she was talking, and he had no idea was she was saying. He had been longing for her for weeks, and here she was, effectively undressing in the kitchen. He felt if he stood there a moment longer he might devour her. *Stop, Aine,* he wanted to say. *I don't care about the lightning, or whatever it is, when you're standing here, finally, hair unbound and feet bare.*

"Aine," he interrupted gently. She started. The name was new, after all, and she wasn't used to it. It dusted a pretty blush across her cheeks, and he felt that another minute and he might do something to really make her blush. *Have mercy, Aine. I'm only a man*, he thought. "I'm leaving for the night." Now she looked positively flabbergasted. *You have no idea, darling girl.* His bark of laughter seemed to startle both of them. "Forgive me. Goodnight." He reached for the hand that wasn't holding the stockings and allowed himself the consolation of kissing it, soundly.

He glanced up at her long enough to convince himself that she would be fine, said a firm "welcome home," and fled out into the night.

❦ 27 ❧

What is love? 'tis not hereafter;
Present mirth hath present laughter;
What's to come is still unsure.

W. SHAKESPEARE, *TWELFTH NIGHT*

I**T TOOK HER A WHILE** to sleep that night, for two reasons. The first came as she was slipping between clean sheets and turning down the lamp. A ghostly vision of a bonfire burning on a far hill caught her attention. A lump rose in her throat and she resolutely climbed into bed, closing her eyes to the vision. She could still see it. She broke into a cold sweat, closed her eyes more tightly, and thought of the most recent storm and the walls of water that she had survived to come home to Ronan.

The bonfire wavered, and she thought she could make out the stern of a far-off ship, or a thousand of them. *Well,* she thought tiredly, *if Helen ends up grounded on a shore somewhere for lack of a Light, I think I can live with the outcome of the Trojan War.* She chuckled nervously as she pulled the covers up to her chin, feeling like she was spitting directly into a gale with that irreverent thought. *I didn't mean it,* she thought. *Well, maybe a little.*

She shook her head at the primitive signal Light burning on a hill. "No," she murmured, heart thrilling to the wild power of choice. In the next moment it was gone, and she was left with the overwhelming second thoughts she imagined would now be part of her life for the foreseeable future.

The second thing that kept her awake was that the reason for Ronan's abrupt departure finally sank in, and when it had, she blushed in mortification. What must he think of her? *Does it matter?* she thought, but the impropriety of their situation was becoming quite clear. Even though the inspector had come and gone in her absence, there was the matter of the look in Ronan's eyes when he'd bidden her goodnight. It was on these thoughts that she both drifted to sleep and woke in the morning.

As Wisdom had said, their souls had been a long time approaching one another, and now that they had found each other, and Aine understood her time was limited, there was no reason to wait.

She threw open the front door to find him already outside, dressed in his blue uniform, cheeks wind-nipped. They stared at one another for a long moment, until a smile spread beneath his beard, and she couldn't help but answer it. "Walk with me?" he asked.

They made their way, side by side, down to the shore, walking along the narrow path, huddled together against the morning breeze. The cry of gulls overhead echoed in the clear air, and Ronan found her cold, ungloved hand somehow within his own. She slipped it in without artifice as they walked, and he smiled and tightened his grip over hers. She had a lifetime of love to give away, and it was currently all directed at him. *She has a lifetime of not being loved to make up for as well,* he thought soberly.

They walked a short way along the seashore, watching sandpipers scurrying back and forth ahead of them. The sandpipers chased the waves on the shore as they receded, and then ran quickly on their stick legs in the other direction as the waves flowed back. Aine thought they were endlessly amusing, and he listened to her laugh as they ran back and forth.

Ronan watched her as she watched them. He wanted to catch her, kiss her, keep her. He wanted to give her his body and take hers. He wanted to share his whole existence with her. *Just say it,* he thought. She disentangled her hand and walked ahead a short distance, glancing back at him with a smile over her shoulder. There are moments in any life that should rightfully be frozen in time, if only life were just. Ronan of the Light wanted this one, when his beloved was so carefree, a spark of mischief and laughter in her eyes, framed as she was by the cold morning sky and the deep blue of the sea, her love written unashamedly on her face.

"Aine," he said, his voice more gruff than he'd intended. He cleared his throat, but she had run ahead again and was now following the nearest sandpiper, chasing the waves up and down the beach like a playful girl, her skirts whipped around her, her curls lifted and tossed by the wind. He took a deep breath, heart pounding, hands shaking. He felt the thrill of the essential moments that in the aggregate, strung together like a strand of pearls, make up a life well lived. *Just tell her,* he thought.

Aine suddenly smelled cherry blossoms and saw before her a ghostly vision of the Sumiyoshi Toudai rising majestically beside the Suimon River. The cherry trees were in full bloom, and they waved just above her head. Instead of stepping into the translation, she paused. She remembered tossing and turning the night before after turning down the assignment. Her heart pounded, and she closed her eyes and took a deep breath, laughing at the sheer wonder of the choice.

To be so free! She could shake her head and stay precisely where she was, walking on the beach with Ronan. Or she could step forward into that vision and go visit that familiar Light, and perhaps its familiar keeper, knowing there was a path home! She opened her eyes and took in that dark Light and the house behind it. She thought of the need of the keeper at that Light and of his pain the last time she'd been there. She didn't think of the keeper behind her, or if he needed her.

Ronan saw her still in her tracks, tilt her head to one side as if considering a new puzzle, and then throw her head back and laugh. It was a joyous sound that carried in the clear morning air, and he stepped forward, an answering smile on his face. Then she was gone.

"No!" he cried, and though he knew it was futile, stumbled forward to the spot where she had just been, the echo of her voice fading from the air. "Aine!" he cried. There they were, her boot prints, ending abruptly by the shoreline. One was a full print, made with all her weight, and the other was fainter, as though she had just stepped down. He fell to his knees beside them, his body shielding them from the encroaching sea. The sand was cold beneath his knees, and moisture soaked quickly into the fabric of his pants, chilling him.

"Aine!" he cried again. The wind snatched her name from him, the silence after her laughter unbearable, broken only by what remained: raucous gulls, the waves washing in and out, as inexorable as time, and his panting breath in the cold spring morning.

He looked down at the boot prints and felt as though a sinkhole had appeared in his center and was going to start steadily pulling down everything inside him if he didn't find a way to plug it.

The waves ebbed and flowed beside him, and try as he might to shield her last set of footprints, the waves slipped between and around his legs and started to wash them away. The water carried the bitter cold of the North, and he knelt, paralyzed, staring between his knees at the last visible evidence of her existence.

He numbly watched the next wave steal up beside him and wash the fainter boot print away. He looked behind him, in the direction they had come, and saw that all evidence of their journey had faded, washed into the sea.

He felt his heart trying to slip, to slide into the sinkhole within him. It would be so easy to let it go, to give in to bitterness and resentment. *Is this time it? Is she coming back? A moment longer,* he thought desperately. *I needed but a moment to tell her. Why didn't I speak sooner? What was there to hesitate about? She deserved those words,* he thought. *Why didn't I give them out to her, untidy and out of order? She was within arms' reach!*

"Who could need her more than I?" he cried, tilting his head back to shout at the sky. "I need her!" he yelled, anger welling up inside him. "Thief," he choked. It didn't make him feel any better.

Perhaps I'm not strong enough for this. Had it only been moments ago that she was dancing along the seashore, his life so full of joy, of her?

He had been about to ask something impossible of her. Ask her to give herself completely, to be with him. To stay. *It's impossible,* he thought. *I can't ask it of her, because she can't give it. Can she give it?* He didn't know. *I'm not strong enough to ask it,* he thought. Her intentions couldn't keep him company in midwinter.

What had he expected? A marriage where they worked side-by-side tending the Light? Where they washed dishes together and he watched her read in the deep armchair next to his? Where he held her warm body next to his every night until—what? Until death? As far as she was concerned, he'd already died.

Yes, he thought, his face bowed against the brutality of the sea breeze. *That's exactly what I expected.* He clenched his jaw against the painful cold in his lower extremities from the seawater.

It was unutterably painful, to be the one left behind. How was he supposed to bear waiting while she went and he stayed? He glanced down at her last boot print. Of course there was no trace of her left. The sea had slipped between his legs and washed her away.

Frozen in place, he let the cruel breeze touch his face and set the tears he had unwittingly shed aflame against his cheeks. *She doesn't belong to you,* he told himself harshly. *She comes and goes. Let her go.*

Sumiyoshi Toudai, Ogaki, Japan, 1743

S HE WAS ON THE NARROW Road again, the one that led to the
Deep North, and the cherry blossoms were in full bloom. The
short, dark Sumiyoshi Toudai squatted by the bank of the Suimon,
and Aine felt a spring in her step as she pushed back her wide silk
brocade sleeves and walked around the side of the building to the
door waiting ajar at the back.

As she pushed her sleeve back, twisting her wrists to free them
from the fabric, a low-hanging branch caught the tender skin on the
inside of her arm. She gasped, more in surprise than pain, as she felt
the still-new sensation of her skin splitting, the sharp knife of pain
from the branch slicing her fragile skin. She was coming to see that
human pain always occurred in moments like this. When her attention was focused on something else, pain reached up and nipped at
her ankles, whining for attention.

Aine kept her sleeve free of the small cut, holding the joy she felt
in the translation close and blocking out the sensation of the cut.
Instead, she thought, *I have a choice. I'm here because I have a choice.*
Her heart lightened and she stepped forward.

The acts of removing her shoes, padding inside in her socks, and
finding the keeper kneeling waiting for her in the back of the small
house felt in themselves like a ritual. She hardly made a sound,
but his bowed head came up at her soft footfalls, and he smiled,
his unseeing eyes warm on her. The air was heavy with the grassy
smell of sencha, and before she could speak, he had risen with liquid grace from his seat, and in a couple of ground-swallowing strides
that almost had her doubting his lack of sight, he folded her into an
embrace.

His strong arms enveloped her, and in contrast to the previous
time, he did not have a bird-boned feel to him at all. In fact, Aine

realized, she was the one who felt small and slight. She leaned into his shoulder, breathing in the scents of rapeseed oil, cherry blossoms, and sencha, mingled with his own human scent. It wasn't home, but it was a comfort nonetheless, and she felt a strange kinship with this man to whom she had been called back a second time.

He took a long, trembling breath and drew back from her so that she could see his strong, smoothly shaven jaw, his dark straight hair combed back neatly from his pale skin, and his lips curved into a slight smile. Gently, and slowly enough to give her time to pull back had she wanted to, he bent his head and reverently kissed her forehead, before opening his arms and drawing away.

She stood, frozen to the ground, while he walked back to his seat and held out a hand to her, inviting her to sit across from him. "Welcome home, dear one," he said softly.

Her feet carried her forward and she ungracefully knelt across from him at the low table, relieved that she didn't immediately knock over the bowl in front of her. *To see that look in another's eyes,* she thought. She thought she had seen it the night before, when Ronan named her. It was a look that focused all the whirling planets and bright stars in the cosmos into a single person, and crowned her queen.

She steadied her breath and watched him fold back his sleeve from a strong, pale wrist to pour the green-gold tea. It steamed fragrantly between them, and she breathed deeply of it, heady with the scent and the bittersweet joy he emanated. *I choose to be here with you,* she thought, her eyes smiling at the man across from her. They sipped their tea slowly, taking their time with the ritual, and Aine's eyes caught again on the keeper's face when he lifted his tear-filled eyes to her, honoring his beloved with his tears. This time, her shoulders relaxed, her brow unfurrowed, the knot in her middle loosened, and—glory be—she wept with him.

Loon-Call Light, Maine, 1910

After the tea, she willed herself home, and realized she was only a few strides from where she and Ronan had been walking. She turned in a half-circle to find that he was still there. *It must not have been long*, she thought happily.

He stood gazing out to sea, hands tucked into the pockets of his uniform. Her step faltered when she noticed his hunched shoulders, back tensed as if anticipating a blow. She thought, fleetingly, that it must be difficult to be the one left behind, and wished that there was some way she could have told him before she left. It was all so new, and she hadn't had time to think it through. She hadn't been the one left behind before, so she only knew the difficulty of forever *going*, rather than that of waiting. She must have made a small sound, because his head snapped up and whipped around, his gaze catching and focusing on her. Her greeting died on her lips at the fierce look in his eyes.

"Aine?!" he exclaimed. It sounded to her like a question, though she didn't have time to think how to answer it. In a moment he had twisted his body around and stumbled toward her as though shoved from behind by an unseen hand, and she was tackled into a sloppy embrace.

"Aine," he breathed, and crushed her close, so that there wasn't space enough for a spring breeze between them. He leaned back long enough to fumble with his gloves, which he stripped off, and dropping them unceremoniously in the sand at their feet, he scooped her face between his broad, warm palms. Aine caught her breath at the concentrated determination on his face.

"Don't disappear," he commanded, and brought his mouth down on hers.

She tasted of both the faraway grassy sweetness of sencha and of home at the same time. He angled her mouth to his and kissed her again.

Mind blank, Aine stood, frozen with the shock of his warm mouth on hers, while the chill morning breeze raked at all the places not shielded by his warm body. She closed her eyes and felt the wind against her forehead, his warm palms cupping her cheeks, his mouth devouring her own. His taste was foreign to her, sweet but with a hint of salty sea, framed by the scratchiness of his rough woodsmoke-scented beard. She brought a hand up to his chest, feeling the quick rhythm of his heart beneath her fingers.

He pulled her in closer and gentled the kiss, so that it took less, but asked more. He drew back slightly and brought his forehead to hers, heart racing as if it could pound straight out of his chest had she not been pressed against him to hold it in place.

He took a couple of deep breaths, their faces close together. "Aine, Aine, Aine," he murmured, and slanted his mouth over hers once again.

The second kiss stormed her defenses and scaled her walls. The third left her warm, her outer self stripped away like the gloves he had discarded in the sand at her feet. She had never felt so breached, or so safe.

"Ronan," she breathed, and his arms tightened around her.

He drew back a second time, the hands cupping her face stroking and smoothing her hair back, running through it to her shoulders, and setting her back from him gently so there was a forearm's width between them. The air rushed between their bodies and Aine felt the chill of his momentary absence, but it didn't dull the warmth he had lit within her. Her face shone with it, and she fairly glowed at him as he gazed intently down at her.

"So," she said shakily, attempting a wobbly smile. "Was I gone as long as all that?"

He said nothing for a moment, his eyes so somber on her that she nearly couldn't hold his gaze. "A lifetime," he murmured. "Or an hour," he added, attempting a smile back, but not succeeding.

"Aine," he began haltingly, "would you . . ." He stopped, swallowed, and turned away from her for a moment, to look out to sea. He composed himself and tried again. "Would you do me the . . ." he stopped, his throat working. She watched him swallow dryly, and winced a little.

He ran his fingers through his hair to the base of his neck. His hand lingered on the back of his neck for a moment, and then a look of resolve tightened his features.

He set his shoulders as though against a task, and before she knew what he was about, he bent to his knees in the sand before her. Wide-eyed she gazed at his broad hands splayed against his thighs for a moment, and then understanding finally dawned in her eyes. "Aine," he said in a voice he willed to be strong and sure. "Would you do me the honor of marrying me?"

"Ronan," she said softly, and fell to her knees in the sand with him. "There's no need to—"

"You were happy a moment ago," he murmured, reaching out and framing the side of her face with his wide palm.

She covered his hand with her own and shook her head. "I'm happy now. Please don't feel that you must make promises or pledge yourself in any way. Not for me."

"I want to," he told her gently. "I need to."

She took in the lines of his face, so newly precious in her life, and suddenly remembered that she hadn't told him yet.

"Oh!" she exclaimed. "I have something to tell you," she said, suddenly shy and unsure.

His hand tightened on hers. "Are you well? What is it?" he asked, scanning her face.

She shook her head, momentarily wordless, fumbling for a way to begin to tell him her news. He gripped her hands tightly, as though he thought them birds ready to take flight. She took a deep breath. "I'm going to age now, Ronan."

"What?" he asked, bewildered, his head jerking back, his grip on her loosening.

"I've been given a choice, I mean. Between continuing as I am, without a will—" She laughed as his grip again tightened on her hands.

"Or?"

"Or I can stay, and age."

She's already decided, he realized, heart racing as he took in her furrowed brow, awaiting his reaction. *What would it be like,* he wondered, *not to age? To be unsusceptible to cold, disease, and time itself? Would I give it up for a woman?* He was uncertain, but then again, he had not lived her life. *And it is her life, isn't it?*

"Aine," he breathed, and framed her face with his warm palms. "You'll stay. And age." He pressed a soft kiss onto her upturned mouth. "With me."

"Ronan," she murmured, returning his kiss, "it's not so simple."

Of course not.

"I will still be presented with work, though I can choose whether to take it now."

So she left of her own will just now, he thought, stung. "How will you choose which work to take?" he asked her, finding his voice.

"It hasn't been long," she warned, "but I try to choose the ones I think have a true need."

What makes a need true? he wondered.

"But you'll stay," he finally asked.

"I'll try," she replied, "but you need make me no promises. What if I choose to go somewhere and am somehow detained? Or what if I'm injured there and unable to return? What if I . . ." She swallowed. There was no shame in it, only sadness. "What if I die in another time, and you just keep . . . waiting?"

What if, indeed? he thought. Hadn't he agonized about it in the interminable hour while she was gone? He had spent the weeks she was tending the Colossus thinking of it. It made no sense. *Life with you makes no sense, Aine,* he thought, *but neither does it make sense without you.* He had tried to reassemble the puzzle in his mind to cut her out of it, but it made a bleak picture. *It's madness either way.* He could choose the safety of a life without her, or the certain pain of love with her.

He said nothing for long enough that she believed him when he finally spoke. "You'll go when you must, and I'll stay, and I'll hope for your return."

She shook her head weakly. "I don't know how much time we'll have."

This time he waited long enough that she thought he'd changed his mind. She warred between wanting him safe and unhurt and wanting him to fight for her, selfish though it might be. *Don't change your mind,* she thought urgently. *I would brave death to be with you, Ronan. I'm doing so now.*

"I know it's uncertain, Aine," he started quietly. "I would be lying to say it doesn't strike terror into my heart. It was agony to wait on you the last time, not knowing if you would return." She nodded and closed her eyes. He brushed her hair back from her face. "But Aine," he said, taking her right hand within his own and pressing it to his chest. "It's too late for anything else."

What does he mean, that it's too late? she wondered. She'd never thought in terms of time-poverty, or worried about running out of time or not having enough of it for her needs. She'd never understood why people wrote about time as though it were some cosmic currency, to be used, traded, spent. Why was it never enough when times were good, and interminable when there was suffering? How could the hour be "too late," as Ronan had said? What he meant, of course, was that things had gone too far in a certain direction, and that time couldn't be run backwards to reverse what they had done.

She felt the rapid but steady beat of his heart and knew he spoke the truth. It was "too late" for her as well. He saw the moment she agreed with him, and he sighed.

She gazed into his beloved face for a long minute, her heart in her throat. "It isn't certain," she said softly. She had never looked so young to him as in that moment.

"No, it isn't," he agreed gently.

"I want . . ." She sighed.

"What do you want, my joy?" he prompted, his face somber but his eyes smiling into hers.

"I want all of it, with you," she told him, a blush blooming across her cheeks. "I've never wanted anything more."

"Well, here I am."

"I've never been able to keep the things I want," she reminded him sadly, as though he didn't know.

His gaze lingered on the circlet of heath flowers marked around her neck, and the lightning peeking out from beneath the sleeve of her arm, before finding her eyes again. His hand tightened over hers, covering the lightning there, and pressed it against his heart. Her fingers flattened, feeling how quickly it beat beneath his calm exterior.

"I'm not a thing, I'm a man," he told her firmly. "And no matter when or where you are, you keep this," he said, motioning with his chin to their two hands held over his heart. Her fingers curled within his and she sighed.

"Aine, darling girl, will you stay, if you can, and be my wife?"

Her eyes blurred with tears, and she blinked hard to clear her vision. "You love me," she told him quietly. It wasn't a question.

"Yes," he said, heart racing beneath her fingers.

She gave a watery sort of laugh and inched forward, wrapping her other arm around his neck and burying her face against him. She had almost no breath left in her, but she nodded and whispered her reply to him. His eyes closed while he absorbed the relief and felt the new weight settle on his shoulders. He drew her closer until his forehead rested against hers, their hearts beating wildly together.

Between one heartbeat and the next, the sand under their feet became warm, the wind against their faces soft, and the sun overhead brightened.

Ronan opened his eyes to find himself gazing into Aine's clear eyes, sparkling with wonder and excitement.

She eased to her feet and reached down to help him up as well. *What is this place?* They were on a new shore, soft white sand beneath their bare feet, the sea stretched out before them, glistening under a full, warm sun. There was no Light, no house, and no one as far as the eye could see.

A warm, honeyed breeze rifled through Aine's hair. He started when he noticed that her coat and stiff boots were gone, and in their place she wore a gown of seafoam green. Her hair curled about her shoulders. He glanced down and absently noticed that he was wearing some finery of his own, but then he became distracted by her bare toes curling into the sand.

Ronan took in her relaxed face, her calm brows. "Where are we?" He shook his head. "When are we? Is that a better question?"

"No one has ever translated with me before. I have been here before, though," she said slowly. "I've met the Keeper of All Lights here, though . . ." She trailed off. "I'm never certain if it's a dream."

"It's no dream," he replied. He looked from her to the beach around them, but didn't let her go until he caught sight of the Woman behind her.

His arms dropped away and his face stilled. Aine knew who he'd seen before she turned around. She grasped his hand in hers and, turning to Wisdom, bowed at the waist.

Ronan was momentarily frozen in place as the Woman came closer, her gown and hair moving in the breeze but her face a calm, immovable presence in the midst of the motion. He quickly bowed from the waist as he'd seen Aine do and watched in amazement as the Woman approached Aine with a smile, her feet seeming barely to skim the ground.

"You've chosen well, daughter," she said, in the most fluid, melodious voice he'd ever heard. "Do you take this man, both inside and outside of time?"

Ronan turned his head and caught the flush rising up Aine's neck, but she cleared her throat, and her voice was firm when she replied, "Yes."

The Woman turned to him. "Ronan of the Light." He heard his name from her lips and felt it from the top of his head to the soles of his feet, and it seemed to shake something loose inside him. "Do you understand that you will both die, and that your time together will be uncertain? That she will choose to go where and when she is most needed? That if she chooses not to go, she will live in uncertainty of the consequences of her decisions?" Aine's hand tightened in his.

The Woman turned away to give him a moment and faced Aine. *You do realize what it means, that he has called you back to himself more than once? That though there were other, more dire, circumstances elsewhere and in other times, his need is the greatest?*

Wisdom waited silently, her calming presence unhurried. *He needs me,* thought Aine. Had there ever been a more sobering thought?

Let it anchor you to the earth, said Wisdom, and Aine nodded mutely. Wisdom turned to Ronan.

"She will go, and I will stay," he said simply, humbly. Aine stood taller at the strength and conviction in his voice. He sounded so very sure.

"And you will not go with her," said the All-Keeper, "though you are here with her now."

He nodded.

"And your time will be limited, and she will often be gone when the need is greater elsewhere."

He nodded again.

"And as she has buried you, so will you bury her," finished Wisdom, her voice grave and final.

Glad he was holding Aine's hand, Ronan clasped it more tightly. His fingers trembled, but his grasp remained strong. He held onto her while the silence lengthened.

Finally, he cleared his throat and tried to speak. Nothing came out. He nodded instead.

"It will not be an easy life, and I cannot tell you how much time you have," continued Wisdom. "Do you take this woman, knowing all of this?"

The question was not for her, but Aine wanted to answer for him, though she had no voice in that moment, and love could give but one answer. *No* was the logical answer, the response that made sense. Why choose a woman who couldn't stay, who brought uncertainty, and who would surely leave sorrow in her wake? She understood, though she had not experienced it before, the depth of his love, and understood—with shame in her heart—that it would be difficult for him to turn away from her. Surely over the years it would be the merciful thing to do, for both of them?

In that place out of time, Ronan stood tall, the warmth of the sun on his back, its presence somehow a comfort. Though he had not noticed it before, the sea had slowly reached the place where they stood. A wave lapped against his bare feet, the water soft and warm. He knew that he could pause in this place and think. *Maybe I can just stand here,* he thought, almost deliriously, *and just hold her hand for all of eternity, pretending that I am unsure of my decision.* The Woman raised her brows at him, the hint of a smile on her face. *Of course,* he thought. *Forgive me, my Lady.* She inclined her head.

You give me little choice, he told her silently. *You know my heart. Surely some joy is better than none.*

If there was another, the All-Keeper asked silently. *If there was another woman that you would meet at some point in the future that you could make a simple life with? One who could provide you with a family and help you keep the Light, would you let this woman go?*

He waited for the catch.

There is none, my child.

He stood under the warm sun, his feet wrapped in the caress of the sea, and closing his eyes, bowed his head. The hand that held Aine's felt traitorous, as though he had already betrayed her. It was such a small hand, though he knew it to be so capable. He hated this conversation, and it hurt his head to stand there exchanging words with the Woman, but he felt that he had to defend Aine in this place, or he would never feel worthy of her.

He looked back up at the Woman. *Isn't there always uncertainty, when one gives a heart into another's keeping?* he asked. *I can't betray this woman because I fear uncertainty. She belongs with me, for however long we have, if she'll have me; I've chosen her.* His hand tightened purposefully around Aine's, and he felt her grasp his more firmly in return.

"Very well," said Wisdom aloud, an appraising look in her eyes. The sun continued to warm him, and the sea continued to soothe him, and he felt that his head was less foggy for a moment.

"So you take this woman, knowing all of this?" asked the Woman again. He wrinkled his brow, puzzled, feeling as though he had already answered her.

Yes, he replied clearly.

"Do you want to give her the word? So she can hear it?" asked Wisdom gently, reaching for Aine's right hand. Aine released her left from his grasp gently, and flexed it, smiling a little, as though to get the circulation back into it. He stood for a moment, and then it struck him, as Wisdom placed Aine's right hand in his own and he realized that his beloved was blushing prettily up at him, what she was asking.

He looked down at their hands, clasped together, and his heart expanded with happiness, then suddenly felt fuller, heavier, with responsibility. He glanced over at the Woman once more and said a brief, heartfelt *thank you*, before tucking Aine's hand more deeply into his grasp and looking down into her trusting eyes.

"Yes," he said, his voice deep and strong, carrying out across the sea. "Yes, I take this woman."

The All-Keeper stepped back, the sun shining brightly, the sea surrounding them. Ronan looked down at their joined hands for a moment, then he tilted Aine's face up and brought his mouth down over hers, breathing deeply of her, tasting the salt of her happy tears. His mouth was soft, gentle, questioning, and when he drew back her face answered with wonder and joy.

~: 28 :~

A real friend . . . exults in his friend's happiness, rejoices in all his
joys, and is ready to afford him the best advice.

HERODOTUS, THE HISTORIES

Loon-Call Light, one week later

THE WIDOW McLEARY, AGED THIRTY-FOUR, was, in most
of the town's estimation, far too young and pretty to be living
alone without a man. She tried to ignore the glances and knowing
looks she received at the bakery, the bank, the café on the corner,
and the greengrocer's. *Small-town minds,* she would often mutter to
herself. She was, however, through a rather unfeeling twist of fate,
quite lonely, for she had loved her husband, and he her, and she had
awoken some months after his death to realize that it was unjust,
and that she hadn't quite counted on this, and that she didn't much
prefer to be alone in her thirties, without children, receiving pitying
glances from the small-town minds who lived around her.

She had married Joshua when she was nineteen and he twenty-one,
in a frilly dress in a small church, and they had been each other's first
loves. All the neighborhood girls had envied her, because she was

lovely in the first blush of her youth and was marrying the catch of the town. She and Joshua had muddled through those first few years, learning each other and growing into adults together. They had been so normal and happy.

She squared her shoulders. There were few options for first husbands, let alone second ones in town, and none that gave her much pleasure to think about. She didn't want to be alone, but neither did she want to give up her self-respect either to look after Patrick Morgan's brood of six hellions or to lovingly tend to old Sean O'Rourke's gouty feet. Which left Ronan of the Light, as they called him.

Ronan was a hard one to pin down, and she had tried on a few occasions to catch his eye as he came to pick up large sacks of rice and flour from the mill or nurse an occasional beer. He was a quiet bear of a man who never said an ill word against anyone, and he seemed not to have a tendency toward cruelty. Her stomach roiled at that: was she honestly narrowing down her list of prospective partners based on whether they had too many children, too many medical conditions, or were able to control their tempers? In any case, Ronan seemed, for such a large man, quite gentle, and she had seen him on more than one occasion break up a brewing fight with a gentle word or a warm, heavy hand on the shoulder of a man who was drinking too much.

She decided that today would be the day. She carefully sifted and measured and trimmed until the perfectly-shaped rhubarb pie—one of several, for she never went to all that trouble to make just one— was ready to slide into the oven. Her hands shook as she tidied up the kitchen. *There's no need to be nervous,* she thought. *I'm just dropping by*—she laughed a little at that. If anyone couldn't be dropped in on it was Ronan of the Light. He lived so far from the rest of them as to make that impossible. There could be only two reasons to go that far: either to drop off his mail, of which there was next to none, or to deliberately bait him with a pie.

He wasn't stupid, and she was tired of being alone, and of being lonely, for she now knew they were two different things. She hated the loneliness and she craved connection, *and*, she thought, shrugging into her coat, *perhaps he's lonely too. At the least, perhaps I can make a new friend.*

The hike up to the Light was no easy task in her Sunday shoes, which pinched at the toes a bit. She rounded the last bend, straightened her skirts, smoothed a hand over her hair, and stepped onto the path, the pie in her right hand. The Light stood tall behind the keeper's cottage, and she imagined fixing the small space up, putting flowers in a jug on the kitchen table, being a warm presence for this man, who could be nothing but lonely here at the back of nowhere, with naught but the Light to occupy his hands. She stepped lightly up the path.

As she rounded a corner she heard an odd sound, and if she hadn't known better, she would've thought it was a woman. Giggling. The pie slipped out of her hand as she glimpsed with open horror, through the window of the house, Ronan of the Light kissing a woman. She gasped and whirled around, desperate to get away, but her face heated and she froze in mortification when a voice laughingly called to her to wait.

The woman, who the widow McLeary immediately decided had altogether too much hair, ran lightly up from the house to catch her, Ronan following at a more sedate pace. Her gaze skittered away from the look on his face. His eyes trailed the woman with satisfaction, and the widow looked away from both of them.

The woman stopped in front of her with a comical little skid on the path. "Please don't go!" she cried. "We so rarely have visitors." She took in the flushed face of the widow, and something seemed to startle her. Her hand came up, unconsciously, it seemed, to her heart, and she gave a small cry. Her face broke into a large smile.

"I beg your pardon," said the widow McLeary stiffly. "Do I know you from somewhere?"

The woman stood dazed, flushed, and speechless for a moment but snapped back with a shake of her head. The smile was still there, and the widow couldn't account for it. It was huge, welcoming, and completely out of place. "You don't know me from anywhere," she said definitively. If the widow hadn't been mortified at being caught on the path, she might have noticed the tears welling up in Aine's eyes and really wondered at the exuberance with which she was being greeted.

As it was, the widow McLeary was much too horrified to give it more than passing notice. Aine's eyes fell on the pie. "Oh, you've brought pie!" she cried, a hitch in her voice. She glanced back at Ronan and then carefully picked up the once-perfect pie, which had fortunately landed filling side up under the towel the widow had covered it with. Other than some of the filling spurting up from a fissure that had formed in the crust when it was dropped, it wasn't much the worse for wear.

The widow didn't know where to look or what she hated more: the pie, which she despised herself for baking and wanted to snatch out of the woman's hands and fling into the ocean, or the loving glances that excluded her. She certainly couldn't look at Ronan, for his eyes would be all too knowing, whether the woman with him knew or not.

She had the momentary and perverse thought that she wanted to wipe out Ronan's happiness and fancied that she could have the power to do that, perhaps with a few well-placed words. She imagined, for an instant, hinting at a liaison or a long-term relationship, some understanding between them that could erase the abominably assured look from this woman's face and make Ronan as lonely as she was. When she glanced back into the woman's eyes, though, she realized they weren't young and stupid, as she'd assumed based on the giggle she'd heard. They looked ages old, and they were not only knowing, but also compassionate and full of welcome as they gazed on her. Besides, the widow had never been a spiteful woman, just a lonely one.

She couldn't lift her face, and waited for a moment, her cheeks blazing, until the woman's hand came into her view. It was held out in greeting. She glanced up and the woman took her hand in hers. She glanced from her to Ronan, who didn't seem to have any words to offer.

Finally she spoke up. "I'm the widow McLeary," she forced through lips suddenly dry in a voice full of dust. She glanced at Ronan quickly. His eyes were on the other woman, waiting to take her cue. "I uh, have just come to bring you a pie." She paused lamely.

The woman must have felt that Ronan was not going to help with any introductions, so she clasped her hand and said, her voice gentle, "I'm Aine."

Ronan finally stepped close behind her and spoke up. "My wife," he clarified, in that deep voice that she had heard so rarely.

Suddenly, her reason to be there seemed even more sinister. It was one thing to visit a single man with a pie. But a married one! She nearly put a hand to her forehead, then realized the woman, Aine, was still holding it. She glanced up and felt Aine's eyes on her; they held no recrimination, only understanding.

"What is your name, Mrs. McLeary?" asked Aine quietly. *Claire*, she thought, *my darling friend. How I've missed you. You told me you would be lost when next I saw you. I'm so sorry for your loneliness, dearest.*

There was a long pause, while the widow's hand remained limp in Aine's grasp. The widow absently noted that Aine had calloused hands. Finally she said in a nearly resigned voice, "Claire."

Even anticipating it, Aine stiffened a bit. Claire didn't notice it, but Ronan did and stepped closer behind his wife. "Please, Claire," said Aine, her voice hitching on the name. Her tone was pleading and unnaturally high for her. "Come inside. I'll put some tea on to go with this beautiful pie. We so rarely have visitors."

Claire looked up and found Ronan finally looking at her, his gaze impassive as usual, but not unkind. A small smile played on his lips. Desperate to end the embarrassment, she nodded mutely and allowed herself to be led up the path into the tiny kitchen that had most definitely felt a woman's touch recently. There both she and her pie were made much of by the mistress of the house.

Claire, thought Aine. *My dear friend.* She understood now why Claire had swept her into an embrace when she'd seen her long ago, in the future. Aine led her into the kitchen and put the kettle on, wishing she could instead hug her and draw her into a chair by the fire, where they could have a good long chat to catch up. Aine composed herself. "Now," she said, settling across from Claire, secretly marveling at the reddish-gold color of her hair, her clear, unlined skin, and the brightness of her blue eyes. She was so young. "Tell me: how are things in town?"

Ronan disappeared during the eating of said pie, making a brisk comment about something Light-related, ignoring Aine's sardonically quirked brow at the already completed task, and then making himself scarce. Neither woman looked up. They had an awkward chat about life in general and the Light, and avoided mention of Ronan.

They danced around the topic for several moments before Claire asked, in a voice that cracked a little, "How long have you been married?"

"About a week," replied Aine.

The other woman's eyes widened. "A week!" she repeated faintly.

It wasn't the reunion Aine had wished for, but she was up for a challenge, and she missed her friend. So she cheerfully ignored the sags in the flow of conversation, the pensive look Claire leveled at the wildflowers on the table, and the feeling of being figuratively held at arm's length from her friend.

At the end of a short chat, Claire made to leave, and Aine,

desperate to hold on to her a moment longer, said, "Mrs. McLeary, will I see you again?"

The other woman, flustered, paused in the act of slipping her arm into her coat sleeve.

"Oh, well, of course we shall see each other in town and . . ." She trailed off.

"Will you come back, for tea?" persisted Aine, her eyes eager on the other woman, who looked like she wanted to finish throwing on her coat so she could run down the path to town.

"Oh, well," said Claire, flushing. "It is quite a ways to the Light, as you know," she began.

Aine nodded, and the crestfallen look on her face must have touched something in the other woman, because Claire decided then that she *could* be friendly to her, though there wasn't any particular reason to be.

"But you must come down to the cottage when you're in town, of course," added Claire, decisively. As she said it, she realized she meant it.

Aine's face brightened into a wide smile and she impulsively reached out to take Claire's hands in her own. "Thank you," she said warmly, her voice oddly affected. "I would like that very much."

Claire, having had enough of the exuberance of her new acquaintance, said a brief goodbye and found her way to the door, where she stepped into the waning afternoon light, her toes pinched in her shoes on the path back to town.

Aine began a tentative friendship with Claire McLeary. She couldn't think of her as Claire of the hearth quite yet. The relationship was hesitant on Claire's end and secretly enthusiastic on Aine's. Claire seemed to suspect her motives for the friendship at first, and Aine couldn't very well explain that her motives *were*, in fact, suspect. Aine, impatient with the tentative teatimes and stilted conversation about the townspeople, wanted to shout, *You see Claire, we're already friends, in the far future, so all of this is just a formality. Couldn't we skip ahead to that point already?*

Less than a week after offhandedly inviting Ronan's new bride to her home for tea following the pie she had unintentionally brought to her, Claire was surprised to find her offer taken quite seriously. On Thursday morning Claire opened her front door to find an eager Aine with a basket containing, to Claire's secret horror, a loaf of hearth bread baked with more enthusiasm than talent. *Poor Ronan.* Claire accepted the hard loaf with an indulgent smile. *I should let her keep making this awful bread for him*, she thought briefly, but with wicked glee.

Nevertheless, she ushered Aine in with grace, took her coat, and settled her on an armchair. "I'll just put the kettle on," she said, breezing out of the room.

Aine looked around eagerly. The wind chime above the door was missing, but the entryway did seem to hold a respectable jumble of scarves and coats. The walls held a couple of formal paintings, but the colorful one of the blue cat curled around a pile of books was missing. The house was rather less cozy now than it had been—*than it's going to be.* Aine took a deep breath, and the smells of the kitchen off to the left of the sitting room reached her: warm, yeasty, fresh bread. *Ah*, she thought, *there's the heart of this home.*

"Have you lived long in town?" asked Aine as Claire rejoined her, settling into the armchair opposite her while the kettle boiled.

"I moved here with Joshua when we were newly married," she began. "He kept an apiary here."

"Oh?"

"Yes, and I still—" her head snapped to the window and she stood, crossing to it in short, angry strides. She leaned her head out, and Aine could see the rigid line of her back as she held herself stiffly. "You children get out of there!" she yelled, her voice breaking a little. "I told you not to touch that!" Aine heard a shriek and the sound of small pattering feet, but couldn't see past Claire to the culprits.

Claire returned to her seat, her shoulders stiff, a frown marring her face. "Those wild, unruly—" she broke off abruptly, clenching her fists in her lap and closing her eyes for a brief moment, composing herself. "As I was saying," she started, "I still keep the bees, out back." She composed herself for another moment, and Aine said nothing.

"Joshua taught me," Claire said more conversationally, and they chatted for a while about this and that while they had their tea, Aine trying to forget the angry set of Claire's shoulders as she yelled at the children. She had never heard her gentle friend raise her voice at anyone, and she had always been bighearted toward the neighborhood children.

Their conversation eventually circled around to Claire's baking. "I do bake bread at times, and I've been thinking of selling it," Claire said offhandedly, and Aine looked up sharply.

"Well," she said firmly, "I do hope they pay you enough for it. That bread is miraculous."

Aine said it with such offended sensibilities on Claire's behalf that the woman felt she had somehow made a friend, though she thought a pie should not have endeared her to Aine quite so well. She was also so thrown off that it didn't occur to her to wonder how Aine had ever tasted her bread to form an opinion of it.

She smiled at the ferocity of the statement and shrugged. "Well, Dahlia has been saying she wants to sell real bread. Those loaves they sell are . . ." She shuddered and trailed off. Aine nodded approvingly, a smile on her lips. "I don't suppose people want to buy hearth bread, do they? Don't most just bake their own?"

Aine shook her head resolutely. "No, they don't. Claire, you should get a fair price for your bread when the time comes."

Startled, Claire laughed at her new defender's vehemence. "Well, she has been saying for years she means to open . . . I suppose when she does I'll think of a price."

Aine met her eyes evenly and stated a number.

Claire's eyes widened. "Why, that's highway robbery!" she exclaimed with a half-laugh.

"It isn't!" insisted Aine. "Not for good hearth bread. And don't you accept a penny less!" She glanced at the clock on the mantelpiece. "I have to run to help Ronan with the Light. Do come by when you've got some time!" She was out the door before Claire could think to make a reply.

~: 29 :~

Loon-Call Light, Maine, 1910

RONAN CUPPED HER CHEEK IN the palm of his hand and she leaned, as always, into his warmth. "Change whatever you like in the house, lass. There's a little money." It had been years since Margaret, and he had a vague idea Aine might want to add . . . something.

She looked up at him through her lashes, and he took in her unadorned face before he felt the curl of her smile against his hand. She turned and took a lengthy look around their small home. It was a long enough perusal that he slipped a finger into his collar, imagining new upholstery, rugs, stiff-backed chairs and dollies. But still. He would endure it, to give her any small comfort.

"Maybe I'll put up some curtains to filter the morning light in the kitchen," she said mildly, a smile playing on her lips.

He nodded, trying not to exhale too forcefully. He kept waiting for the massive wave, the tsunami that would wash away the small pond of his life, but he found instead that she was a live coal that had sizzled into cold water, and now the water was warm and comforting around them both.

Some days were better than others. Most of the summer months were filled with joy, and each day was a new revelation. Ronan and

Aine kept their lens faithfully. He, as promised, had informed the inspector that there was a new Mrs. Ronan of the Light, and had received a letter of congratulations in the post.

Though their lens was of medium size and their Light not tall, Aine had fallen hopelessly in love with both it and her home, and she told Ronan as much as they walked home from town in late morning. The sky had begun to darken and she could feel a coming afternoon storm.

His usual tart reply, which she had anticipated, never came. He simply smiled at her.

"Well, aren't you going to tell me that it's not our Light, but yours?" she asked, baiting him with a laugh.

His smile faded a little, but didn't leave his eyes, and he said lightly, "A man doesn't joke about his happiness, Aine." He took her hand, which she readily slipped into his.

She said nothing but let his mood sweep over her, along with the coming storm clouds.

"Tell me why you love our Light," he asked, glancing at her. They were coming up the lane to the Light and it rose up from the path in front of them, tall and proud.

She felt his warm gaze and tightened her grip on his hand. "Well," she started, "it's neither too big nor too small. The Saint Augustine Light, for instance," she said. "I remember half-expiring getting to the top of the two hundred and nineteen steps." He smiled at her, his fingers warm around hers.

"I stopped to look out the window at the view halfway to the top and lost track of time. By the time I realized it, the blasted oil had nearly solidified!"

He laughed aloud. "Head in the clouds," he murmured, chidingly, "and not even a book in sight." She shook her head at him, smiling, and they unclasped their hands and went into the house.

Neither of them said it, but their Light was also not big enough to draw many tourists. Aine loved their lens and cleaned it carefully for hours. True, some people went for the massive first-order lenses, but she found them flashy, and besides, she and Ronan didn't have eight hours between them to clean one daily. She liked their little lens, and more importantly, she liked the solitude it afforded them, being less of an attraction for visitors. Tourists had begun to descend on light-stations like locusts in plague-like proportions during the summer months, devouring the scenery, the history, and the solitude. They were, in a word, pestilent to a man long used to his solitude, but Aine didn't mind.

"What else?" he asked. They had left their supplies from town behind and were making their way down the path to their little skiff, moored on the small dock. The wind picked up, and he watched her look out to sea with restless energy while he pushed them away from shore toward the buoy he had set out. She had big plans for their evening meal.

"What else what?" she asked, distracted by the movement of his shoulders as he palmed the oars and began rowing. He caught her staring and grinned, making short work of the trip. He pulled up alongside the buoy, and they secured the boat together.

Aine tried to lift the lobster cage out of the water, but found to her chagrin that it was too heavy. She grunted against the heavy load, the metal of the cage biting into her palms. The muscles in her shoulders cramped, and as the moment stretched, Aine felt the singular discomfort of once having been able to do a thing, and then having grown unable to do it. She glanced at Ronan.

"May I?" he asked. She nodded without looking at him, her face ablaze. Ronan reached over her shoulder, lending her a hand and his strength to draw the cage out of the water. They set it down together, arms aligned, her back cupped against his chest. The silence was acute, though gulls filled the air, crowding the cage to see if they might snag supper for themselves in the confusion. He could feel her tense body and hear her sigh, and though he didn't know what she was feeling, he sensed her distress. He released his hold on the metal cage, flicked the cold water from his arm, now wet to the shoulder, and with his dry palm brushed the hair from her neck. He slipped his arm around her middle and drew her more closely against him.

Aine released the cage and leaned back into the protective embrace, her body relaxing against him. She took a long breath and blew it out, and he held her while she passed the internal milestone. Finally, holding her own wet arm away from her body, she turned in his hold and lifted her face to him. His lips found her forehead and passed softly over her brow. She leaned back and offered him a tentative smile.

He searched her eyes until he found the answer he was looking for and murmured, with studied nonchalance, "I still can't understand why you want me to catch lobster for you."

Aine glanced down at the red imprint of the cage on her wet palm and deliberately shook off the creeping melancholy. She focused on the beautiful day, the fact that they were both whole and healthy, and the way he was looking at her. She thought of the meal they were about to share beneath the apple tree. *So what if I can't lift a heavy lobster trap anymore? I have this day, and this man.*

Ronan eyed her, gauging her mood. "It's peasant food, Aine," he continued, stepping back with a small smile. He reached down, and grunting, shifted the cage in the skiff and repositioned himself to row them back to shore.

She willed herself to feel the excitement she wanted to feel about their catch and smiled at him, the smile expanding within her as she went through the motions. When it reached her eyes Ronan felt the tightness in his chest ease.

"I love lobster," she told him enthusiastically as they wrestled the two large lobsters into a potato sack when they reached shore. "And what a snob you are, Ronan! I'll have you know it won't always be peasant food. It's about to become quite popular in restaurants. They charge a pretty penny for lobster at the turn of the next century."

"Restaurants!" he exclaimed. "This prisoner food? By God, but the future sounds grim."

She smiled secretively at him. "You'll see."

Gingerly carrying the sack of lobsters, he asked, "What else do you love about me? I mean, what do you love about the Light?"

"Well, it's tall," she began. "And dark, and handsome." She glanced over and found him grinning behind his beard. "And does this amazing—"

"All right, all right!" He laughed and held up a hand in surrender. "How about the Light?"

She laughed as she took in his intent focus. "I like that it's not a tiny Light, like some, and that it has a view." She thought for a moment. "I've tended *vippefyrs* in the Nordic lands."

"What's that?" he asked, alert.

I will never tire of this, she thought. *His interest, his willingness to listen: they will never grow commonplace. As to that, the commonplace is the only thing that could break my heart anymore. The Light, the man, the loon calls, the supper dishes, and the tea by the fire. What else in the world is there?*

"Vippefyrs," she answered. "They're tipping lights. They were triangular-shaped navigational aids in the 1800s. You couldn't climb them, but they tended to be in beautiful places. They had an open flame in a basket, operated by a pulley."

"That sounds dangerous," commented Ronan drily.

"You're telling me!" She laughed. "I nearly lit my hair aflame!"

"Well, yes," he agreed, keeping a straight face. "With that hair."

She chuckled, but something about the look on her face made him pause. "Lass, I'm teasing you. You know that?" he added more gently, reaching out to finger a stray curl that lay against her cheek. He waited, heart in his eyes.

235

"It's not that, Ronan, really," she said. She reached for his free hand, and he offered it readily. "I love being teased by you. It just reminds me of something."

She now knew that the comb she had slipped into her hair had been made for her by Ronan. The comb that had forever turned her hair into a tangle of curls. She didn't think much about her hair, except that it was on her head and protected it from the sun, but she thought often of her beloved, whittling the comb alone. She thought of him dying alone, and of the way in which she had buried him. *How different that burial would have been had I known! How did I not know?* Her hand tightened its grip on his. *How could Claire not have said something?* She glanced at him, taking in his serene face as they walked hand in hand. *When my hands prepared your body, how did I not recognize you, beloved?*

She didn't blame Claire. It wouldn't have served anyone. It would only have made things even more awkward when she finally met Ronan, and he her, that first time. It was better this way. Still, when he teased her about her hair she couldn't help but think of the comb tucked like a secret in his palm, and of his figure slumped at the small desk in the lantern room.

"Please," she said, gentling her grip on his hand. "Please keep teasing me about it. It's just a memory I can't banish. It has nothing to do with us now."

"All right, lass," he said.

At her request they boiled water with a few spices in a large pot, and she showed him how to cook the lobster. His eyebrows rose at her explanation. "It's normally canned, isn't it?" he asked. "Not that I eat it!" He smiled over his shoulder at her as he sliced bread.

"Canned lobster is an abomination," she informed him primly, a smirk tilting her lips. She carefully melted butter in a piece of crockery over the hot stove.

They sat under the apple tree at midday, clouds gathering, their underbellies heavy with portent. They lingered as long as they dared, with the coming weather, and she taught him all about preparing lobster the correct way, and he had to concede defeat and admit that it wasn't entirely hopeless prisoner food.

"Hmm." She eyed his empty plate meaningfully.

"Anything else about the Light?" he asked, trying for nonchalance.

It means something to him, she realized. Her strong, handsome husband was looking at her eagerly, with a boyish expression of anticipation on his face.

"Well," she went on, smiling, "I love our small home, and the books and running water, the windows looking out on the garden and the sea." His eyes never left hers, reading her face carefully, watching for any sign of discontent. "I love the flowers that grow in spring, the asters, the goldenrod." A genuine smile curved his lips as she built momentum.

"I love the morning glory vines on the north corner of the house. I love the bayberry and purple thistles. The blue violets this summer. I love all of it, Ronan." *I love you.* The message was clear, meant for him to see. That look on her face made him feel taller than the Light, and he drank in the sight.

"I love the loons year-round, and the birds that visit," she continued. "The sandpipers, the swallows, the blackbirds. I love to put out seeds for them. I even love the squawking gulls."

"You go too far, woman," he teased, laughing. "Now I'm not sure if I believe anything you've said! No one can love those infernal creatures." She laughed at him while the clouds sagged darkly above them.

They gathered the plates and went inside as the smell of the coming storm settled like a damp cloak about their shoulders. *It's going to be a beauty*, Aine thought, and she could feel it building in the air and inside of her.

Ronan settled by the fireplace with a book, but it was a pretense.

Storms *did* something to his wife, he'd realized in the few miraculous weeks he'd been married to her.

He looked up to see her glance outside, a small, secret smile tugging up her lips. *My joy*, he thought, as she kneaded bread by the window, pushing hair off her forehead, leaving a smudge of flour. She caught him looking and he held her gaze, searing a little blush onto her cheeks until she smiled and ducked her face back to the dough.

Never mind the nuisance of the roof-shingles he would have to repair, or that her carefully tended garden might drown. He knew how she felt about powerful storms. She would wait all day for them, hurrying to get as much done as possible. She always tried to bake something on those days, though, heaven help him, her bread was still hard and lumpy. He smiled a little at that. She was by no means a baker, but it made her happy.

When at long last the anticipation had built to a peak, when the sky finally cracked for her, she would plaster her body against the glass and watch the rain slice the air, the smell of baking bread warming the inside of the house like the haven it was.

Some days she would hurry outside and rip the sheets down from the clothesline as the first drops fell. He loved when she wasn't fast enough, when she came back into the house flushed, laughing, and wet, her hair damp and her arms full of half-wet linens. He loved it more when she was really caught in it, and he would hear her scream his name, and he would run to rescue her, bundling her and the linens in his arms against the driving rain. His lips curved up at the thought. Not today, though. Today she was inside, waiting with her face to the window in those last few moments before the sky came down for her.

It started with a shower, and she opened the thick wooden front door, leaned against the jamb, set her head against it like a lover, and watched as the first drops came down hard onto the soil, steaming the air, the smell of damp earth rising. He watched her, her breaths

238

rising and falling in excitement, elated by the power of the storm. The wilder and more bruising the better, he'd noticed, as it built in fury outside. And God in heaven, but when lightning would strike, he could nearly see it course through her, raising bumps all along her slender arms. He saw her finger the mark of the lightning on her right wrist where it disappeared under her sleeve.

And God help him, he would try to leave her in peace, enjoying the storm, but a man had his limits, and she was practically vibrating in the doorway, and he wanted a part in her happiness. So on this day, as he had on others, he slipped behind her, wrapped her carefully in his arms—loosely, so she could step away if she chose to—so that she leaned back against him, rather than the doorjamb, and started at the nape of her neck.

If he was resourceful, she was generous. He traced the shape of the lightning on her body from tip to tip, while the house trembled from the force of the storm outside. Later, she tucked herself like a cat in the chair beside him, the same secret smile on her face. He waited, knowing she would soon pull something from the oven, something imperfect, but they would share it between them with some sharp cheese, and it would be perfect somehow.

And when the lump in his throat cleared, he would pray, trying to hold her loosely with his mind instead of cracking her ribs with the force of his embrace, as the rain pelted the glass sideways, and the sky occasionally cracked with lightning—he would pray that she would stay. *Stay, my joy,* he would say silently, his eyes soft on her. *Stay.*

~: 30 :~

Loon-Call Light, Maine, July 1910

SOME DAYS WERE MORE DIFFICULT. A week after the storm, Ronan watched her from the front door as she optimistically combed the beach for shells and other treasures.

She eventually wandered back up to the doorstep and held out two handfuls of shells. He eyed the smudge of tears on her smooth cheeks and cupped his hands beneath hers so she could spill the shells into his palms. She wiped her hands against the folds of her skirt and looked up at him, the light reflecting in her eyes.

"Did you leave?" he asked quietly.

She shook her head, a plea for absolution on her face. "I didn't want to," she told him in a small voice. He knew she worried when she didn't go. She feared leaving a ship marooned without a Light, a sailor struggling to swim to shore, or a keeper ill and incapacitated without aid. She had imagination enough for multiple confessions of guilt.

He didn't reply but looked down into his cupped hands, and she followed suit. There were common cockles, clams, and scallop shells, and she had found an intact sea star. "I found a large knobbed whelk, like the one you drew for me," she told him, a little breathlessly.

"Did you? They're rare."

"Yes," she replied simply. "I left it behind. Someone else can have it. I'm happy with the ordinary ones." Her voice cracked. "I like this little wooden pebble." She pointed into his cupped hands. "It makes me think of forests beneath the waves."

"Aye, it's pretty," he replied lightly, not taking his eyes from her. "I saw you down there, dressed like a little jay bird earlier," he said, smiling down at the top of her bent head.

She lifted her face and flashed him a watery smile that held no hint of apology. "The summer is so short, Ronan." *And joy so improbable*, she thought.

He smiled, and it reached the corners of his eyes. "Stick legs," he teased, and she laughed through her tears, as he meant her to, cheeks burning but her heart so full.

"Are you happy, darling girl?" he asked softly, his hands full of shells.

Am I happy? she thought. *Is happiness supposed to hurt?* She ducked her head, squeezing her eyes closed. "I'm almost afraid to say it, Ronan," she managed, voice full of tears.

"Well, that's all right then," he said lightly, and bent his head to take her mouth with his own and draw her inside, where there was warmth, and life.

He made much of her finds after supper, soaking them in water to rinse them off, and helping her sort and catalogue each one. "These are bivalves, or cockles," he told her, pointing out their hinges and ridges. There were iron-grey ones and dove-grey ones bleached by the sun, and every shade of pink. They sorted them together, then he moved to the gastropods. "These are complete as one unit, you see." His hands, large and calloused, were cautious with the little bits of shell.

Remarkable, she thought. *How gentle he is.*

"This is a scallop." He pointed. "And these are clams—you see that fan shape?"

She stared at the top of his bent head, dark as a seal's pelt, while he continued. "This is a cone. You see this slit?"

"Yes," she said to the top of his head.

"You can tell how old a cockle is by counting its rings." He showed her. "Here's the first year, and the second. This one is three—are you paying attention, lass?" he demanded, unable to keep a stern look on his face.

"Of course," she replied primly. "What's this one?" She pointed to a conical shell with sharp ridges.

"It's a whelk, as you well know," he said, his eyes full of laughter.

She shook her head helplessly, a smile blooming on her face, and then she laughed, unable to stem the happiness within her. She let it bubble up from the well inside her that was so, so full.

He watched while she laughed, and then waited as her laughter abated and turned into a single sob, and then he waited through the quiet tears. He dusted his hands free of sand, wiped them against his trousers, and reached out to cup her face. She wept into his palms, the tears running down his arms and wetting his elbows propped among the seashells.

"Aine," he murmured. "Aine, my darling girl. You're here now, sweetheart." He stroked his hands into her hair and drew her off the chair and into his lap. She continued to weep, and he began to kiss her gently, unhurriedly, willing his calm into her, though he felt the same impending sorrow she did.

"Oh, Ronan," she cried brokenly. "Look at it all," she said, her hand sweeping to include the both of them, the shells, the house, the beach, the loons, the Light. "All of it," she gasped, between progressively longer kisses. His kisses were wet with the salty tang of both ocean and tears. "Oh, Ronan," she wept, and desperately, not knowing how else to fix it, he lifted her in his arms.

"You're here now, Aine," he said, voice hoarse, and offered her all he had: his love, his quiet, brave strength, his whole self in the present moment.

It was afternoon when he lay beside her and stroked her hair away from her tear-streaked face. "Why don't you take the bicycle down to see your friend Claire?" he murmured, fingers sinking into her curls, cupping her head in his hand.

"I don't know how to cycle," she replied, frowning.

He smiled. "I'll teach you soon."

"Besides, Claire isn't my friend," Aine continued peevishly, but leaned into his palm.

"Isn't she?" asked Ronan, all innocence.

"Well, she is, but she doesn't know it yet," said Aine, feeling put out and tired.

"Ah," said Ronan, "well, don't you think she might need some enlightening on the matter then?"

Claire answered the door an hour later, wiping her hand on a towel tucked into her apron.

Her hair was caught up in a bun, sleeves rolled up past her elbows, and she had a smudge of flour on her right shoulder. Her face showed genuine pleasure at the company, however, and Aine's heart lightened as she hung her wrap and followed Claire into the cozy home.

"I was just kneading some hearth bread to set aside, if you don't mind giving me a few moments," said Claire over her shoulder.

"Oh, were you?" asked Aine eagerly. "I've tried ever so many times to get it right." She laughed without self-consciousness. "My bread is awful!"

Surprised at her frankness, Claire looked up from the table. She gave a quick bark of laughter and shook her head as she turned dough out onto the lightly floured surface. "It's just a little hard because you over-flour it. Don't fuss over it."

Aine sidled up to the table next to her. "Is that it, do you think? I've made about every mistake in the book at this point. I've poured boiling water on the yeast."

Claire laughed aloud, a foreign sound to both of them, and Aine momentarily forgot her melancholy from earlier, a grin spreading across her face. Claire had apparently not had a good laugh in a while, so Aine continued, encouraged.

"I've gently laid the dough to rest, rather than what you're doing now," Aine added, pointing at the hearty pounding the dough was receiving at Claire's hands. The other woman threw her head back and laughed again.

Aine continued, smiling. "I've also packed the flour down as hard as I could, you know, to add more of it."

Claire had to wipe at her face with the fabric at her shoulder. "Well, that's your main problem, you know," she told her, eyes alight with laughter.

"That's what Ronan thinks," said Aine.

"Yes. Look." Claire walked over to the bag of flour sitting open on the table and fished out a cup. "If you scoop like this—" She dipped her hand into the bag, coming up with a brimming cup, which she leveled with a finger and held out to show Aine. "You get a heavy cup of flour." She dumped the contents onto the table into a little mound. "But," she continued, "if you fluff the flour and sift it, you get a much lighter cup." She waved Aine over and showed her how to sift and fluff the flour so it was a fine small mound. She scooped, leveled, and dumped it out next to the first cup. "So you see," she said, smiling, "one is lighter, more full of air. And so is the loaf of bread, eventually."

"Wonderful," said Aine, transfixed by the two side-by-side piles of flour. "I'll try it!"

Claire smiled at her excitement and then began scooping the flour back into the bag.

"Would you like to knead with me?" she asked, glancing sideways at Aine.

"Oh, yes, please!" said Aine, laughing, and rolled up her sleeves. "I've always wanted to learn."

"Really?" asked Claire. "Didn't you learn growing up?"

The question, innocently asked, nevertheless pinned Aine to the sink, her back to Claire while she washed her hands. Aine flinched, the cold water running over her palms. As nonchalantly as she could, she answered over her shoulder, "No, I didn't get a chance to. I was . . ." She hesitated, drying her hands and turning back to Claire. "I was an orphan," she finished mildly.

"Oh, bless you," said Claire, not looking up from her kneading. "It must have been hard on a little one. Did you have other family, then?"

Aine cast about for an explanation that wouldn't be too premature. "Of sorts."

Claire nodded. "You seem to know your way about a lighthouse, though."

"Yes," said Aine. "I grew up with a sort of adopted family, on a lighthouse." *Or hundreds of lighthouses*, she thought.

"Oh," said Claire, looking up, eyebrows arched in surprise. "What a romantic childhood." Her smile was wistful.

Before Aine could think this over or ponder the fact that she couldn't remember her childhood, Claire motioned her over and buried her elbows-deep in flour.

"Now," started Claire, "like this." She showed Aine how to knead the dough so that her arms didn't tire, and her back didn't ache, and the dough ended up at just the right consistency.

"See," said Claire, holding out a ball of dough in one hand and poking it with a finger of the other. "See how the dough gives just this much? That's enough. You don't want too much, but less than that and you'll end up with a hard lump."

Aine nodded, taking it in. She held her own ball of dough up for inspection, and Claire declared it a success.

A cat jumped onto the table lightly, delicately avoided the flour while picking its way to the opposite end, and leapt off. Claire rolled her eyes and smiled in an exasperated manner after it. *How can she love that cat?* wondered Aine. It was a different cat from the last time, long ago. *They die so quickly.*

They put the dough aside to rise, covered it with cheesecloth, and set about cleaning up. As they worked, Claire chatted on about her own childhood, which had been spent on a farm with a large garden plot.

"It sounds wonderful," said Aine, her turn to be wistful. "It's so normal, and . . . steady. It's such a constant, solid life."

"Oh, a farm is one of the most uncertain places in the world," said Claire. Aine's eyebrows lifted and she crossed her arms unconsciously over her chest. "It is," insisted Claire. "You can't guarantee the sunshine or the rain, or keep the frost and pests away."

She paused to put the flour away in the pantry. Aine could hear her rummaging around in the small room off the kitchen. "You only do what you can, really. You furrow and plant. You weed and tend. You keep a weather eye out and watch for pests. You can't plan entirely. There is always uncertainty in farming. You just plant and pray."

Aine nodded thoughtfully, leaning against the table.

"It's life in general, I suppose," mused Claire. "You plant and pray, but there's naught else to do if something dies in the ground or the frost comes early."

"Like Joshua," put in Aine.

Claire froze in the act of opening a cupboard, her face half hidden by the small door. "What do you mean?" she asked stiffly.

Aine's heart raced, wondering if she had spoken too freely, if she had presumed on a future friendship and rushed the current one.

She cleared her throat in discomfort. "I only meant that your Joshua's death was like an early frost."

The silence in the room was deafening. Claire's face was now fully hidden behind the cupboard door, and the only thing Aine could hear was the pounding of her own heart. *I didn't mean to hurt you,* she cried silently, and then realized Claire had said something. "I'm sorry, what did you say?"

Claire cleared her voice and closed the cupboard door. Aine's heart hammered in her ears. "I said you're right," repeated Claire. "I'd never thought of it that way, like an early frost. That's just what it was. A senseless, unaccounted-for, devastating early frost. And just when I had put my tender seedling in the ground." She frowned, shook her head as if to banish an unwanted vision, and turned back toward Aine. Claire leaned against the table across from her guest, who suddenly appeared older than she had moments before.

Claire finally murmured, in a soft voice, "You think you have a sure thing, like a dependable crop or a family, and then life happens along and freezes your seedlings to death in the ground."

Both women were silent for a moment, and then Aine spoke up. "What does one do?" she asked. "About the uncertainty, I mean."

Claire shrugged, leaning more heavily against the table. "I don't know," she replied honestly. They both stood in silence a moment longer. "I do know that practicing sorrow in advance doesn't lessen the pain a whit when it does come. The blow is no less startling or painful if you expect it."

Aine thought this over, this idea of practicing sorrow. She remembered a line by Wendell Berry she had read years ago. *I come into the peace of wild things / who do not tax their lives with the forethought of grief.* Had she been doing that? Taxing her life with the forethought of grief? She thought of how uncertain she felt in her new life and how easily breakable her body was.

She thought of the fragility of her relationship with Ronan, despite how sure she felt of him. Wasn't everything uncertain in the end? Her life, her translations, her life's partner. Even the Lights were on a ticking clock in a sense, heading toward automation and oblivion. Every loon-call was uncertain; behind every haunting wail was the possibility of it not being returned, of the call hanging tragically in the air, one mate forever waiting for an answer that might not come.

She thought of Ronan holding her earlier and telling her "Aine, my darling girl. You're here now." *Indeed*, she thought. Could that be the answer? To be rooted solidly in the present? *Is it possible to live with such depth and breadth in the present moment that there can be no sorrow when the present moment is past?* She glanced up and was about to open her mouth to say as much to Claire, who was still lost in her own thoughts, when she glimpsed it.

Just beyond Claire's kitchen were a dark abbey and a Light. There were no people at its base, but she could smell, as though in a faint dream, the scent of incense. Without thinking, she said, "Claire." Her eyes were unfocused. "I can explain this." Claire glanced over at her, a question on her tongue, but Aine was gone.

Saint-Mathieu Light, Plougonvelin, Finistère, France, 1696

SHE SAW THE ABBEY AND the cross standing proudly beside it. Her eyes scanned the compound for the tallest structure and caught sight of the abbey tower rising sharply against the clear grey sky. The smell of putrid fish oil was mingled with the scent of incense, and she could hear, off in the chapel, the voices of the Benedictine monks chanting the midnight service. She closed her eyes for a moment, focusing to hear them better. It was a high, ascending chant, somehow lifted to the heights by deep, resonant baritones and basses. She loved the sound of men singing in concert. She glanced up again. Well, she could leave them to their chanting while she tended the lantern for them.

With some difficulty she was able to locate the entrance to the tower and let herself up the cold stone steps, scratching her palms on the inside of the tower more than once in the dark. She found a glass lantern at the top, the smell of fish oil overwhelming the incense at this distance from the chapel. There were three successive rows of lanterns. She sniffed around until she found the store of fish oil, and mentally blocking her sense of smell, she made the quickest work she could of lighting the copper lanterns. The light from the lanterns was a bright glow within the tower, but Aine knew without a lens it couldn't actually be seen very far out to sea.

Perhaps it'll help someone, she thought, stepping out of the stifling lantern room into the cool air of the small balcony outside. She rubbed her soot-stung eyes with the back of a sleeve and took several lungfuls of the cleaner night air, ears straining for the sounds of the midnight service.

The monks continued their chant, and she thought of their private toil, lifted on incense, tendrils drifting up and out, secretly reaching up, lighting and lifting the world. She looked over her shoulder at the lantern she had just lit, with its plumes of fish-oil-stinking smoke and the meager rays that could barely be seen from shore, and shook her head, a wry smile on her lips. Her eyes stung, her hands were scraped, and she was starting to feel faint from the fumes, but she had done her small part. *I have a small part to do*, she thought.

She stood and closed her eyes to listen to the deep voices of the monks in the chapel, then willed herself home.

❧ 31 ❧

THE NEXT DAY, RONAN STOPPED on his way down to the lobster trap and, catching sight of her, squatted next to where she
knelt weeding in the garden. Her hands were covered in dirt and her
hair was caught up in a bun, but strands had escaped to plaster themselves against the nape of her neck in the heat of the day. She looked
up, smiling at him, her easy grin catching him unawares yet again, no
matter how many times he prepared himself for the blow. He rocked
back a little on the balls of his feet, and put one hand down onto the
soil between his knees to steady himself.

His face was somber, all mirth suppressed, except for his eyes,
which were incapable of looking at her with anything but tenderness.
"Well, wife," he said, "I'm off to retrieve your lobsters. As you can
see—" he spread his hands out to the sides, palms up in supplica-
tion— "I've been reduced to fishing for prisoner food."

"What you're fishing for, Ronan of the Light," she told him sassily,
"is a kiss."

"Ah," he said lightly, "you've found me out, then."

Her eyes scanned his beloved face, her grin insuppressible, and
kneeling between his legs, her hands still in the dirt, she leaned
forward and kissed him, her lips curved into a smile. "I love you,

husband," she told him, her delight so unshaded that she could see the answering flush rise on the nape of his neck.

"Yes," he murmured, pressing his lips together, as if to hold her kiss against them. "I must feel some way about you, woman, or else how would you explain this?" He indicated the net.

She continued to smile up at him, and then something over his shoulder caught her eye. She gasped softly, bringing a sodden hand to her chest, heedless of the dirt against her clean linen. He quickly turned, still in a crouch, putting out a hand to steady her, but ready to rise and meet whatever had put that look on her face.

He saw only the house, and the Light rising up sharply behind it, both backed by a bold summer-blue sky. He turned back to her.

Aine's gaze was fixed past Ronan's shoulder to the towering lighthouse of Alexandria, which rose precipitously from the small island of Pharos. It was sometime before the three successive earthquakes that had sent the tower into the depths of the harbor, and it rose in three concentric tiers, each one smaller than the last, its pale limestone walls reflecting the glare of the North African sun. She could feel the heat of the summer day, the smell of fish in the harbor, and . . . she squinted. She could just make out the statue at the top of the Light. The textbooks had always been unclear about whether it was Zeus or Poseidon, and she'd forgotten to check last time she was there. A faint line of smoke rose from the towering heights, and many people, as tiny as ants in the distance, scurried about the base. Her body leaned forward a little, and the Light became less ghostly, more solid, and the heat of the sun more intense. Then she remembered what was before her: Ronan, the Light, the cottage, the buttery lobsters under the apple tree, and the slide of his foot against hers in the middle of the night. With only a little regret, she made up her mind. There were plenty of people there, and the Light looked to be burning brightly. Decision made, the Light, the island, the smells, and the heat all vanished as though they had never been.

Ronan watched her as she knelt, arrested, her eyes a glassy green that reflected the cloudless summer sky above. She blinked forcefully, sending a tear that had trembled on the tips of her lashes down her smooth cheek. She shook her head, sighed, and focused back on him.

"Where?" he asked.

She reached out a hand that neither of them noticed was dirt-covered, and he clasped it in his. She gave a short, wistful half-sigh, half-laugh and said faintly, "The Pharos."

His grip unintentionally tightened on her hand, and his eyebrows rose until they disappeared in his hair over widened eyes. His mouth hung comically open. It was enough to break the draw of the ancient Light over her, and she let out a laugh and leaned forward to kiss his gaping mouth.

"*The* Pharos?" he asked incredulously, setting her back so he could look into her eyes. "The one in Alexandria?"

She nodded.

"In *ancient* Alexandria?"

She nodded again.

"Why in the world wouldn't you . . . ?" He motioned with his hand, waving her away, into the sky, into time.

She sobered, but the smile still softened her eyes. "Well," she began seriously, "I've been looking forward to that lobster since all of yesterday, and don't think for a moment that I trust you not to eat it all before I—"

"Oh, off with you," he exclaimed, exasperated, his body leaning at a disbelieving tilt away from her, though his hand in hers remained gentle.

She tipped her head forward, until her forehead was touching his. Quietly, without looking at him, lest the blush burn her freckles away, she said, "Ronan, dear heart, there's no other place or time I'd rather be."

Summer burned on, and they scraped the outside of the Light and repainted it meticulously with a wide brush, Ronan hanging from a rope-and-board cradle made expressly for that purpose. Aine hated to see him dangling in the air like that, on such an unsound-looking contraption, and told him so in no uncertain terms. He laughed in her face, and when she protested he lifted his eyebrows and summarily silenced her with, "Aye. And the Colossus of Rhodes? Who was struck by lightning during an earthquake that sent *that* tumbling into the sea?"

Aine continued to translate away when she felt she was needed elsewhere, though Ronan's heart remained firmly lodged in his throat the first dozen or so times. The Neist Point on the Isle of Skye was followed by St. Abbs Head in the Firth of Forth, the Tower of Hercules in Spain, and then a fire on a hillside so long ago she expected to see Viking vessels slip silently through the early morning fog. The translations happened in quick succession, and she came home safely so many times that he began to breathe a little easier. He had nearly become comfortable with the idea when, toward the end of summer, she came home injured.

Aine came up the path, her left arm cradled in her right, a tense-jawed grimace on her face, and he ran out to meet her.

"Aine, what happened?" he gasped, giving the arm a wide berth.

"It's fine, Ronan," she reassured him quickly, though the sight of blood seeping out from between the fingers cradling her forearm made him sick to his stomach.

She told him, as he gingerly cleaned her wound, of how she had fished a sailor out of the sea near the Aquitaine in France and had scraped her arm against the side of the boat dragging him into it, since she couldn't swim him to shore. It was something she would not have hesitated over *before*, but now . . . her heart had pounded at the danger of it, and the fear she felt pulling him in, his clothes heavy with seawater, and the sharp, stinging pain of the salt water entering the gash on her arm.

Ronan's lips compressed into a thin line, brows tightly knit, his anger spoken plainly in his silence. He cleaned her wound with the care of a surgeon, winced at her discomfort as he disinfected it with a small amount of alcohol, and then carefully bound it with clean linen strips. He was distant and withdrawn during their supper and answered her questions about the goings-on in her absence with near-monosyllabic responses, reminding her of a shelled creature grown suddenly shy of harm.

In late afternoon, when he did not join her for tea, she found him out back splitting wood over a stump. The yard was littered with hacked blocks of wood. She glanced over at their abundant winter woodpile and sighed. She approached him from behind, watching as he swung the axe up and over his right shoulder, high overhead, and then with more force than necessary brought it down on the small block of wood. The block split halfway down the middle, and she watched him bring his booted foot up to pry his axe free.

He'd shed his jacket, as he was wont to do, and she watched as he brought the axe up and over again, and down with enough force to neatly cleave the block of wood. Ronan breathed heavily, his arms beginning to tire, a trickle of sweat snaking down the center of his back. She must have made some small sound, because he twisted around and caught sight of her.

She had caught him unawares. His eyes were stark, wild. She saw the effort he made to rein himself back, swiping at his forehead to hide his face from her for a moment, but she sensed his barely leashed anger. Her feet moved forward of their own accord, and

Ronan's shoulders slumped a little as he eased the axe carefully away from her to lean it against the stump.

His head was tilted down and away from her, his eyes shaded from her gaze, jaw tense, his body stiff and distant. Aine kept her bandaged hand behind her back as though she could remove the evidence. She leaned in to catch the smell of woodsmoke in his beard, and her other hand slid between them to the topmost button of his linen shirt.

He swung his gaze down on her, wary and still angry, eyeing her as she fiddled with his button between her thumb and pointer finger. Neither of them said anything, and Aine found herself taking a deep breath, filling herself with the smell of his beard, sweat, and freshly split wood. She worked the button free of the buttonhole, and he stilled, except for his hand, which shot up between them and grasped her wrist. With hardly any pressure at all, he pushed her hand away from his shirt.

Not yet, then, thought Aine, tamping down the sudden stab of hurt. She flushed and drew her hand away to lay it on her chest, over her heart. She could see the skin below his collar, a little paler than the skin on his neck, and it was suddenly too intimate, with his anger trained on her the way it was. She turned away, and he didn't stop her.

He didn't come to bed that night when they had finished silently tending the Light, and that pained Aine more than saltwater to the gash.

It was about three in the morning when she, tired of tossing and turning in the too-empty bed with no warm body to put her perpetually cold feet against, gave up, slipped her robe on, and toed into her boots.

He was looking out to sea, his elbows on the rail of the Light, and turned to regard her steadily, his gaze no longer angry, before looking back out to sea. *Finally*, she thought. She had a sudden flash of remembrance, of another night not so long ago when they had stood just this way, and he had told her to forgive herself.

She stepped next to him at the rail, and he wordlessly put his arm around her shoulders to lend her some of his warmth. Upset or not, he was ever gentle. *What place is there for anger when we have so little time?* she thought. She relaxed into his embrace and waited.

After a time she felt his sigh. He removed his arm and slowly tightened his big palms over the rail before him. "Aine," he began, "my sister . . ." she could see his throat working as he swallowed. "You know she—" Aine put her hand over his rough knuckles. "She drowned," he forced out. "I was responsible for her, and she drowned."

"And you're responsible for me?" she asked carefully.

"No!" he exclaimed. "Well, yes. But also, I—" he broke away from her, his hands clenching and unclenching.

She tucked herself closer against him. In a faraway voice Ronan told her of his beloved sister who had drowned, and how he had searched and searched for her, and of his despair. She had been his responsibility, and he had let her drown. The grief was still fresh, though it had happened years ago, and he still suffered.

"I feel as though I have forgotten more things than I remember of her," he told Aine with quiet horror. "There were days I didn't want to rise from bed but simply huddle under the covers and let the earth spin on without me. I hated myself for being alive and her for being gone. I felt like such a . . . coward." He spit the word out as if it had spoiled in his mouth.

"Did anything help?" asked Aine, leaning against his side. He unbent enough to release one hand from the rail and bring her into the circle of his arm.

"I don't know that it helped, but the Light forced me out of bed."

He bent down to nuzzle her neck, breathing in the comforting scent of her, of home. "I've dreamt of her many times, Aine," he said, straightening and turning back toward the sea. A strange look came over his face, and he shook his head in dismissal.

"What?"

"I'm not sure. In my dreams sometimes, it's not Margaret I see, but a selkie."

"A selkie?"

"Yes. An older selkie, her hair going grey. It's very . . . specific." She said nothing, but stood beside him and let him think of his long-ago grief, which colored his dealings with her today. She knew no human strong enough to resist that fault.

"So Margaret drowning makes you worry for me," she asked, turning her face up to his.

"Yes." He tucked a curl behind her ear, his hand lingering to cup her face. His chest expanded on a deep inhale. "And I just worry for you." His broad palm was warm against her cheek. "It would hurt less to take your pain away, lass. It hurts more to bandage you up and send you back out there." He didn't say more, and he didn't have to, but she pressed against him again, and they let the quiet bind them together.

They did not live a loud life. Many of their days were spent in the rhythmic silence of the ebb and flow of the sea, marking time like a grandfather clock, each moment the sound of a wave washing either up or out on the shore. The mornings were filled with slow love, gathering eggs from the hens, and repairs about the Light. He taught her to ride the bicycle so she could zip down to see Claire more quickly. The evenings were long and filled with the manual labor of lugging heavy pails of oil, trimming endless wicks, and climbing the forty-two steps to the top, where they often kept watch together.

They naturally fell into a pattern with their work, Ronan following Aine up the stairs to the lantern room, watching as she reached an arm high overhead and with a wide, sweeping motion of her arm drew the curtain back in an arc from around the windows, bathing the small room with late afternoon light. The slide of the curtains always signaled a new night, the beginning of their labors together, and he always sent up a prayer of thanks while he watched her sweep the curtains aside, then lean her body in to gather them in her slim arms.

She made a turn around the room, filling her arms with the fabric, until the bundled curtains were bigger than she was and she had wrestled them into submission. She tied them together beside the low desk and then looked over at him where he always stood, holding the pail of oil, one foot still on the last step of the staircase, where he waited to be out of her way. Right before the work of their life began, she always flashed him a small, contented smile, as though if she held it longer she would lose her composure, but communicating with her eyes that she was happy and that she was where she wanted to be.

To other folk, Aine remained a ghostly presence at the Light. If you asked the townspeople, they would have told you, why yes, Ronan of the Light *was* married. They would have puzzled over the name of his bride before shrugging apologetically. "It always seems to slip the mind." This was usually followed by "But she's a sweet lass, his wife." People knew she was there, but she was ephemeral, and she wasn't memorable.

Her memory burned brightly only with her family, which included Claire, after a rather awkward and lengthy conversation regarding disappearances while baking bread. Aine and Ronan also had a succession of cats which Claire's mouser Hurricane involuntarily provided them. Aine was careful not to name any of them Mistress or Twitch.

In midwinter, most of the river had frozen over but they still had some sea traffic, so the Light remained operational. Aine curled up with the cat Storm, a gift from Claire, and tried to get away with discreetly tucking her feet under Ronan while he sat engrossed in *The Red Badge of Courage*. He was more or less lost to the world, but he did notice her cold feet and sedately lifted his eyebrows at her, a smile tugging at his lips. Aine wiggled her feet with a grin, and then got up to stretch and get a drink of water.

Outside the window she saw, not the pure expanse of untrodden snow in twilight that she expected, but a small, unlit Light. It looked south, and there was no snow. Unlit Lights meant someone was likely in danger, especially when the translation presented itself in darkness. There was not a soul to be seen, and she dried the cup, her eyes on the scene before her. "Ronan, love," she said over her shoulder. He recognized that tone and was at her side in a moment. His strong arms wrapped around her from behind, pressing her back against his strong chest. Aine kept her eyes trained on the Light, but tilted her head back against his chest.

He leaned down and brushed her forehead with his lips. "Fly home soon, my joy," he told her gruffly.

"I love you too, Ronan," she told him in a faint voice, and then his arms were empty.

El Faro Les Éclaireurs, "Lighthouse at the End of the World," Tierra del Fuego, 2021

The Light was a humble affair, the top and bottom thirds painted red, with one large white band in the middle. The surroundings, however, were not humble. The Light sat on a small island, behind which towered the massive white-capped peaks of Tierra del Fuego. The air was crisp, with a clean bite to it, and Aine filled her lungs with the sweet air, though it was cold enough to sting a little. She wanted to laugh at the beauty of it. It made her feel so alive to stand on that rock, the Light standing guard behind her in the early dawn light.

The island was dotted with cormorants, and the air was filled with the cry of sea lions as they brayed at each other on the rocks. She stood there for several moments, glad to be alive and at this far tip of the world, looking out at the water, the birds and sea lions making a commotion all around her.

She sighed, and with one more turn, taking in as much as her eyes could take, she approached the little lighthouse to see if all was operating smoothly.

She was quite far into the future from her home, she realized. The apparatus was new to her, and she grinned as she saw that there was only one small bulb—electric, she could tell that—that lit the entire Light. The bulb had gone out.

She studied the Light for several minutes, a smile lifting her face at the clever little light bulb that, once it went out, was supposed to be replaced on a rotating wheel by the next little light bulb. *How did that happen?* she wondered, looking around for an energy source. *And why hasn't it happened?* She looked all around her in the lantern room. It was odd not to be choked by fumes or careful to keep clear of the delicate edges of a lens. It was amazing that this Light ran itself, without needing a keeper, oil, a massive Fresnel lens, or meticulous care. It was just a light bulb, electric and—*Ah*, she thought, *there we are. Solar panels.*

She reasoned that the plates fed energy to charge batteries that kept the revolving wheel rotating as each light bulb went out. Everything appeared to be in order. She dug around some more and even found a backup generator that kicked in when the solar panels didn't sufficiently charge the rotating wheel. She examined the wheel closely.

She checked all the light bulbs and realized they had all burned out, but the automatic system hadn't kicked in for some reason. There was a box of supplies by her feet, and she shook her head as she picked out a box of small, new light bulbs. It was, in fact, as simple as that. *Wait until I tell Ronan*, she thought, laughing. She could just imagine sitting across from him at the fire, explaining that the backup system for the electric bulb involved harnessing and storing the power of the sun.

She smiled, and then a sobering thought occurred to her. There was something forlorn about the little Light that had nothing to do with its isolated location. There was no keeper, and she had always felt that a Light without a keeper was somehow impoverished. It was sobering to think that the work she and Ronan did could be done by a few wires and bulbs.

Well, not entirely, she thought, and carefully unscrewed the light bulbs to replace them, one after the other, with new bulbs. The rotating mechanism worked like a charm and the entire system lit itself with a blaze, nearly blinding her with the first flash.

She lined the dead bulbs up in a row—thoroughly confounding the worker who arrived a week later for scheduled maintenance—and stepped out into the chill air. It hit her like a wall, and she shivered happily as the wind buffeted her, looking out onto the glory of Tierra del Fuego, at the end of the world.

~: 32 :~

Loon-Call Light, Maine, 1928

AINE AND RONAN STOOD SIDE by side, their elbows lined up on the rail of the Light. The night was of the rare crystal-clear variety that occasionally came along in late summer, before the leaves fell and the nights lengthened. After they lit the Light, Ronan motioned her to the log, and she made the short entry for the night. Moonlight, their newest kitten, a silvery ball of fluff, curled beside her hand next to the log when she picked up the pencil.

Sea like glass, no breeze, no ships in sight.

"Like glass?" he asked, peering over her shoulder.

"A variation on the 'sea like a mirror,'" she explained. *Beaufort zero and all is well with the world,* she thought. She smiled over her shoulder and kissed him.

They stood side by side for some time, watching the water for any sign of movement, but it seemed destined to be a quiet night. They alternated between silence and listening to the comforting familial hoots and tremolos of the loons at the river bend, which was another type of silence.

Presently, they heard a long wail. Ronan saw Aine shiver out of the corner of his eye and wordlessly turned to gather her in his arms.

He tucked her under his chin and rubbed his cheek against the top of her head. Her hair had just begun to grey, and he thought she looked rather distinguished in it.

"Are you all right, love?" he asked her quietly.

She nodded against him and burrowed deeper into his embrace, her back braced against his chest as they looked out to sea. "That sound," she murmured, but he needed no explanation and tightened his arms around her. Aine held her breath, waiting for the answering wail, for it almost always came: that of the mate returning the wail so that the two could be reunited. The silence drew out between them, the expectant wail hanging in the air, an awful, unanswered summons. When, after several moments, there was no reply, the cry came again, more urgently. Lungs burning, she waited, and then finally let out her breath in a painful huff.

Ronan kissed the top of her head again and turned her into his embrace. He kissed her at length, slowly, as though he had all the time in the world. After several moments, when they came up for air, he succeeded in coaxing a small smile from her. "I don't like it when they wail for their mates and then . . ." She trailed off.

He nodded. "I know, darling girl."

She stood in the circle of his arms for several more moments, and then he brushed her forehead with a kiss. "You ought to go down and get some sleep. I'll join you in a little while."

She nodded in agreement, still feeling the warmth of his lips against her brow.

"Goodnight, my heart," he told her gently.

She smiled up at him. "Goodnight, my love," she said softly. He watched her go, heard her steps on the spiral staircase, and then turned his gaze back out to sea.

Aine made her way down, step by step, counting them under her breath, feeling as content as she had ever felt in her life. She exited the Light at the base, and had taken three steps when the translation

263

presented itself.

She noticed the grey, misty surroundings first and waited with pounding heart for the ghostly image of her possible assignment. There was nothing. She turned to look behind her, and her heart plummeted into her booted feet.

The Loon-Call Light was ghostly, grey, no longer the solid structure she had left only moments before. It felt wrong, eerie, and shrouded in half-light. She stood for a beat, paralyzed with dread, her heart pounding in her throat. She'd been there but a moment when she heard Ronan's voice, from high above her, in an anguished cry of "Margaret!"

She stood frozen, swaying between the past and her beloved present as his footsteps pounded a frantic rhythm down the forty-two steps, and he burst from the base of the Light, his face a wild mask of horror. He tore past her, and she felt the air stirred by his flight. He did not see her, but she could see that his beloved face was young, only a man-child, and that he was unknowingly heading into the defining moment of his life.

~

Loon-Call Light, Maine, 1901

Aine stepped boldly forward into that translation, back in time to her home before it was such. Night turned to day, the sun shone brightly overhead, and she gathered her skirts in her hands and raced down toward the beach after him, her hair trailing behind her. Her feet flew, and she felt like she was made of the summer wind and sunlight. She felt strong, and though it was of a different flavor from what she'd felt earlier that night, her run toward Ronan and his sister also tasted of contentment.

There was no time to think of what to do or how to do it, but only a direct flight to the seashore, where she shaded her eyes and looked out to sea, searching for the two figures she felt sure must be there, struggling in the water. Ronan was farther out than she had anticipated, and there appeared to be an upturned skiff of some sort. Aine took one moment to toe off her boots in the sand and then waded quickly into the shallows. She shivered as the chill of the water seeped into her gown, to her skin. With the spare, efficient movement of a practiced rescuer, she dove into the water, ducking under the first small wave that broke over her, and using quick, slicing strokes, she headed for Ronan and the skiff.

It took her only a moment to understand when she came upon him. "Margaret!" The cry broke her heart. He swallowed a great gasp of air and dove down again. He was under the water for several interminable moments, and then he broke the surface with a great heave. Seawater ran in rivulets down his face, his hair dark and slick like the pelt of a seal, his young face tight with anguish. "Margaret!" came the choked, broken cry. He took another deep lungful of air and dove again.

Aine treaded water near him, her heart in her throat, taking in the desperation and helplessness in his voice. He made the plunge several more times, punctuated by his hoarse voice screaming his sister's name.

Aine knew that Margaret was gone. She knew it in the same way she had known the hundred and twenty-seven had gone, and that the name of the young man on the Colossus had been Argos, and other innumerable small things in her life. Margaret was dead and drowned, and there was naught Ronan could do about it.

"Oh, why am I here?" she whispered, writhing at the sight of Ronan's anguish. Should she dive with him to search? There was no use in the futile search he was making. He would only grow fatigued and perhaps succumb to his despair.

Suddenly, with cold-water clarity, she knew why she was present. "Oh," she gasped. "Oh." *It's too hard.* She faltered for a moment, her arms and legs nearly paralyzed by the thought, and she tasted the salty tang as her mouth dipped below the level of the sea. The sharp brine brought her back to the present, and she began to tread water vigorously.

He dove a dozen times, and then clung to the skiff gasping and weeping openly, calling his sister's name until his voice was the croak of a neck-wrung bird. All through this Aine trod water near him, holding her body in the chilly water with the stillness and clarity of a moonbeam, unseen by the half-crazed Ronan but present in his grief.

Aine felt that sense of stepping into the river of time, felt it slow, felt as though empires rose and fell in the time it took for Ronan to realize that his sister was gone. When he did, he folded his arms against the sloping side of the upturned skiff and wept loud, heartbroken sobs. He still hadn't noticed Aine.

He bobbed in the water and wept for what felt like the remainder of Aine's life. Finally, when the sun had waned and it was time to tend to the Light, she saw him stiffen his shoulders, look out at the horizon, and expand his chest with one more deep breath.

Perhaps he's going to dive one more time, she thought, hoping that somehow the evening would end peacefully. She had a sick feeling in the pit of her stomach about the entire scene that made the apprehension creep up her throat and tighten her chest.

He dove again and didn't come back up for several long moments, and Aine began to worry that something had happened to him, that he had been injured in some way, or that the repeated dives he had taken had tired him to the point that he . . . *No*, she thought, *not that*. Heart pounding, in a few short strokes she was at the skiff, and taking a deep breath, she dove after him.

Ronan was not an unskilled swimmer, and Aine saw immediately what he had done. He had taken a lungful of air and dived as deeply as possible, to what exactly? She could see in the cold water, made murky by the approaching dark and Ronan's descent before her, the soles of his feet as he dove ahead of her. They snapped purposefully back and forth like flippers, trailing bubbles in his wake, cutting a swath through the sea as he dove deeper and deeper.

Is he still looking for Margaret? Aine thought, her lungs burning as she followed him. *Ronan,* she wanted to scream, *Ronan, come back. Come back, she's gone!* He was now only a moment ahead of her, and she followed him closely.

You can't do anything for her! She focused through the burning in her lungs and dove deeper after him. They descended until Aine felt her ears pop and the pressure build tightly within her, until the only thing she could think in the entire world was that her lungs were going to burst. She needed air.

Finally, she had to exhale, and she breathed out in a burst of bubbles that must have somehow caught Ronan's attention, because he abruptly turned his head and saw her.

Surprised, he stopped to stare at her in the murky water. Time stopped entirely as he gazed at her. She wasn't a selkie or a mermaid, but she might have been, with her gown suspended around her as though caught in a gossamer web, her hair trailing behind her. She had startled him out of his single-minded descent, and he paused for a moment, contemplating her. She was pretty, in a mature way, her curls tinged with white, her eyes as green as the forests of kelp and sea grass beneath the waves. She eyed him without wavering, a slightly pained expression coloring her features, and he wondered what would put that expression on a selkie's face. He reached out and touched her cheek and realized, with some wonder, that it was solid, and smooth as the pink curve of a whelk. She leaned into his touch, and he drew back, confused.

Aine focused all of her thoughts on Ronan while her lungs burned for air. Breathing was a singular desire, a need greater than any other, but somehow, her mind was able to muffle its need, to focus her love and all the striving of her soul into this one last arrow, and cock it.

She took a breath, because she could not control her body's need, and it was all water, and she felt it fill her lungs. *Oh Ronan,* she thought, *all your tomorrows, and mine.* Her vision began to darken. Blindly, she reached out and connected with his sleeve.

Ronan thought she was a pretty vision, but he had to go, to find Margaret. He turned away from her, and found his sleeve caught fast in her grip. *Strong grip, for an imaginary selkie,* he thought. And then he saw her go limp in the water.

The horror of the day, the heart-stopping fear of seeing Margaret's skiff overturned in the water, and the sorrow that had led to his foolhardy dive to look for her body all seemed to catch up to him in that moment, and he suddenly felt his lungs burning, burning, burning. They burned for air, and he had never wanted anything more in his life. He was starting to become lightheaded from want of it, and subconsciously, before he had made the decision that though Margaret was gone, he needn't throw his life away, his body had started its ascent to the surface. He had gone a few mind-numbed feet when he realized the selkie still had a finger hooked in the cuff of his shirt sleeve.

Something in him knew she was not a selkie, but his mind could not accept the horror that someone had come into the water after him. Who could have done that? There was no one at the lighthouse. There was no one to know, or see, or help.

Another part of him felt that, though his lungs were burning and every moment must count if he was to breathe again, he must not leave the selkie behind, and so he didn't. He knew he was rising too quickly, and that many who did so did not live to breathe again, but he could not control his ascent; he rose as if rejected from the depths by the sea-god himself, her wrist manacled in his hand.

Before Ronan's seal-black head broke the surface, his vision had begun to darken, and he fought to hold to consciousness as they surged up from the water. The gasp of pure, sweet, cold air as it burned its way down his throat and into his lungs was clear, salvific, and as painful as a lance down his middle. He mindlessly gasped another, and another, and another, until his vision blurred, and the world went black.

~: 33 :~

For God created man to be immortal,
and made him to be an image of his own eternity.

WISDOM OF SOLOMON 2:23

But the souls of the righteous are in the hand of God,
and there shall no torment touch them.

WISDOM OF SOLOMON 3:1

WHEN THE KEEPER OPENED HER eyes, she was on the beach beneath the Loon-Call Light, Ronan's sprawled shape a few feet from her in the lengthening dusk. Her heart leapt and she made to rise to tend to him, but found that she was immobile. It was in almost every other respect an ordinary day, and she could see turnstones picking their way quickly along the seashore and hear the sound of a coot in the distance. She lay for an agony of moments, feeling as though she lingered somewhere within herself, but her body was no longer her own, and she couldn't use it to assure herself of her beloved's safety.

Finally she noticed the faint rise and fall of his chest. *We made it!*

she thought exultantly, a smile blooming within her. *He's safe . . . but Margaret,* she thought sadly. Margaret was lost, as she had always been, but Aine had not realized how close to death Ronan had come in the wake of her loss. She had not known the depths of his despair.

She shivered and thought of all their nights at the Light, or listening to the loons, or sitting by the fire in the little house. *He would have missed all of them. I would have missed all of them.* The desolation of his recent proximity to death was so close, so suffocating, that she felt she must weep, but the tears would not come. They felt dammed up inside her as they had so long ago, before Ronan, when she had lived forever.

Ronan stirred, and the Keeper felt a surge of relief at his movements, awkward and jerky, as he tried to push himself up to his forearms, his face turned in the sand toward her. Sand caked the side of his face, matted his hair and beard, and crusted his lips. Eyes closed, he tried to lean on his forearms to rise but collapsed back in the sand, face first. He tried again, and his body scissored in half on itself, and he heaved, and retched seawater. The Keeper winced, wishing she could get up to help him, but her body remained frozen, her bones as heavy as lead weights sunk deep in the sand.

Ronan rolled heavily onto his side, spent, breathing deeply of the evening air. He closed his eyes and slept.

The Keeper grew restless and impatient of feeling as though her body was not under her control, though she was relieved to see Ronan relatively safe. She thought she might close her eyes and sleep awhile too, but she felt that there was something she must do, and that it was important.

She felt the Woman before she saw her, and though her Light illuminated the entire shoreline, the Keeper could look directly upon her. She felt peace steal over her, and she knew Ronan would be well, and all manner of things would be well. The Woman knelt by the body of the little Lightkeeper and put her hand against the still brow.

The Keeper wanted to stand in the presence of Wisdom, but her body betrayed her yet again. "My Lady," she said, "I did the best I could."

The All-Keeper's eyes on her were full of love and compassion. "Yes, you did," she said gently. "Well done, little Light."

The Keeper felt a mooring within her loosen, but she was still held fast by something. What was it? "It wasn't enough, I think," she said faintly, beginning to forget what it was that she had done that wasn't enough.

"It was enough," replied Wisdom patiently. She brushed the hair back from the cold brow, and the Keeper felt life stir within her for a moment, as though she walked between two translations, both hazy and ghostly, but was unsure which to step into.

"I think I wanted to . . ." the Keeper trailed off. What was it she had been trying to do?

"You did," said the All-Keeper gently.

"Oh, did I?" asked the Keeper. "Well, that's all right, then."

She looked around for the first time since Wisdom had arrived and saw Ronan in the sand a few feet away. "Will he be all right?" she asked with detached interest.

Wisdom considered her question for several moments, and replied, "In time."

The Keeper nodded. "What about the Light?" she asked. "What if there are any ships out tonight? Or sailors?"

Wisdom looked up to the cliff overhead, and with a Word the beacon was lit, and the Keeper saw the first beam cut out across the water over their heads.

"Thank you," she murmured, feeling sleepy, but content.

Wisdom smiled gently at her, and then the lines of her face became grave. "Little Light, there is one more thing you must do," she said, her voice kind but firm.

The Keeper nodded. "Yes," she said. "I know. I feel I will think of it presently, though I'm not ready quite yet. I need but a moment," she said faintly.

Wisdom nodded. "A moment then," she said, and the Keeper found herself on the shore alone, save for the slumbering figure of Ronan of the Light.

She lingered there, between those two translations, the ghostly Loon-Call Light far above her on the left and a new shore on the right. She thought she recognized the new shore, and something in her ached to step into it, but there was one last thing she knew she had to do here first. She dozed and woke to find the beach deserted and Ronan gone. He hadn't seen her.

She waited immobile throughout that day, as the sun climbed in the sky and then set again behind her. She waited, and she thought. Suddenly, she felt the quickening of the river of time around her, and above her in the blue expanse of sky the sun sped in its course, rising and setting a thousand times in the blink of an eye, the sea ebbing and flowing against her body, but not carrying her away. The waves changed, cool and refreshing against her skin, but she saw that the waves breaking against the hem of her gown were full of jade, carnelian, and emerald stones, sparkling in the sunlight, and smaller clear gems that caught and held the moonlight. She waited and she thought, until she remembered what she had to do, and then she did it.

~: 34 :~

Death is a delightful hiding place for weary men.

HERODOTUS, *THE HISTORIES*

*For she is the brightness of the everlasting light, the unspotted
mirror of the power of God, and the image of his goodness.
And being but one, she can do all things: and remaining in herself,
she maketh all things new. . . . For she is more beautiful than the
sun, and above all the order of stars: being compared with the light,
she is found before it. For after this cometh night:
but vice shall not prevail against wisdom.*

WISDOM OF SOLOMON 7:26–30

S HE WAS ON A NEW shore, her hair clean, her body strong and
supple, and once again under her control. She flexed her fingers
experimentally. She was wearing a gown of sea green, and it was
light and airy around her, floating in the warm foam at her bare feet.
Instead of shells she could see gems of every color, some like flecks
of starlight, catching every color of the rainbow, and some the size of
her fist, tinkling in the undertow as they tumbled over one another

and were carried back out to sea.

Against her ankles a wave broke, and as she stepped forward with her right foot, she felt a stone beneath it. She stooped down to pick it up. It was smooth, white as snow, and it had a single word on it. She passed her thumb over the letters, whispering it softly beneath her breath, the syllables melodic with a rightness that was outside time.

"My name," she murmured, and noticed Wisdom beside her.

"My Lady!" she exclaimed happily.

"Welcome," said Wisdom, her voice full of joy. Wisdom looked as she always had, but her Light was undimmed, and the Lightkeeper could look upon her. She felt warm and bright, as if she would never be cold again.

They walked side by side from the shore to a cliff overlooking the sea, and they didn't speak. "All of your questions, daughter," began Wisdom, "you may ask them whenever you wish."

The Lightkeeper smiled. "Another time, perhaps."

Epilogue

Call no man happy until he dies.

HERODOTUS, *THE HISTORIES*

Loon-Call Light, Maine, 1938

RONAN LEANED BACK AGAINST THE apple tree, letting the now-strong trunk take the weight of his back, which, having shouldered burdens for some sixty-odd years, was yet strong and unbowed. He had a few hours of daylight left, and his eyes passed over the house, in good repair after the shingles he'd had the Callahan boy fix the week prior. He missed the potted herbs and smell of baking bread that signaled that *she* was home, and that she loved him. He looked out over her garden, which he allowed no one else to tend, though his knees weren't what they used to be. It was as a proper tribute should be, rows tight and furrows even. In the summer the basil stalks grew so thickly they were wooden at the base, their wavy leaves catching the sun. Her tomatoes grew in an assembly, so fast that he ended up canning most of them so they wouldn't go to waste, though there were only a couple left now as fall deepened. *Nothing will go to waste*, he thought, *because she'll be here soon.*

The thought sent a chill down his spine, but he smiled faintly.

He'd awoken with a head cold and had taken Herodotus down from the shelf, feeling a sense of rightness in his bones. He fingered the lovingly read and reread pages. He rifled them and they fell open on a line she had carefully underlined in pencil: "If a man insisted always on being serious, and never allowed himself a bit of fun or relaxation, he would go mad without knowing it or become unstable." He thought about the last time she had ribbed him about just that. Wrinkles had begun to form around her eyes, her figure had softened, and the shock of grey running from root to tip over her right eye had begun to blur and spread. She had fussed over everything he whittled with chisel and gouge, and the more whimsical his creations, the more delighted she was that he was having a "bit of fun to stave off the madness," as she'd called it.

Before closing the pages of the book, he flipped to the inside flap. With a firm hand that shook only slightly, he dipped his quill and penned his name in a bold slash. He resisted the urge to write something cheeky for her to find later. His hand shook only a little as he reached into his right pocket. He was not cavalier about death, but only ready, for the absence of his beloved was indeed an amputation, and he had been too long without her.

He rubbed the tiny thing lightly between his thumb and first finger. A thrill ran through him. She would love this one best of all. It was a small oak-wood comb for that riot of hair she had. He had lingered over it for the last month, chiseling and carving until a series of small waves danced fancifully on one side, and a vine with small leaves on the other. He'd nearly lost the thing a time or two, it was so small, and it had been a strain on his eyes; but it was done, and it was going to her, as was he.

He held it loosely in his right hand, looking out over his land to the sea. He wished she were here to tell him what to expect, what the other shore would feel like. He imagined it was warm, but not too warm, and sunny in a good, squinting sort of way, but not so that his eyes would hurt. And there would be books. And she would have an oven at her disposal. Perhaps that was asking too much, but the woman had become a wonder with a ready oven.

He swiped at a tear that trickled down his weathered cheek, resting his hand only briefly above where she lay. He thought back to that still night years ago when they had bidden one another good night, and he had found her body washed up on the shore the next chill, grey morning.

He got to his feet, wiping off the soil his moist hand had collected. *But really*, he thought, stretching to his full height, *as long as she is there*. He had lived long enough with his time-slipping wife to know his time had come. "Aine, I'm coming, lass," he said, and turning his face from the ocean, he made his way to tend the Light.

Sherry Shenoda is an Egyptian-American poet and pediatrician, born in Cairo, living in California. She was shortlisted for the Brunel International African Poetry Prize. She lives with her husband and two sons. *The Lightkeeper* is her first work of fiction.

Ancient Faith Publishing hopes you have enjoyed and bene-fited from this book. The proceeds from the sales of our books only partially cover the costs of operating our nonprofit minis-try—which includes both the work of **Ancient Faith Publish-ing** and the work of **Ancient Faith Radio**. Your financial sup-port makes it possible to continue this ministry both in print and online. Donations are tax deductible and can be made at **www.ancientfaith.com**.

To view our other publications,
please visit our website: store.ancientfaith.com

ANCIENT FAITH RADIO

Bringing you Orthodox Christian music, readings,
prayers, teaching, and podcasts 24 hours a day since 2004 at
www.ancientfaith.com